WE ARE THE SMURFS
BETTER TOGETHER!

BY FALZAR AND THIERRY CULLIFORD

ILLUSTRATED BY ANTONELLO DALENA
AND PAOLO MADDALENI

AMULET BOOKS • NEW YORK

Library of Congress Control Number 2021948105

ISBN 978-1-4197-5539-2

Original lettering by Michel Brun
Book design by Brenda E. Angelilli

Represented by:
I.M.P.S. s.a.
Rue du Cerf 85
1332 Genval
Belgique

Printed and bound in China
10 9 8 7 6 5 4 3 2 1

ABRAMS The Art of Books
195 Broadway, New York, NY 10007
abramsbooks.com

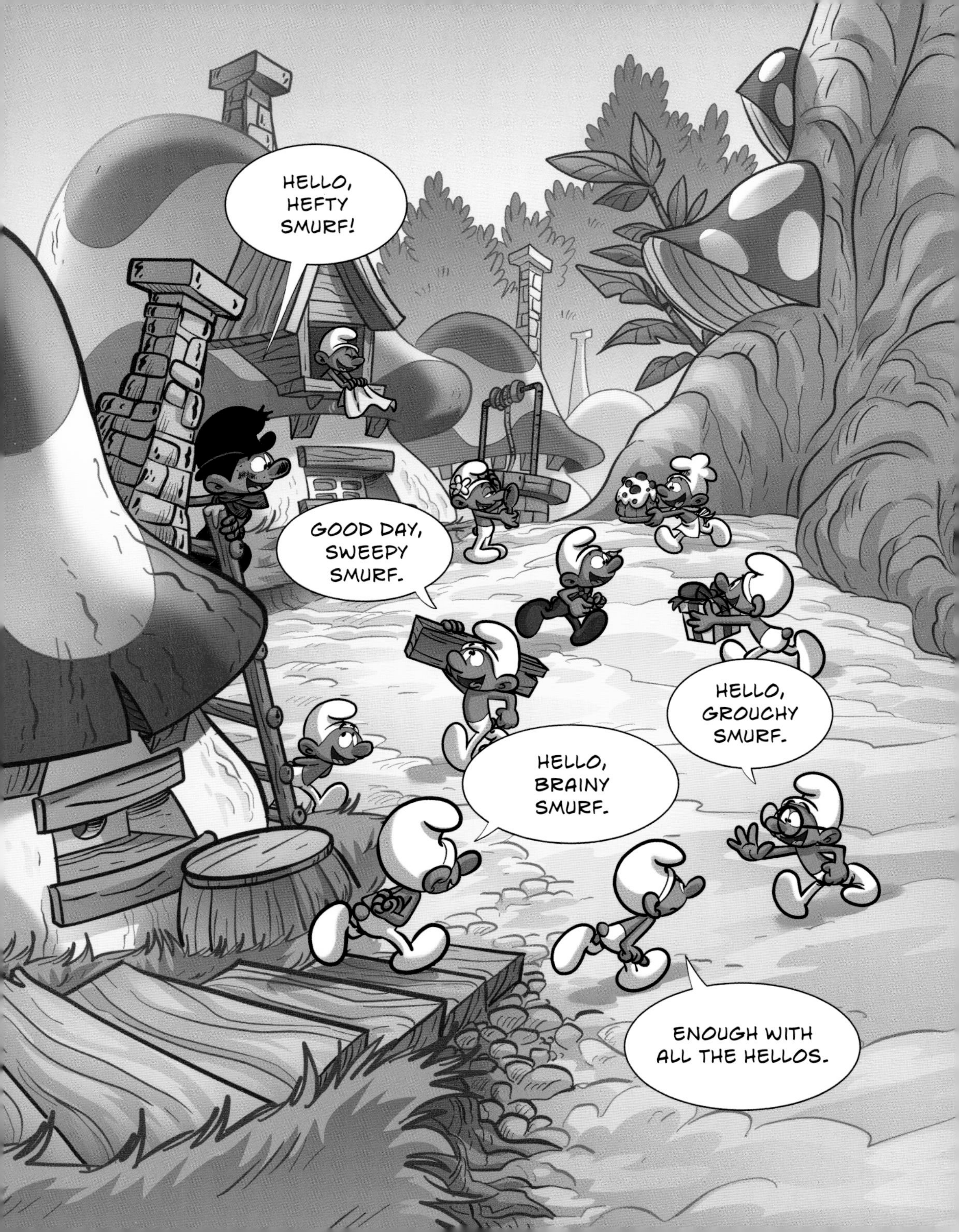
HELLO, HEFTY SMURF!
GOOD DAY, SWEEPY SMURF.
HELLO, GROUCHY SMURF.
HELLO, BRAINY SMURF.
ENOUGH WITH ALL THE HELLOS.

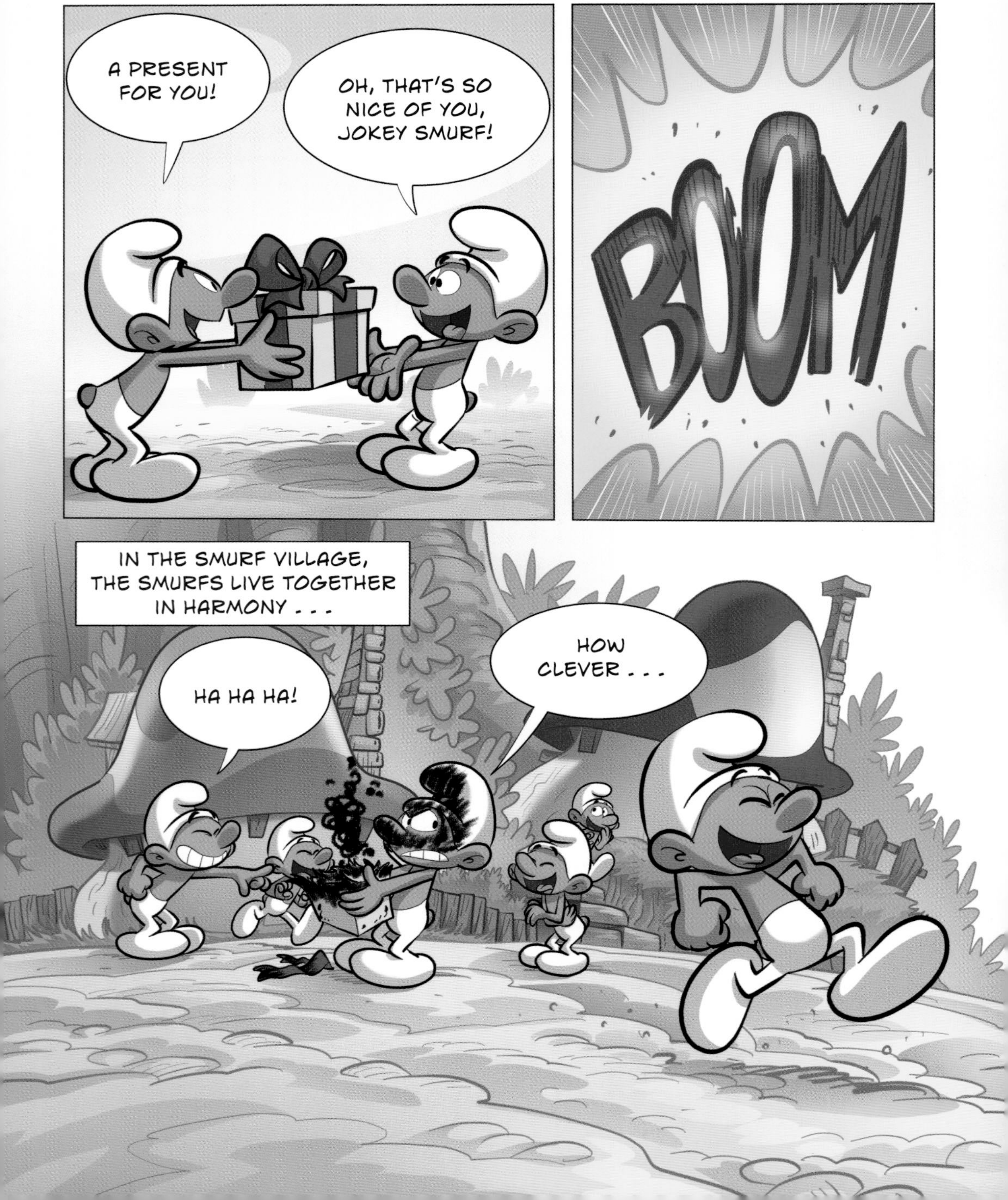
A PRESENT FOR YOU!
OH, THAT'S SO NICE OF YOU, JOKEY SMURF!
BOOM
IN THE SMURF VILLAGE, THE SMURFS LIVE TOGETHER IN HARMONY . . .
HA HA HA!
HOW CLEVER . . .

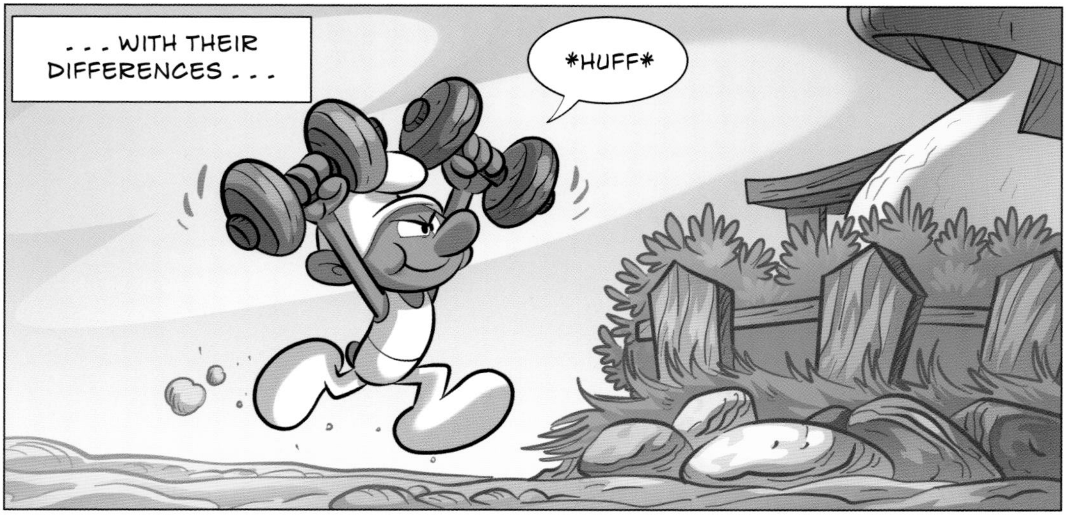
. . . WITH THEIR DIFFERENCES . . .
HUFF

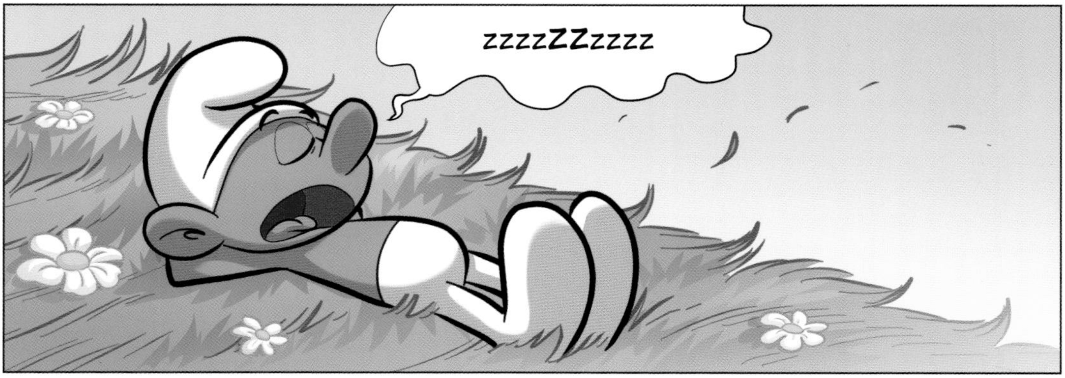
zzzzZZzzzz

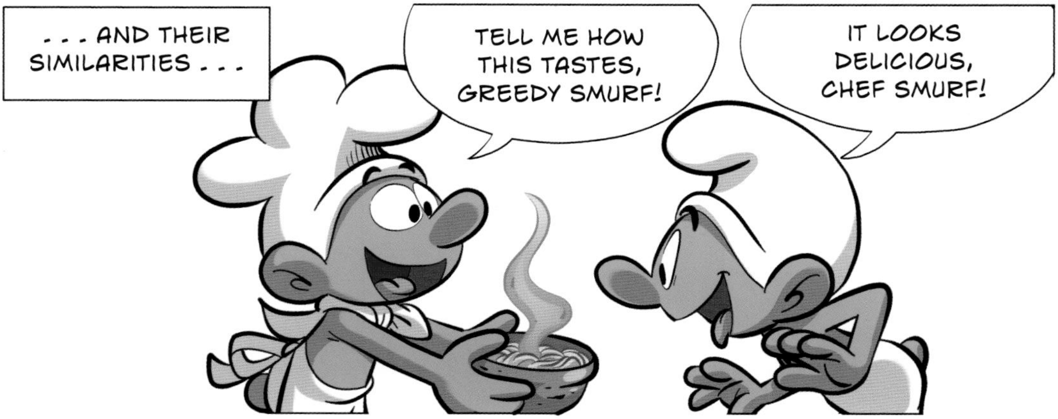
. . . AND THEIR SIMILARITIES . . .
TELL ME HOW THIS TASTES, GREEDY SMURF!
IT LOOKS DELICIOUS, CHEF SMURF!

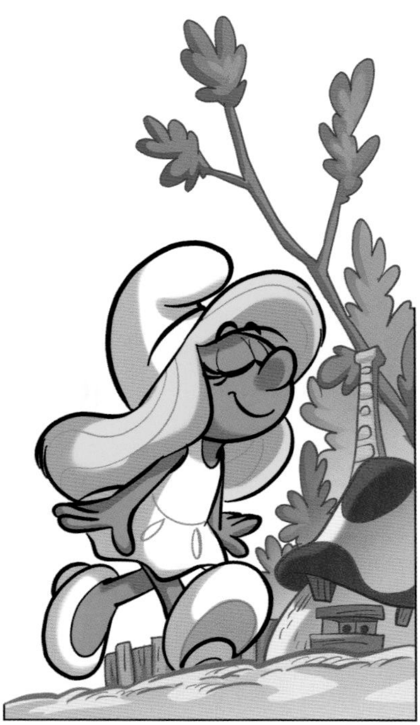

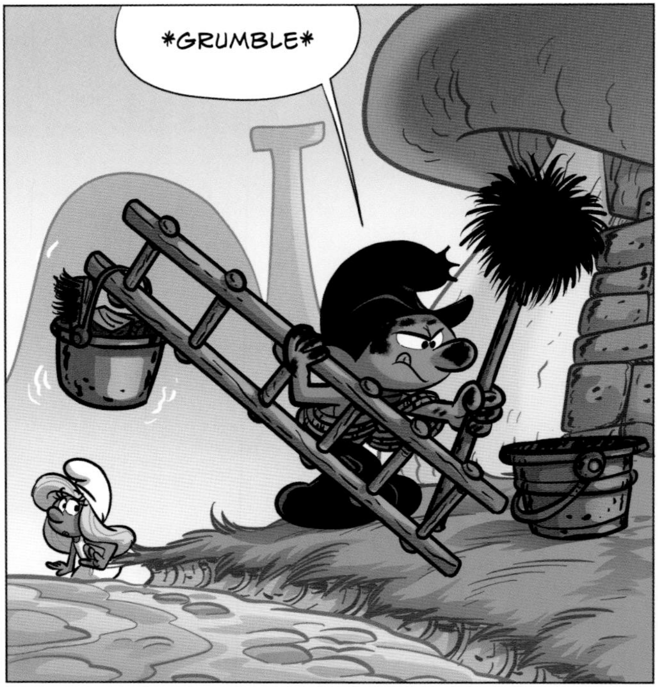
GRUMBLE

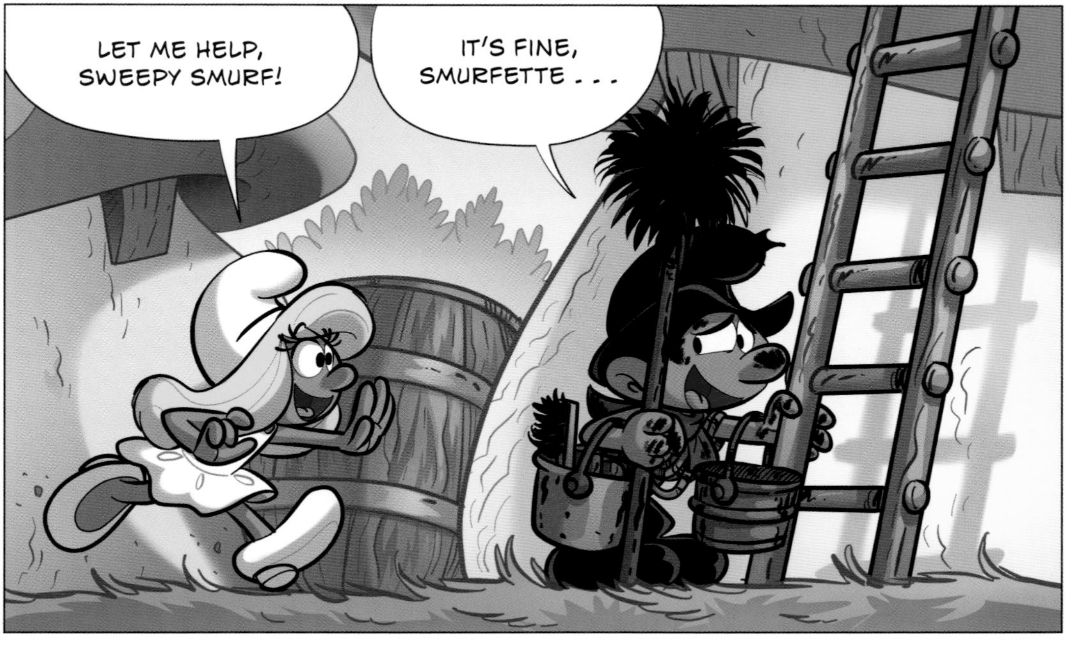
LET ME HELP, SWEEPY SMURF!
IT'S FINE, SMURFETTE . . .

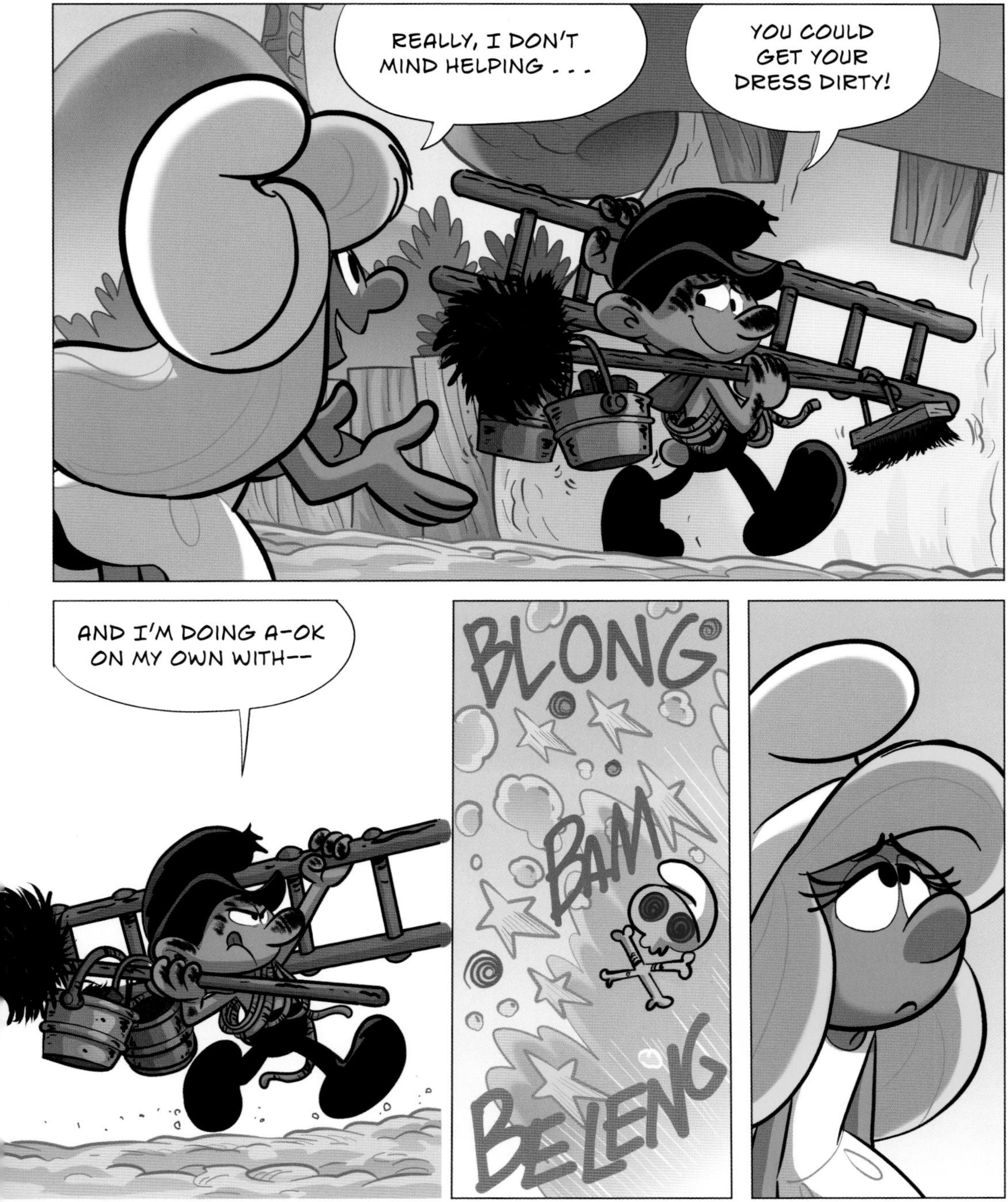
REALLY, I DON'T MIND HELPING . . .
YOU COULD GET YOUR DRESS DIRTY!
AND I'M DOING A-OK ON MY OWN WITH--
BLONG
BAM
BELENG

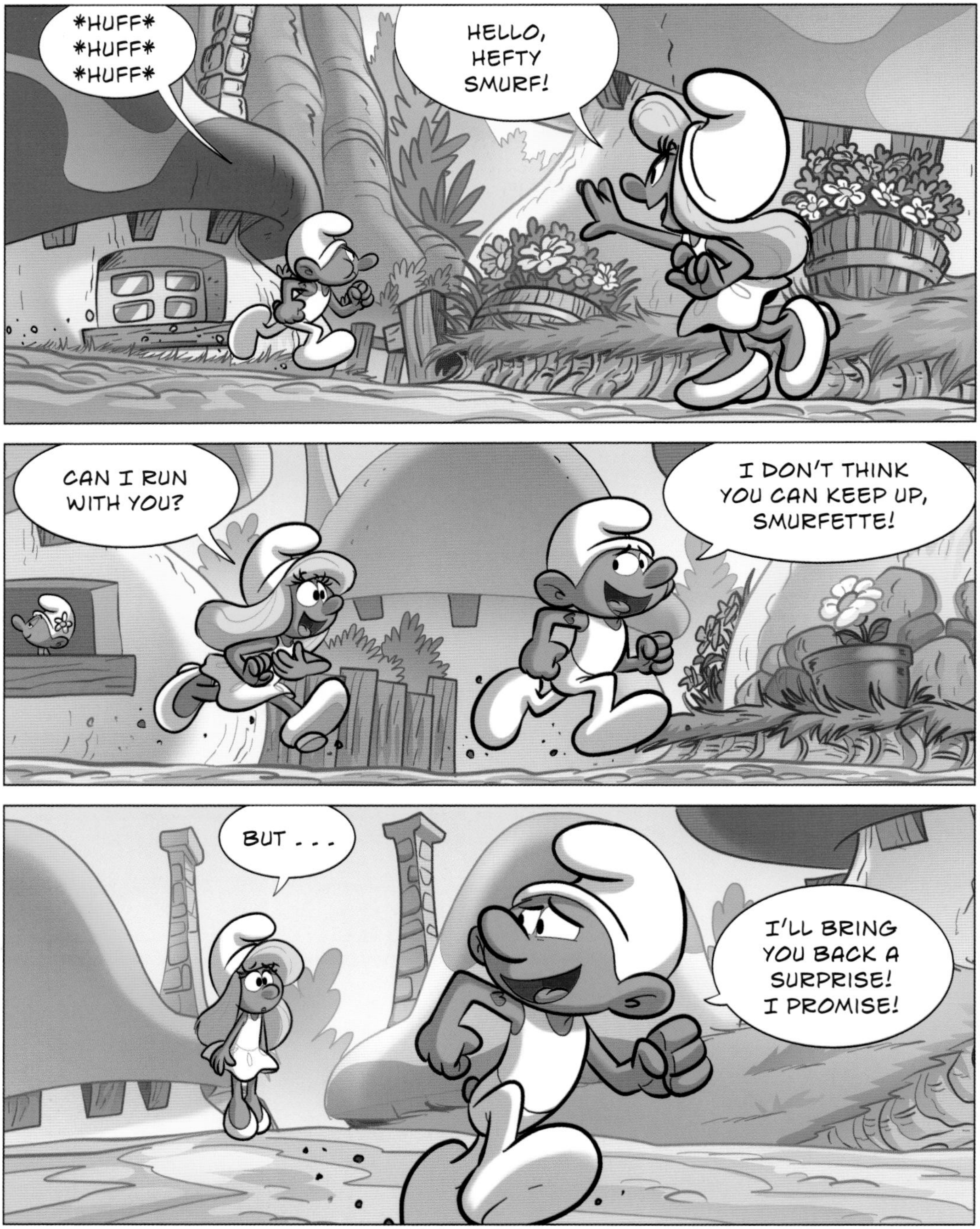
HUFF *HUFF* *HUFF*
HELLO, HEFTY SMURF!
CAN I RUN WITH YOU?
I DON'T THINK YOU CAN KEEP UP, SMURFETTE!
BUT . . .
I'LL BRING YOU BACK A SURPRISE! I PROMISE!

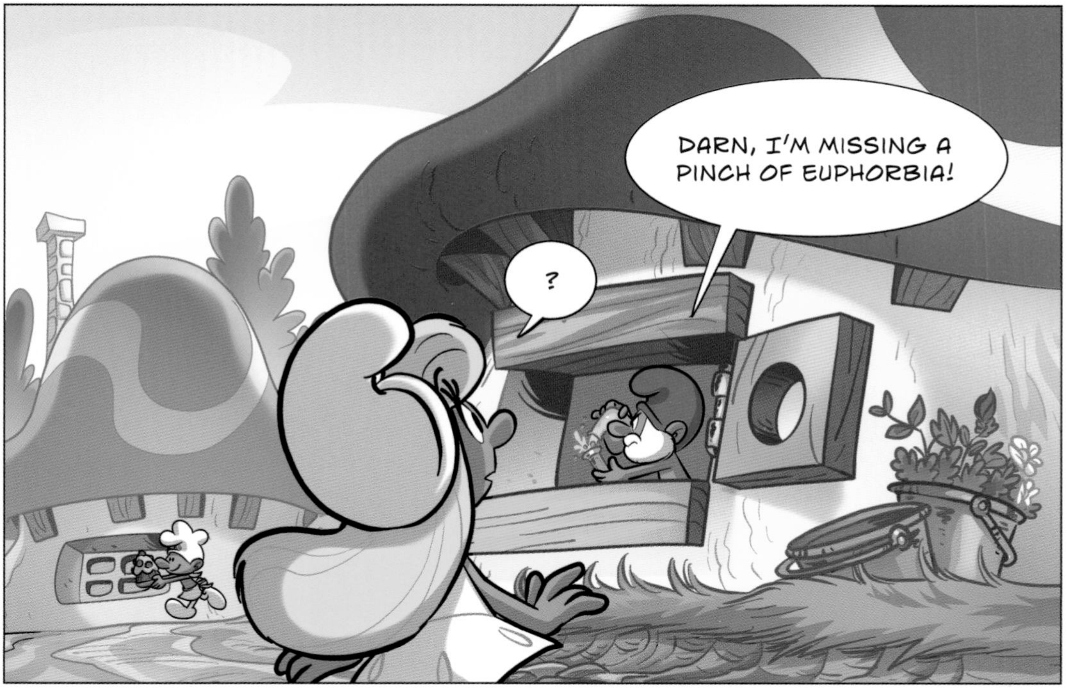
?
DARN, I'M MISSING A PINCH OF EUPHORBIA!

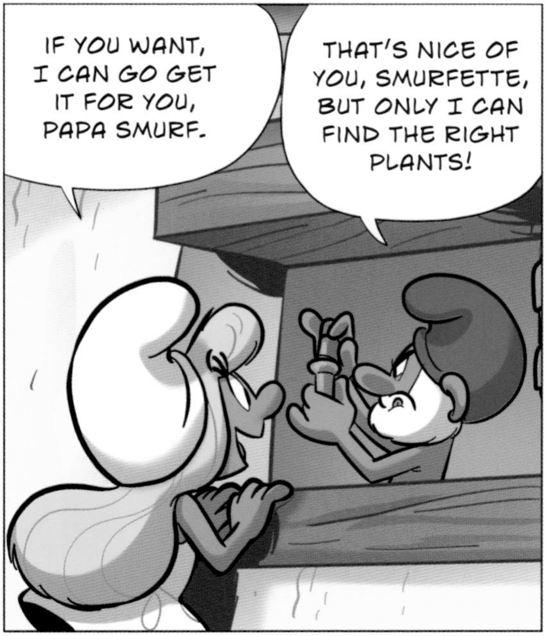
IF YOU WANT, I CAN GO GET IT FOR YOU, PAPA SMURF.
THAT'S NICE OF YOU, SMURFETTE, BUT ONLY I CAN FIND THE RIGHT PLANTS!

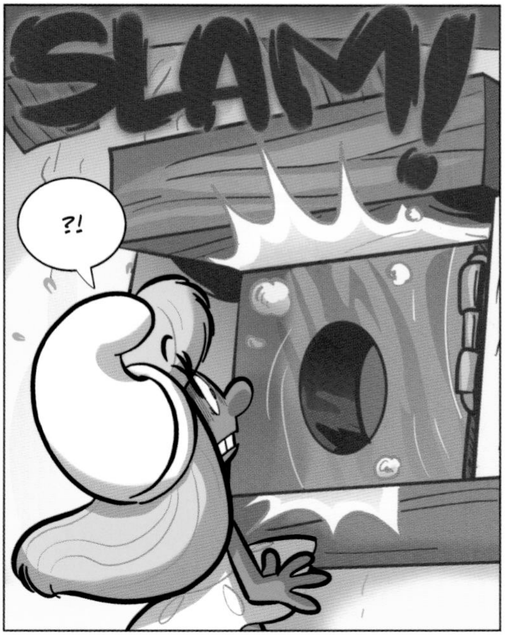
SLAM!
?!

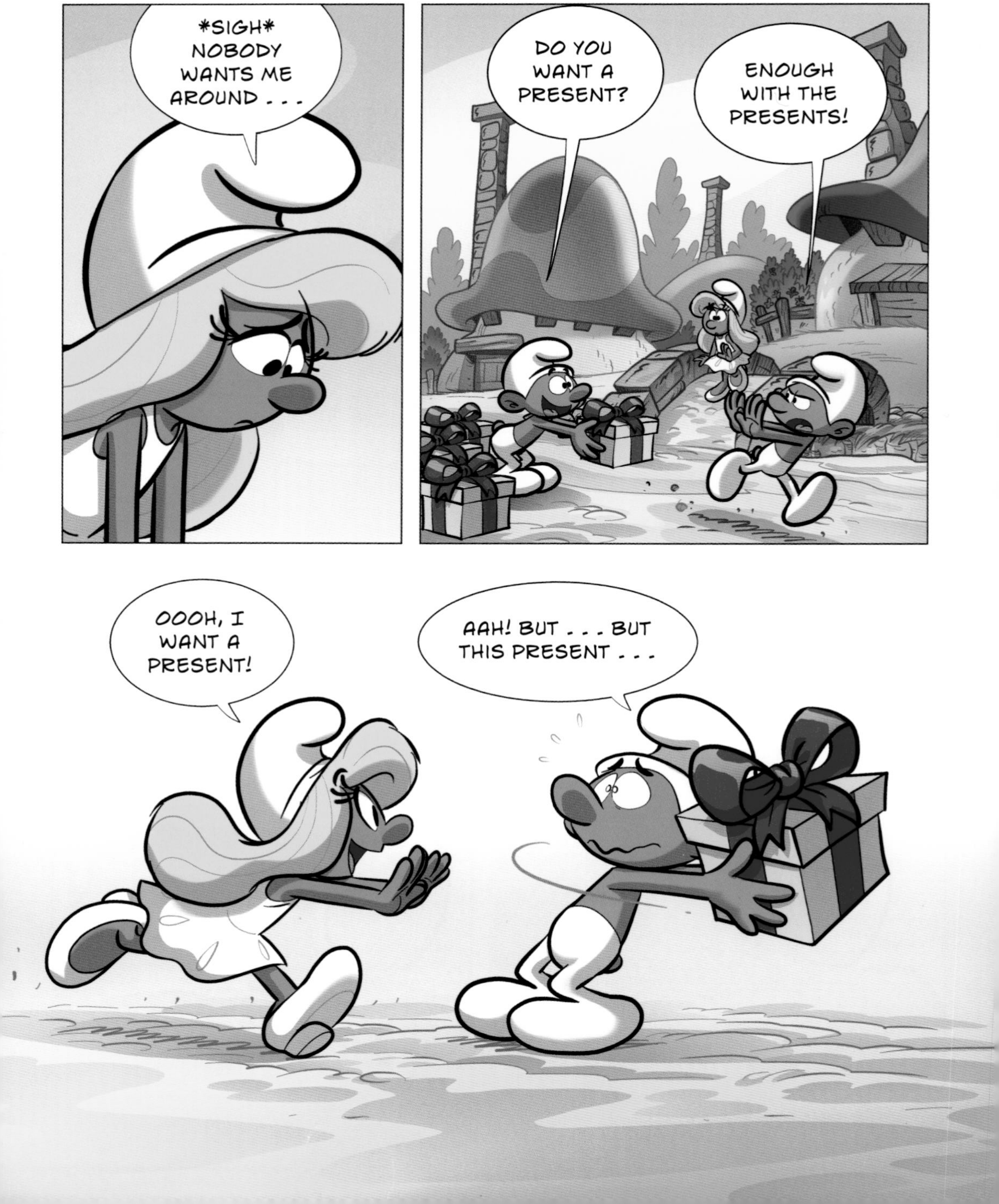
SIGH NOBODY WANTS ME AROUND . . .
DO YOU WANT A PRESENT?
ENOUGH WITH THE PRESENTS!
OOOH, I WANT A PRESENT!
AAH! BUT . . . BUT THIS PRESENT . . .

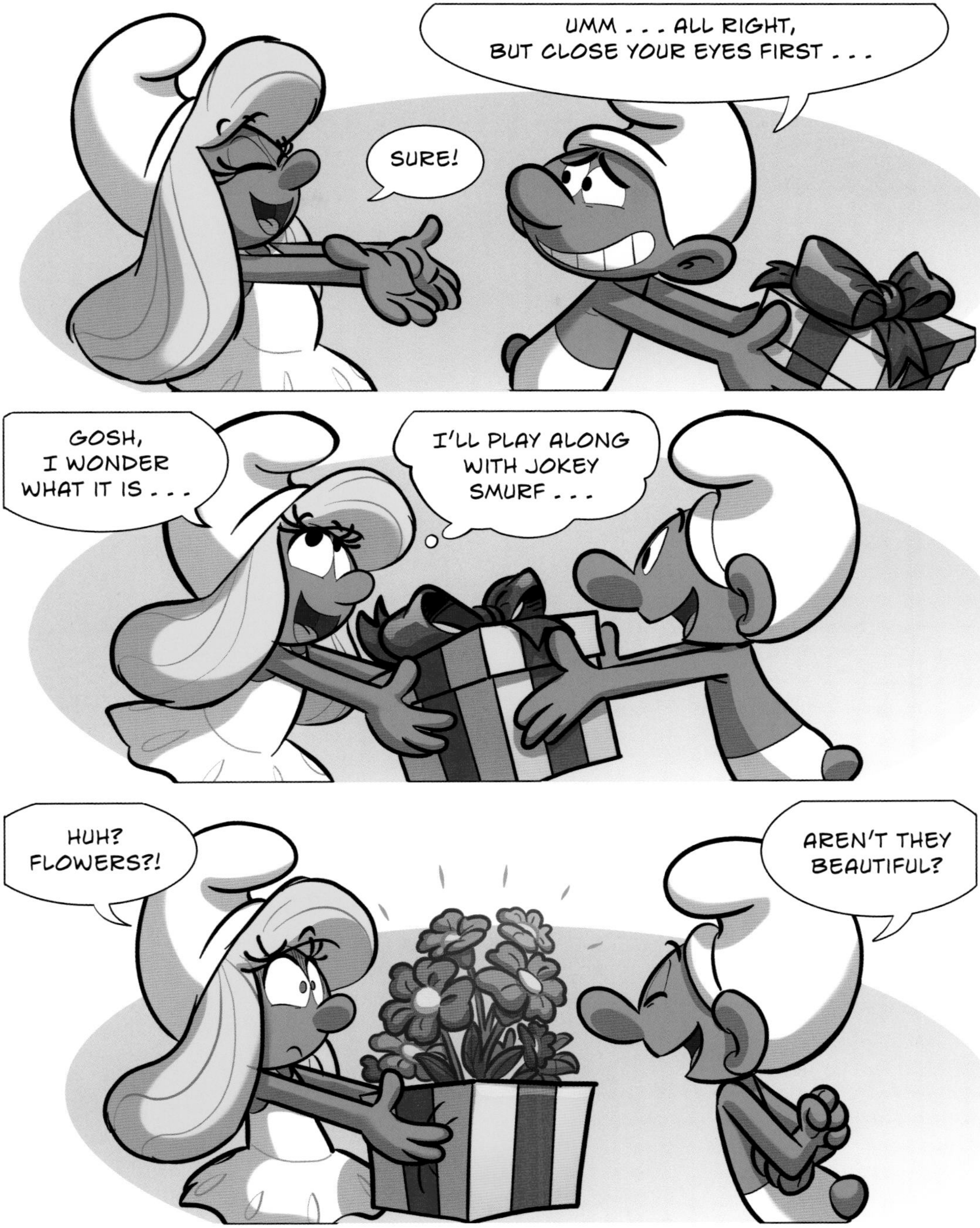
UMM . . . ALL RIGHT, BUT CLOSE YOUR EYES FIRST . . .
SURE!
GOSH, I WONDER WHAT IT IS . . .
I'LL PLAY ALONG WITH JOKEY SMURF . . .
HUH? FLOWERS?!
AREN'T THEY BEAUTIFUL?

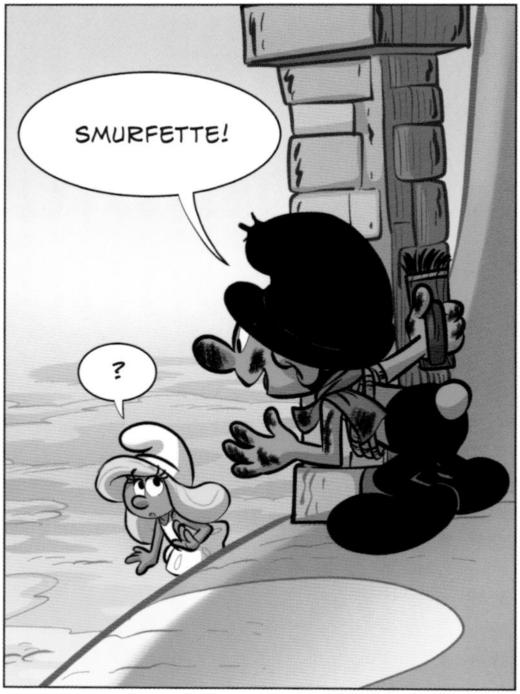
SMURFETTE!
?

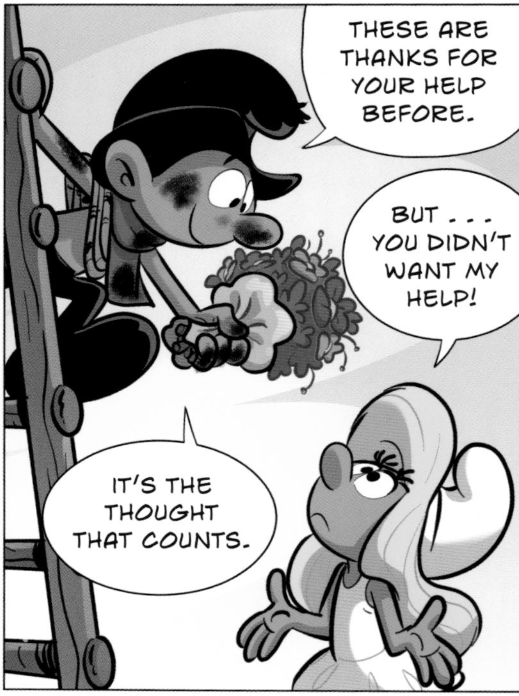
THESE ARE THANKS FOR YOUR HELP BEFORE.
BUT . . . YOU DIDN'T WANT MY HELP!
IT'S THE THOUGHT THAT COUNTS.

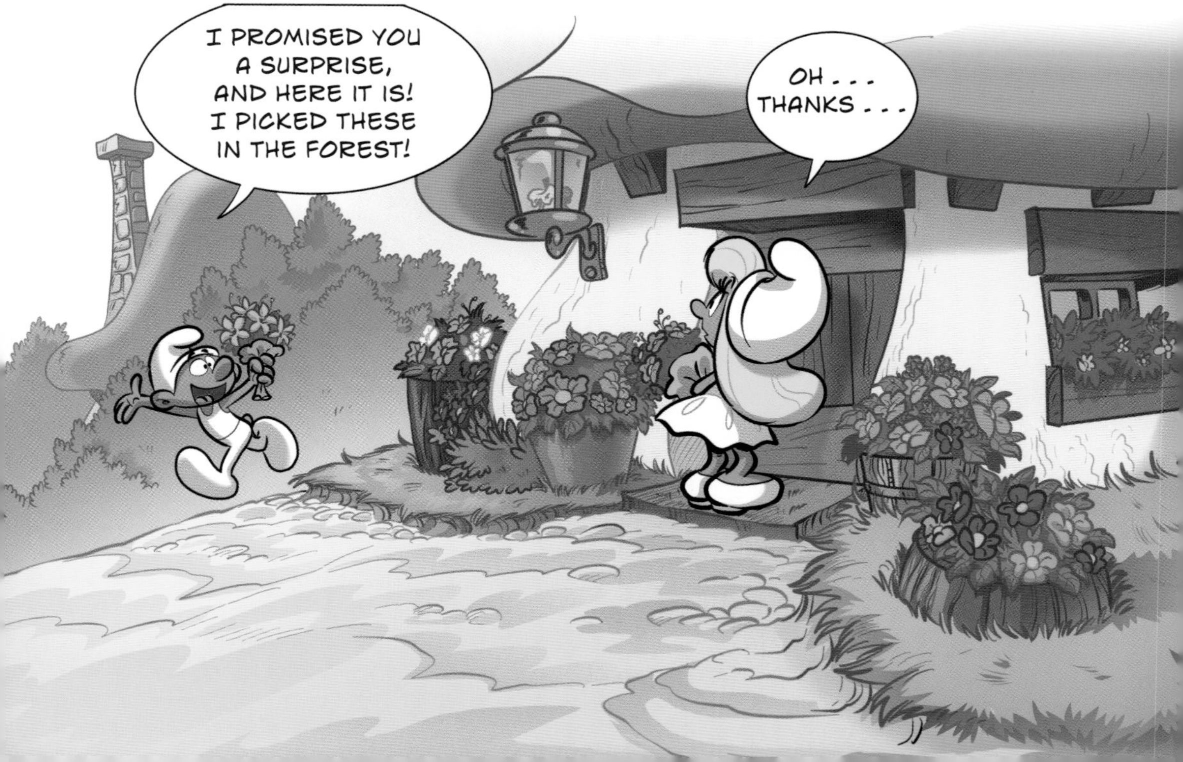
I PROMISED YOU A SURPRISE, AND HERE IT IS! I PICKED THESE IN THE FOREST!
OH . . . THANKS . . .

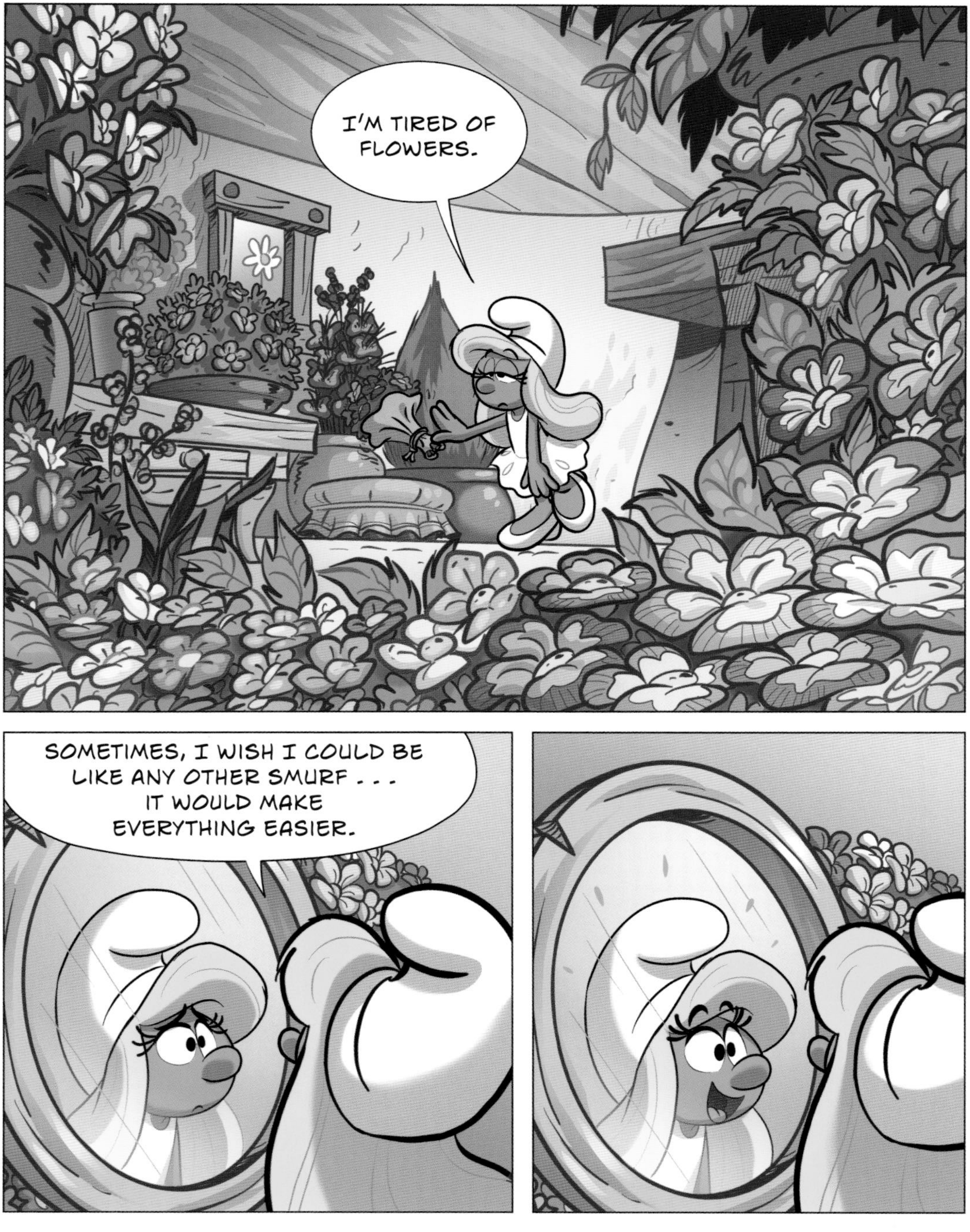
I'M TIRED OF FLOWERS.
SOMETIMES, I WISH I COULD BE LIKE ANY OTHER SMURF . . . IT WOULD MAKE EVERYTHING EASIER.

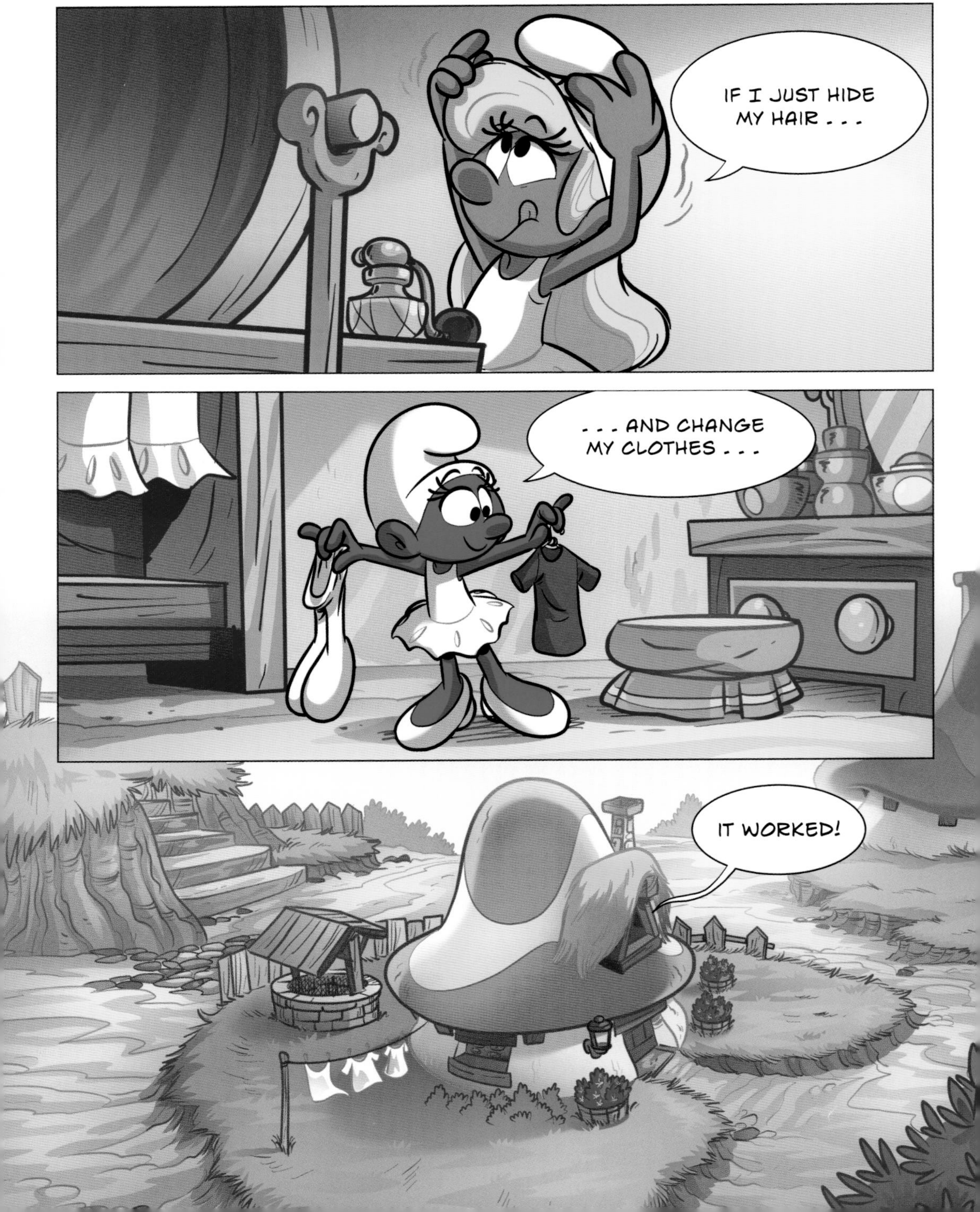
IF I JUST HIDE MY HAIR . . .
. . . AND CHANGE MY CLOTHES . . .
IT WORKED!

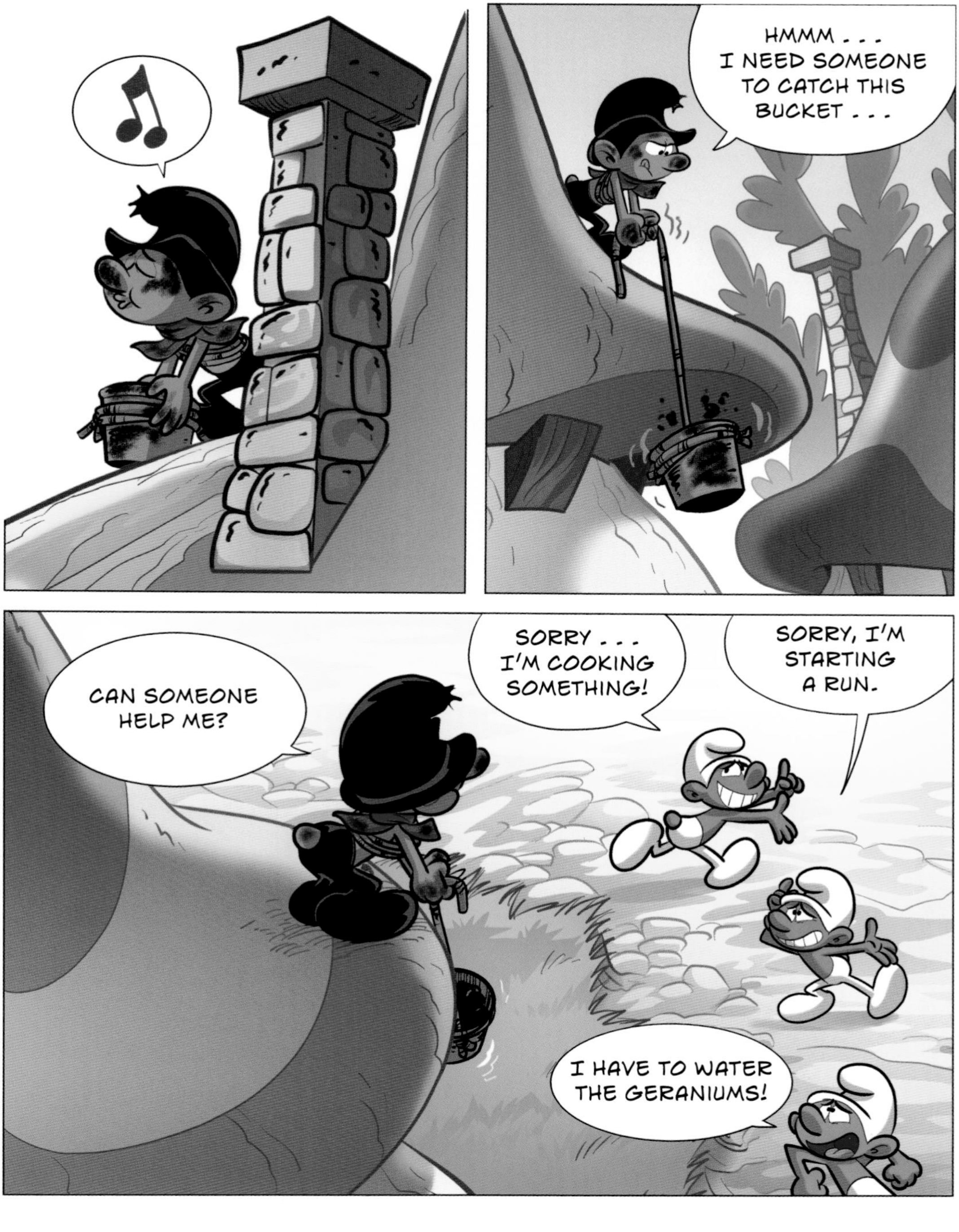
HMMM . . .
I NEED SOMEONE TO CATCH THIS BUCKET . . .
CAN SOMEONE HELP ME?
SORRY . . . I'M COOKING SOMETHING!
SORRY, I'M STARTING A RUN.
I HAVE TO WATER THE GERANIUMS!

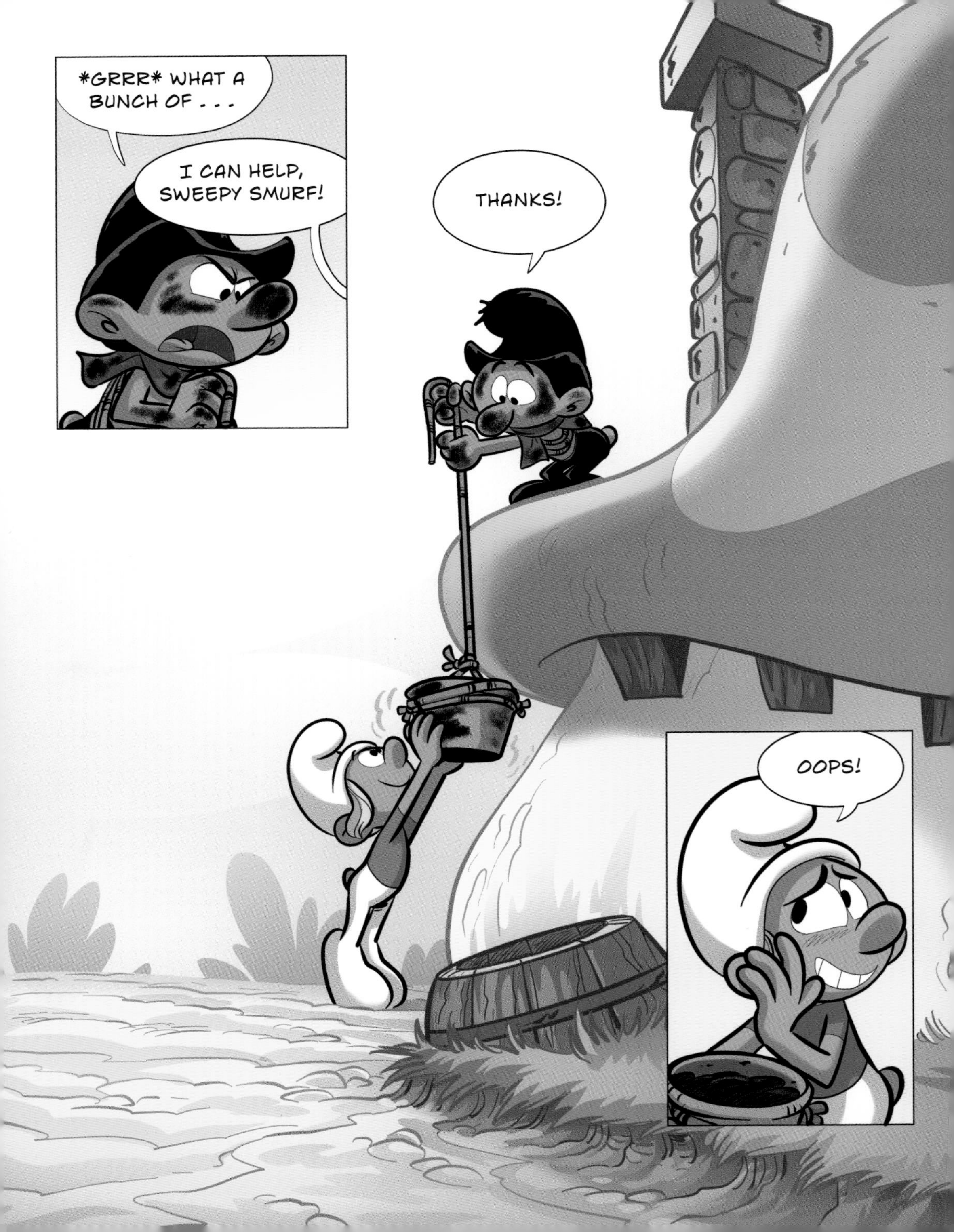
GRRR WHAT A BUNCH OF . . .
I CAN HELP, SWEEPY SMURF!
THANKS!
OOPS!

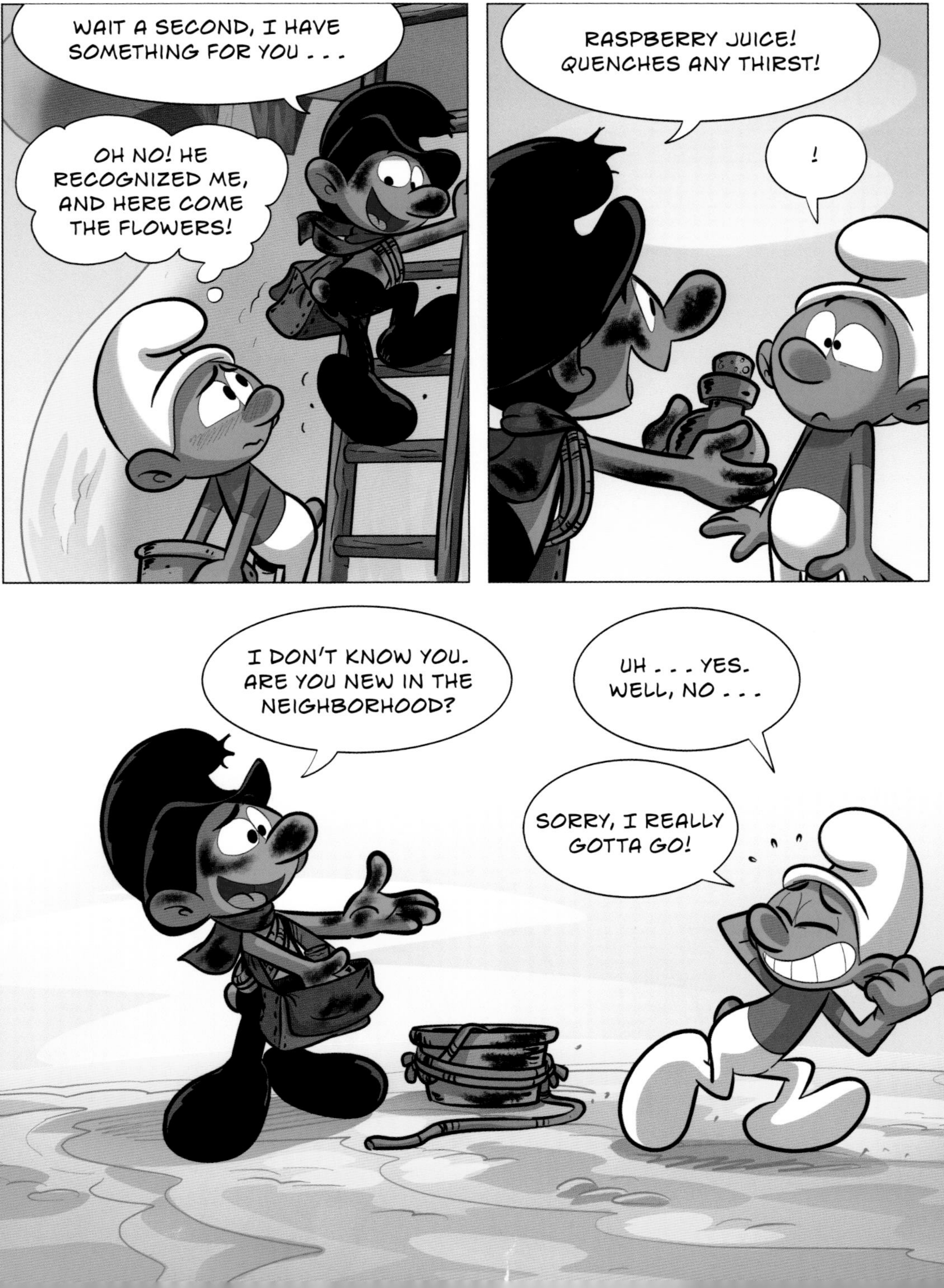
WAIT A SECOND, I HAVE SOMETHING FOR YOU . . .
OH NO! HE RECOGNIZED ME, AND HERE COME THE FLOWERS!
RASPBERRY JUICE! QUENCHES ANY THIRST!
!
I DON'T KNOW YOU. ARE YOU NEW IN THE NEIGHBORHOOD?
UH . . . YES. WELL, NO . . .
SORRY, I REALLY GOTTA GO!

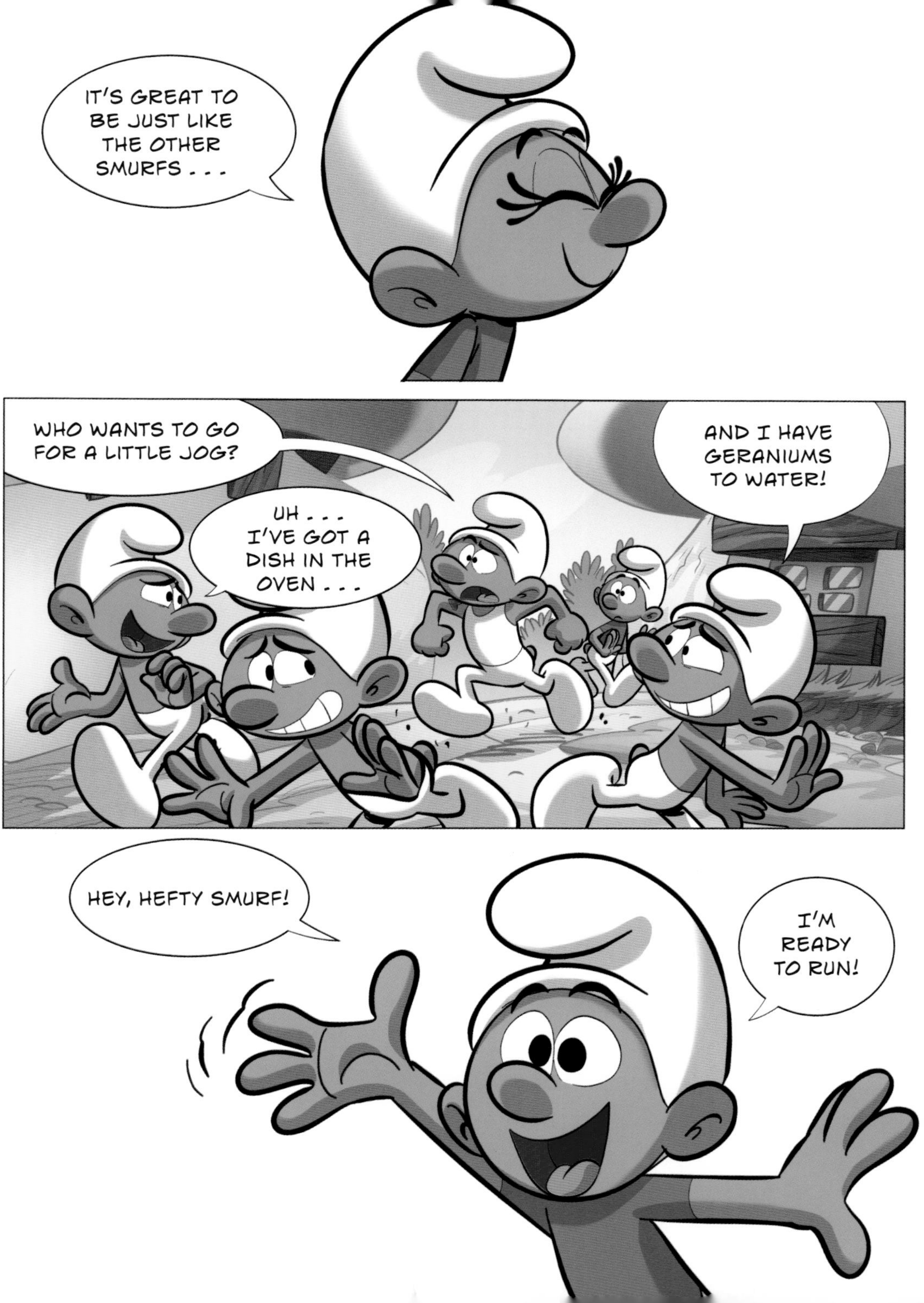
IT'S GREAT TO BE JUST LIKE THE OTHER SMURFS . . .
WHO WANTS TO GO FOR A LITTLE JOG?
UH . . . I'VE GOT A DISH IN THE OVEN . . .
AND I HAVE GERANIUMS TO WATER!
HEY, HEFTY SMURF!
I'M READY TO RUN!

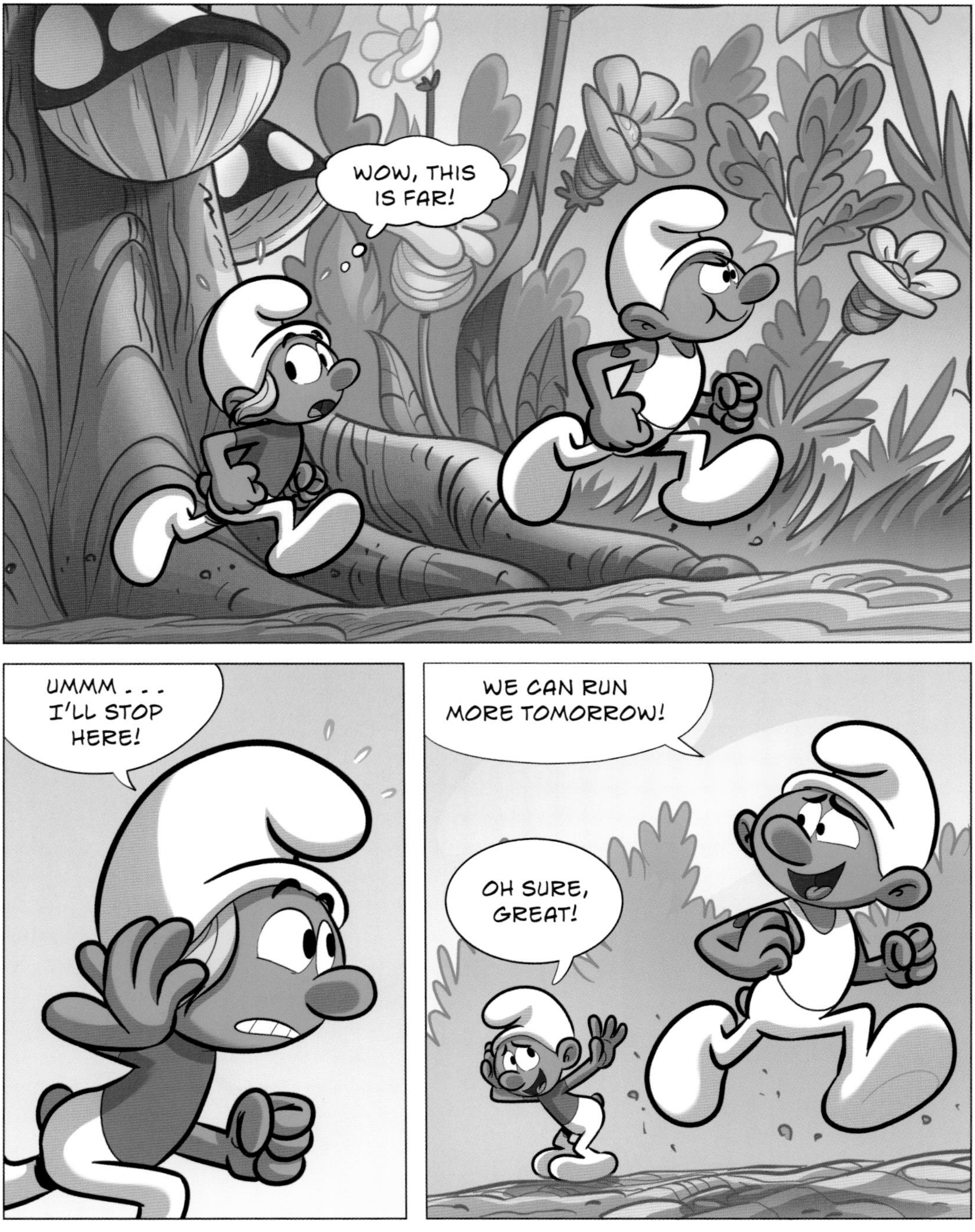
WOW, THIS IS FAR!
UMMM . . . I'LL STOP HERE!
WE CAN RUN MORE TOMORROW!
OH SURE, GREAT!

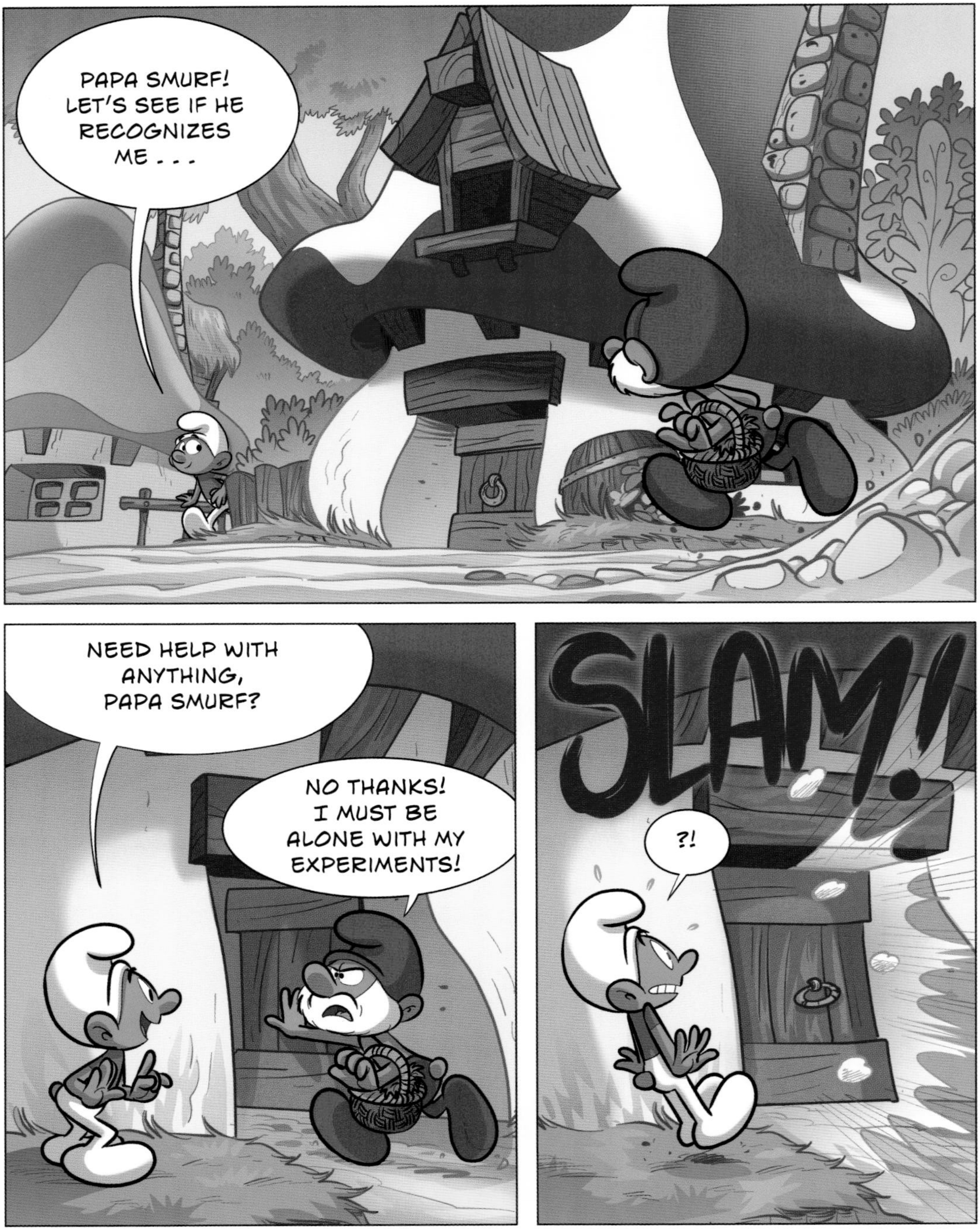
PAPA SMURF! LET'S SEE IF HE RECOGNIZES ME . . .
NEED HELP WITH ANYTHING, PAPA SMURF?
NO THANKS! I MUST BE ALONE WITH MY EXPERIMENTS!
SLAM!!
?!

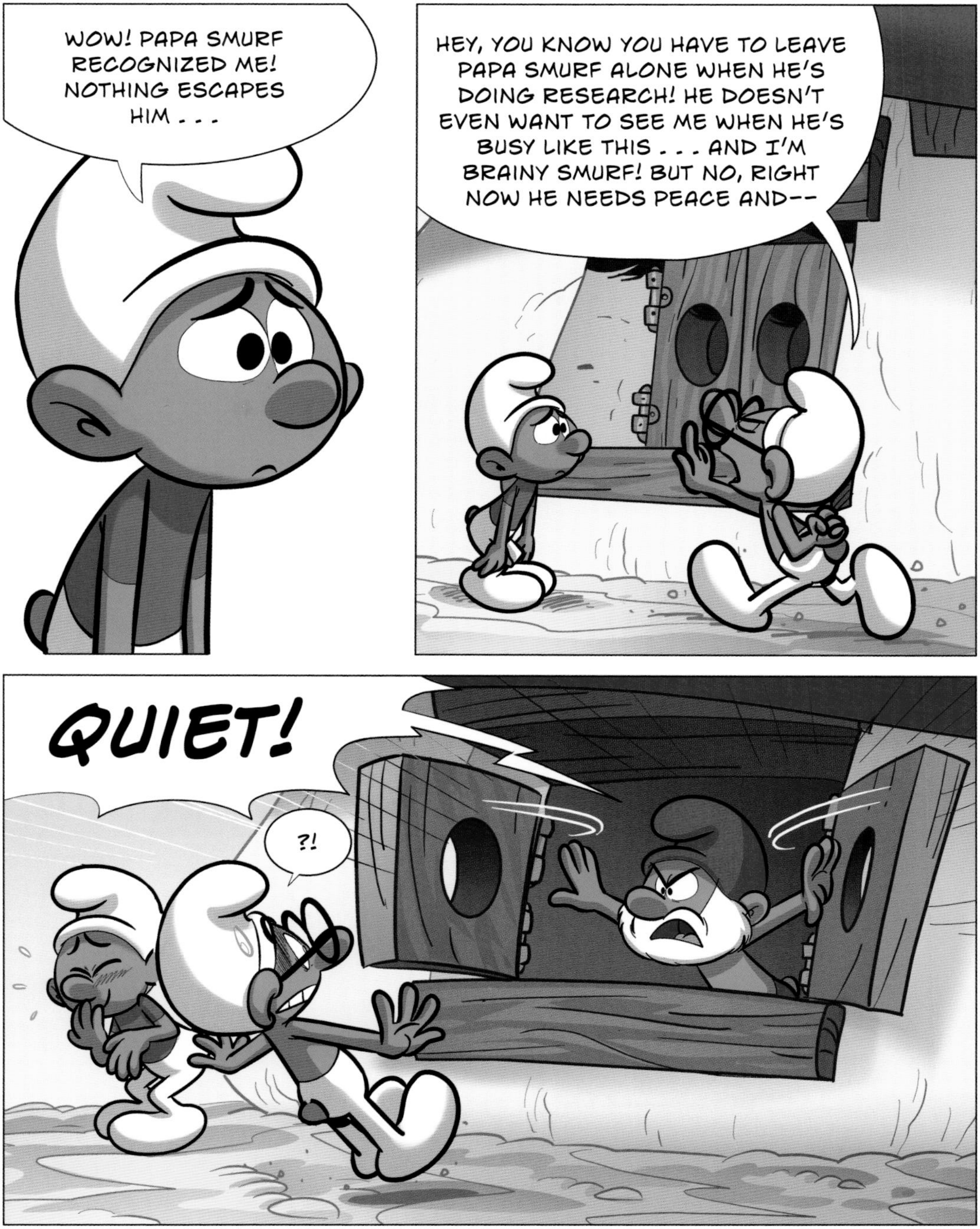
WOW! PAPA SMURF RECOGNIZED ME! NOTHING ESCAPES HIM . . .
HEY, YOU KNOW YOU HAVE TO LEAVE PAPA SMURF ALONE WHEN HE'S DOING RESEARCH! HE DOESN'T EVEN WANT TO SEE ME WHEN HE'S BUSY LIKE THIS . . . AND I'M BRAINY SMURF! BUT NO, RIGHT NOW HE NEEDS PEACE AND--
QUIET!
?!

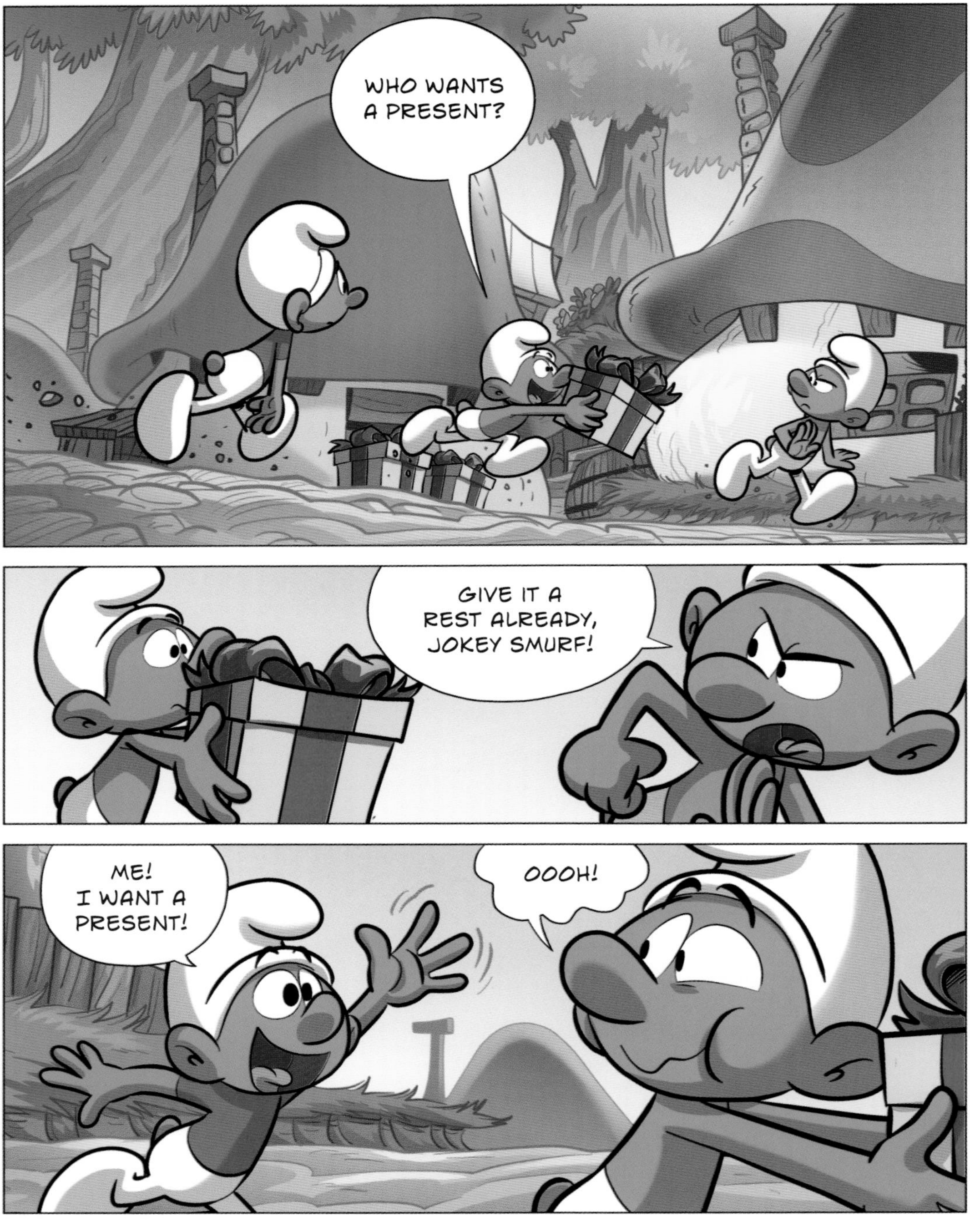
WHO WANTS A PRESENT?
GIVE IT A REST ALREADY, JOKEY SMURF!
ME! I WANT A PRESENT!
OOOH!

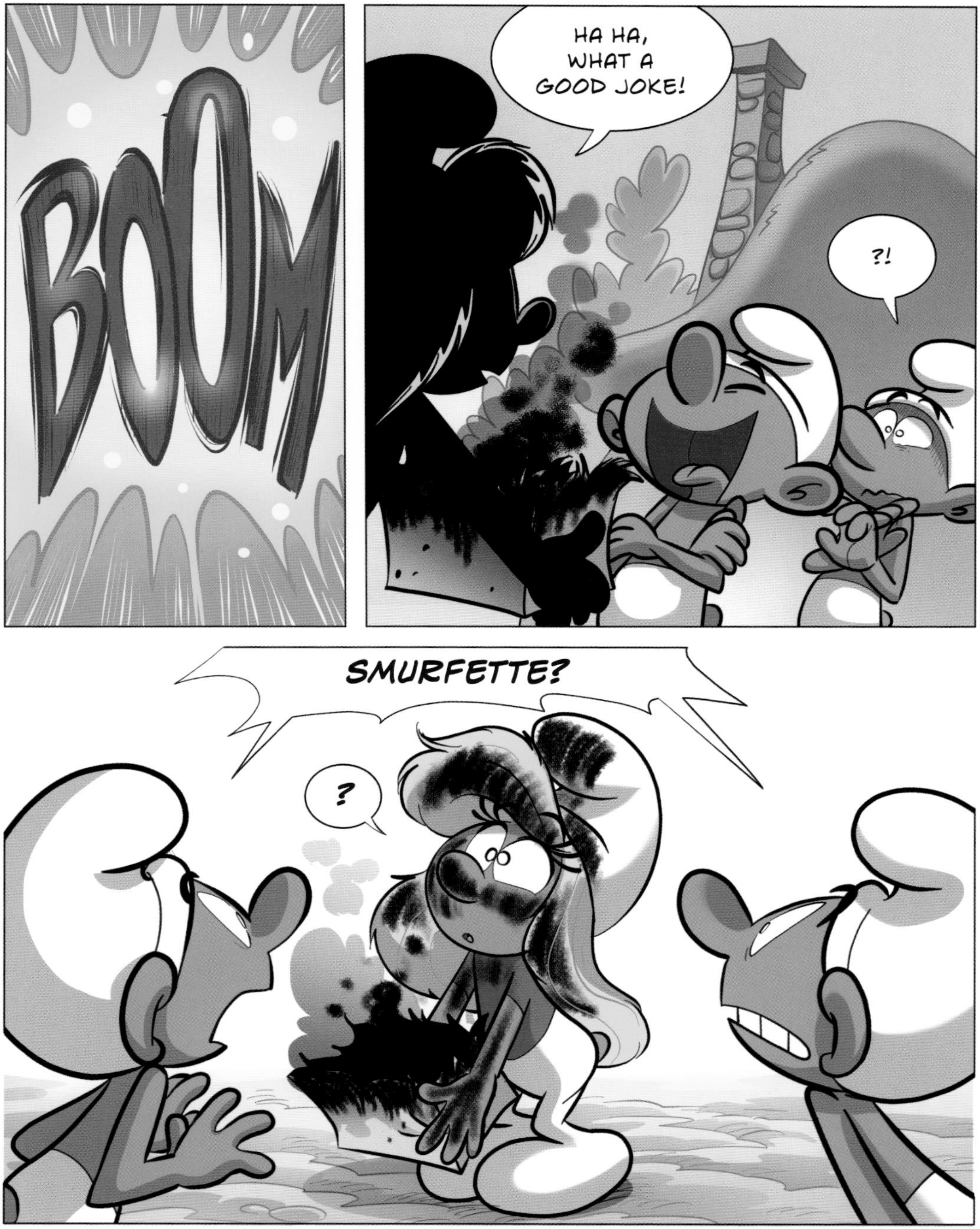
BOOM
HA HA, WHAT A GOOD JOKE!
?!
SMURFETTE?
?

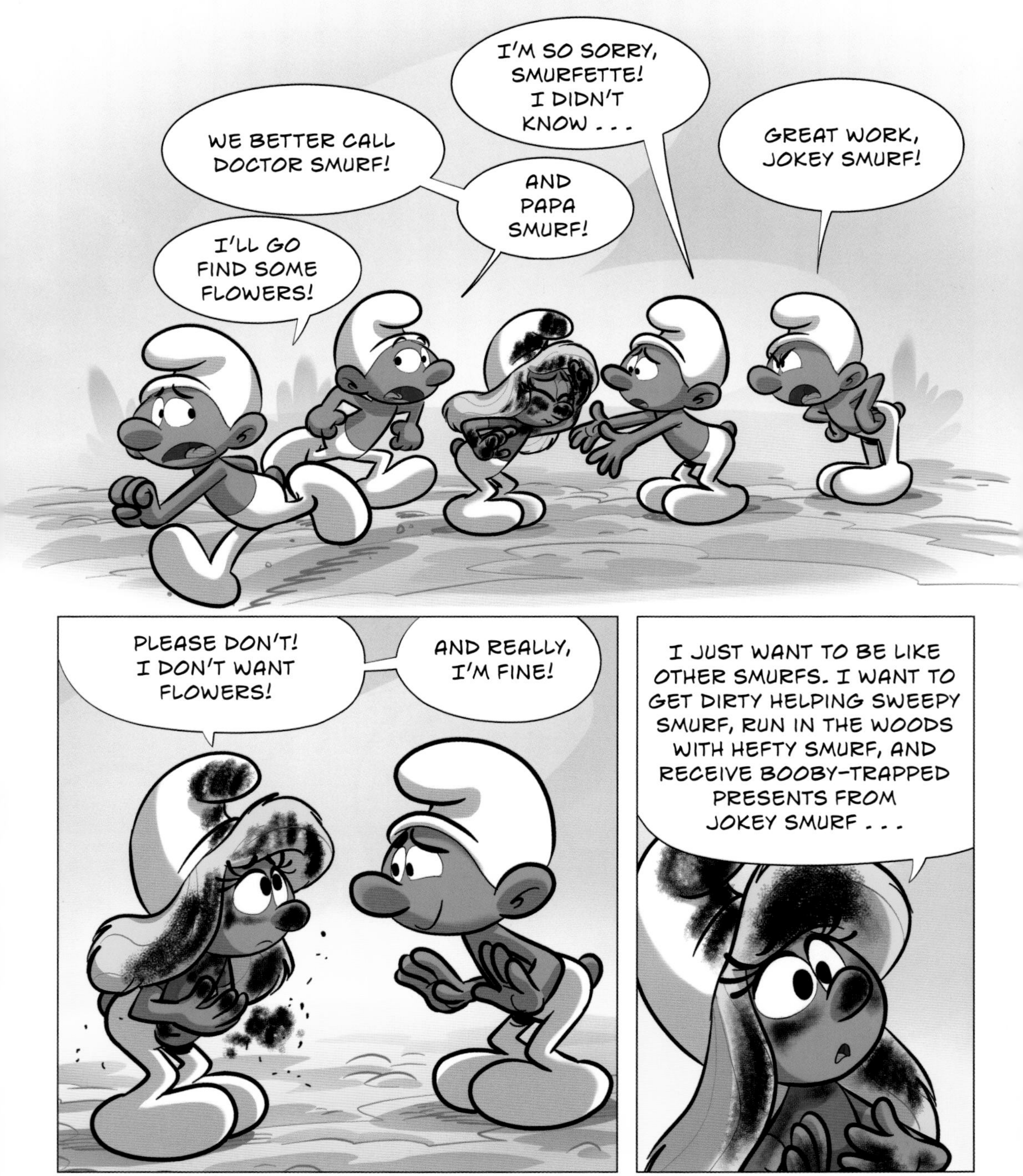
I'LL GO FIND SOME FLOWERS!
WE BETTER CALL DOCTOR SMURF!
AND PAPA SMURF!
I'M SO SORRY, SMURFETTE! I DIDN'T KNOW . . .
GREAT WORK, JOKEY SMURF!
PLEASE DON'T! I DON'T WANT FLOWERS!
AND REALLY, I'M FINE!
I JUST WANT TO BE LIKE OTHER SMURFS. I WANT TO GET DIRTY HELPING SWEEPY SMURF, RUN IN THE WOODS WITH HEFTY SMURF, AND RECEIVE BOOBY-TRAPPED PRESENTS FROM JOKEY SMURF . . .

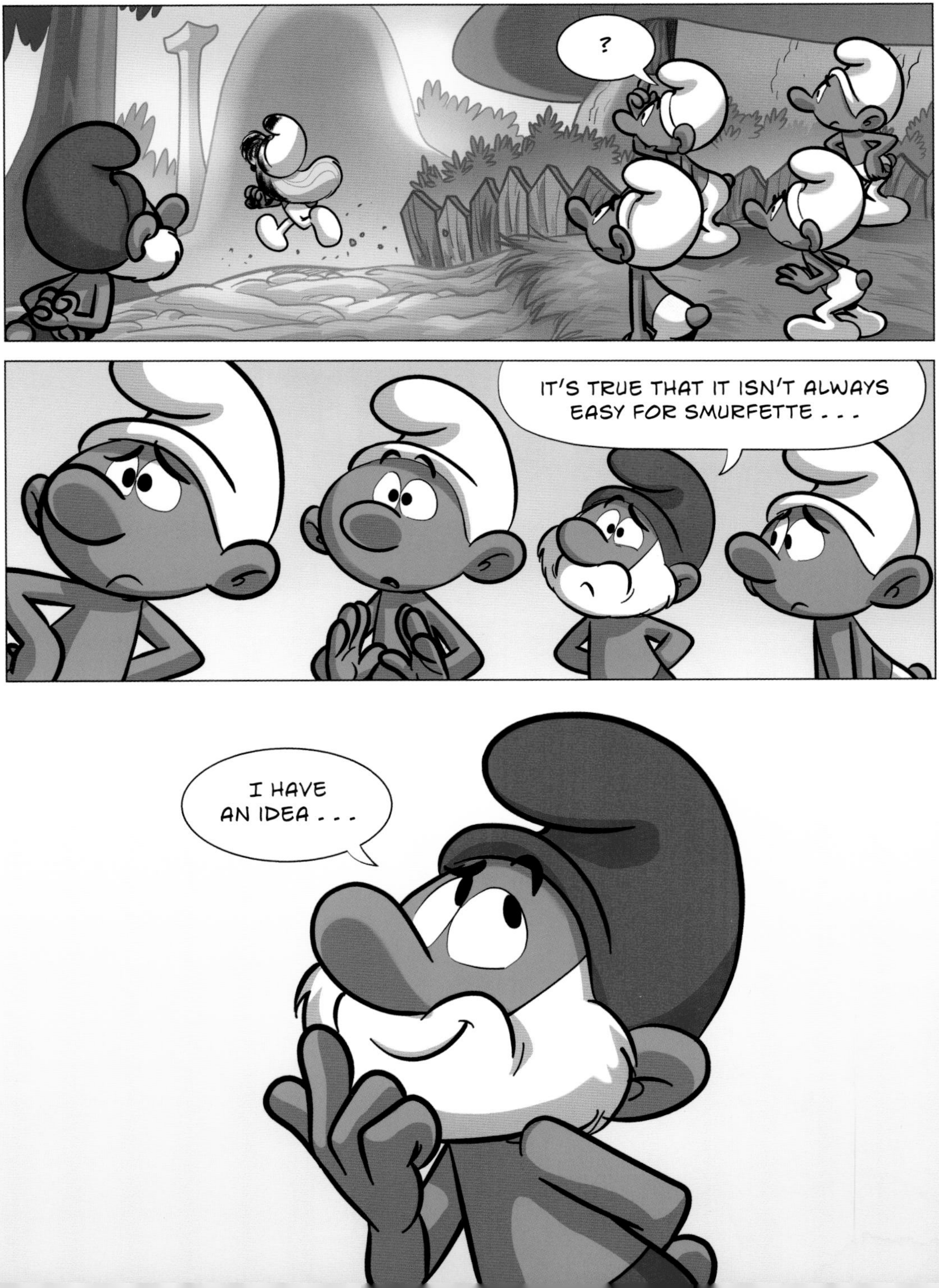
?
IT'S TRUE THAT IT ISN'T ALWAYS EASY FOR SMURFETTE . . .
I HAVE AN IDEA . . .

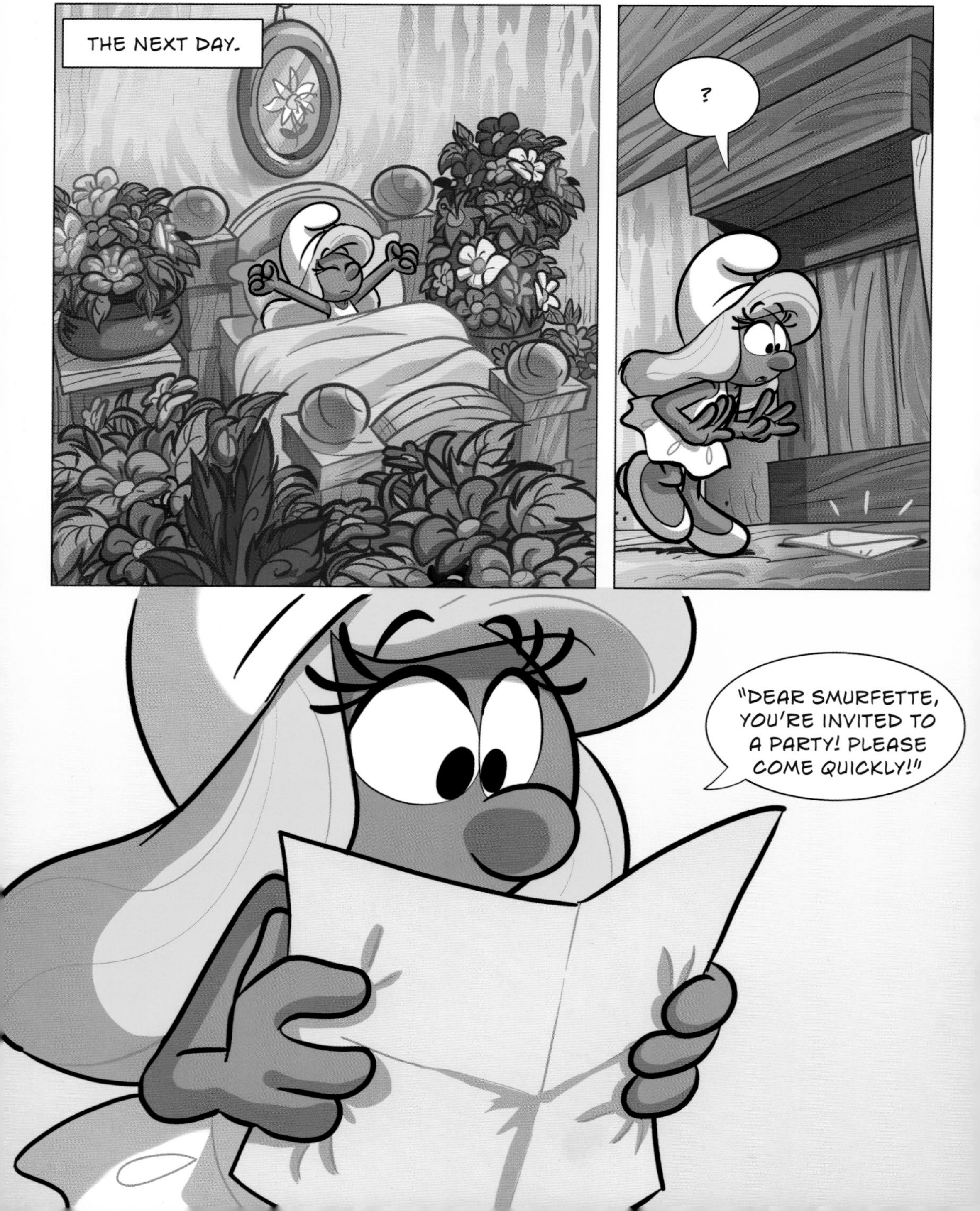
THE NEXT DAY.
?
"DEAR SMURFETTE, YOU'RE INVITED TO A PARTY! PLEASE COME QUICKLY!"

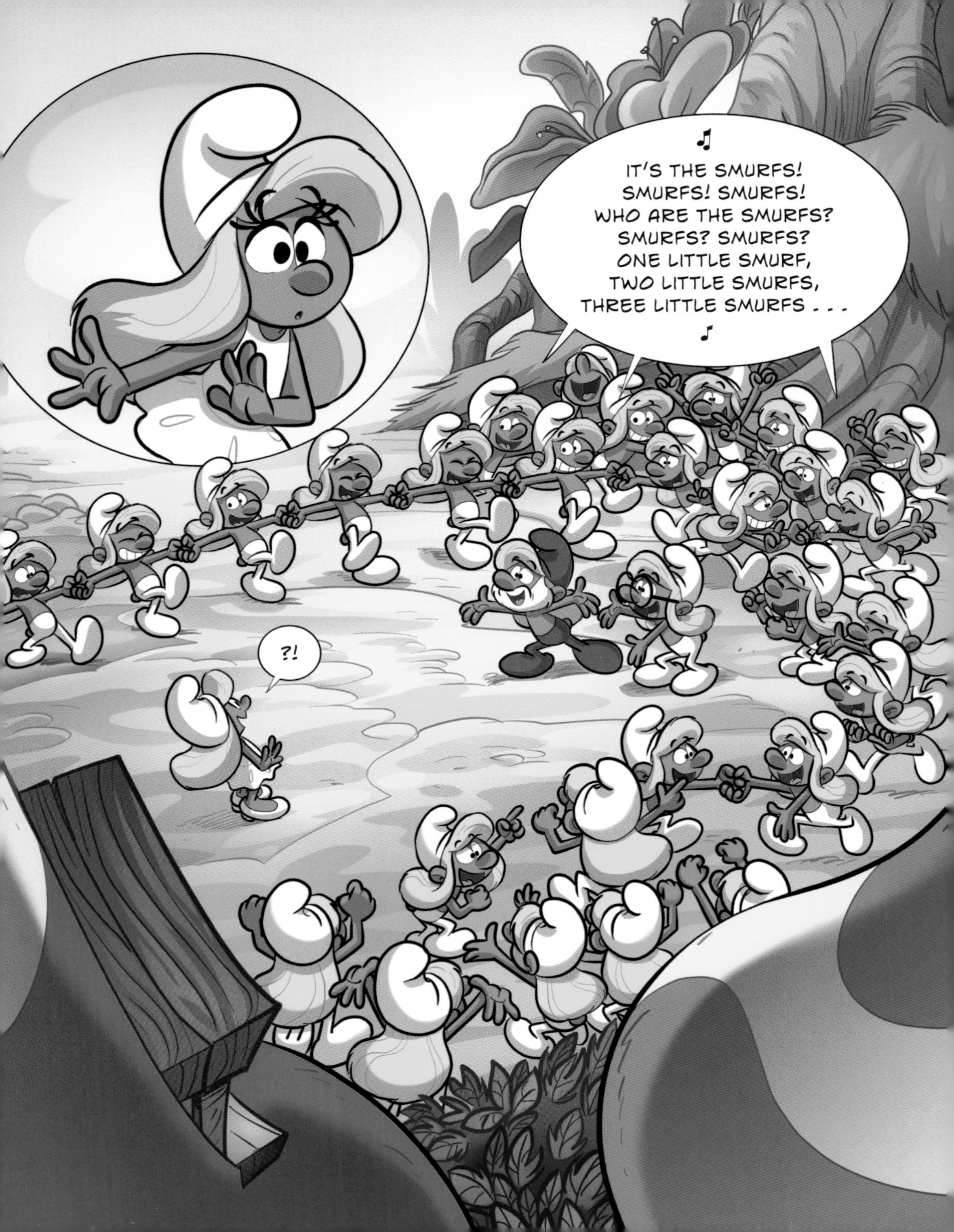
♪ IT'S THE SMURFS! SMURFS! SMURFS! WHO ARE THE SMURFS? SMURFS? SMURFS? ONE LITTLE SMURF, TWO LITTLE SMURFS, THREE LITTLE SMURFS . . . ♪
?!

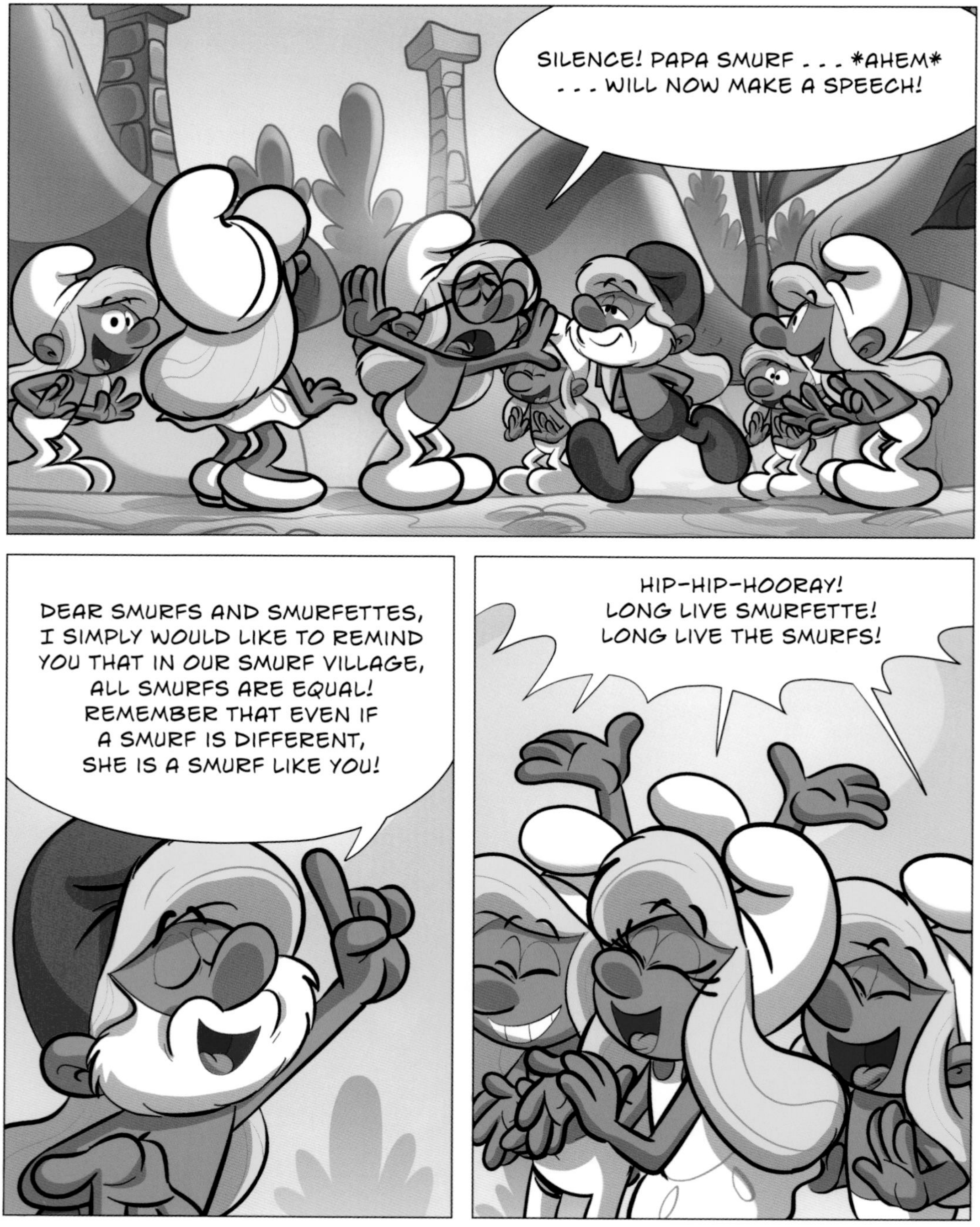
SILENCE! PAPA SMURF . . . *AHEM* . . . WILL NOW MAKE A SPEECH!
DEAR SMURFS AND SMURFETTES, I SIMPLY WOULD LIKE TO REMIND YOU THAT IN OUR SMURF VILLAGE, ALL SMURFS ARE EQUAL! REMEMBER THAT EVEN IF A SMURF IS DIFFERENT, SHE IS A SMURF LIKE YOU!
HIP-HIP-HOORAY! LONG LIVE SMURFETTE! LONG LIVE THE SMURFS!

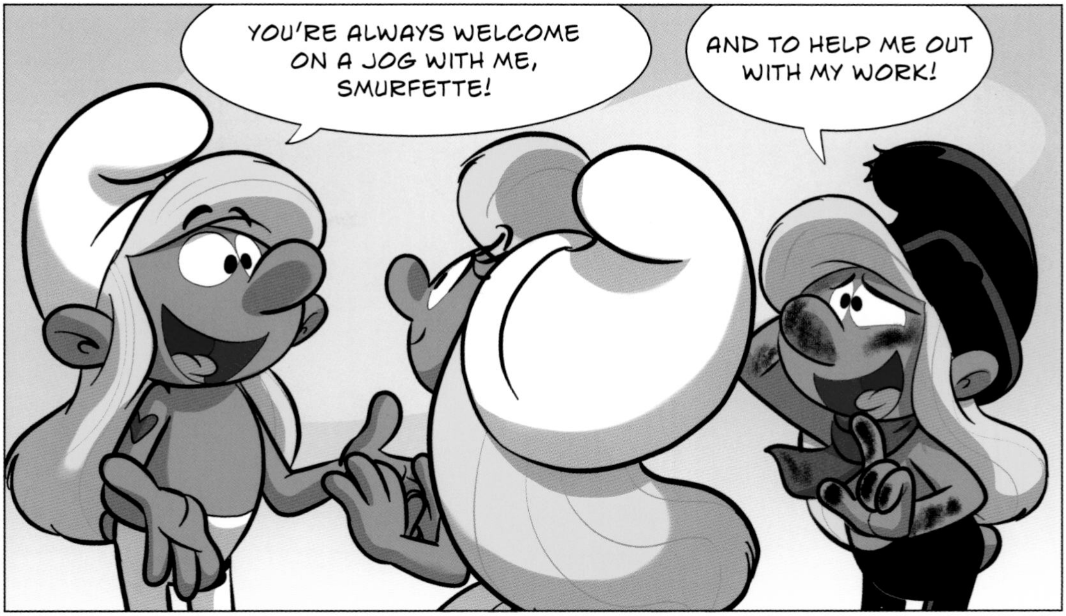
YOU'RE ALWAYS WELCOME ON A JOG WITH ME, SMURFETTE!
AND TO HELP ME OUT WITH MY WORK!

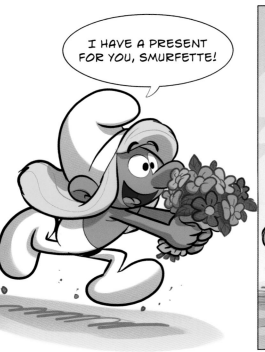

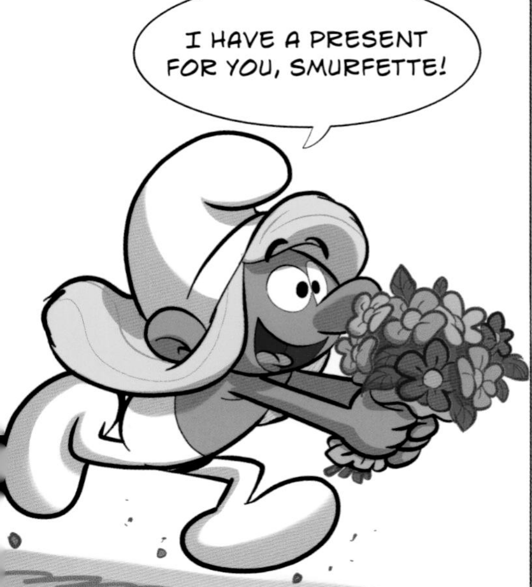
I HAVE A PRESENT FOR YOU, SMURFETTE!

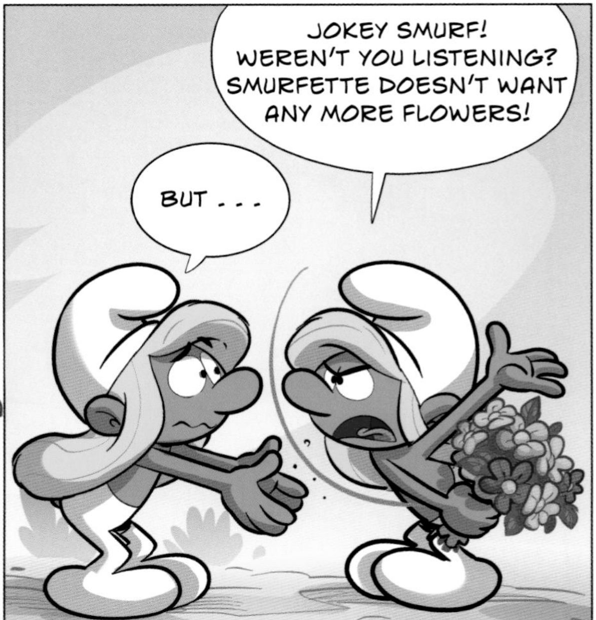
JOKEY SMURF! WEREN'T YOU LISTENING? SMURFETTE DOESN'T WANT ANY MORE FLOWERS!
BUT . . .

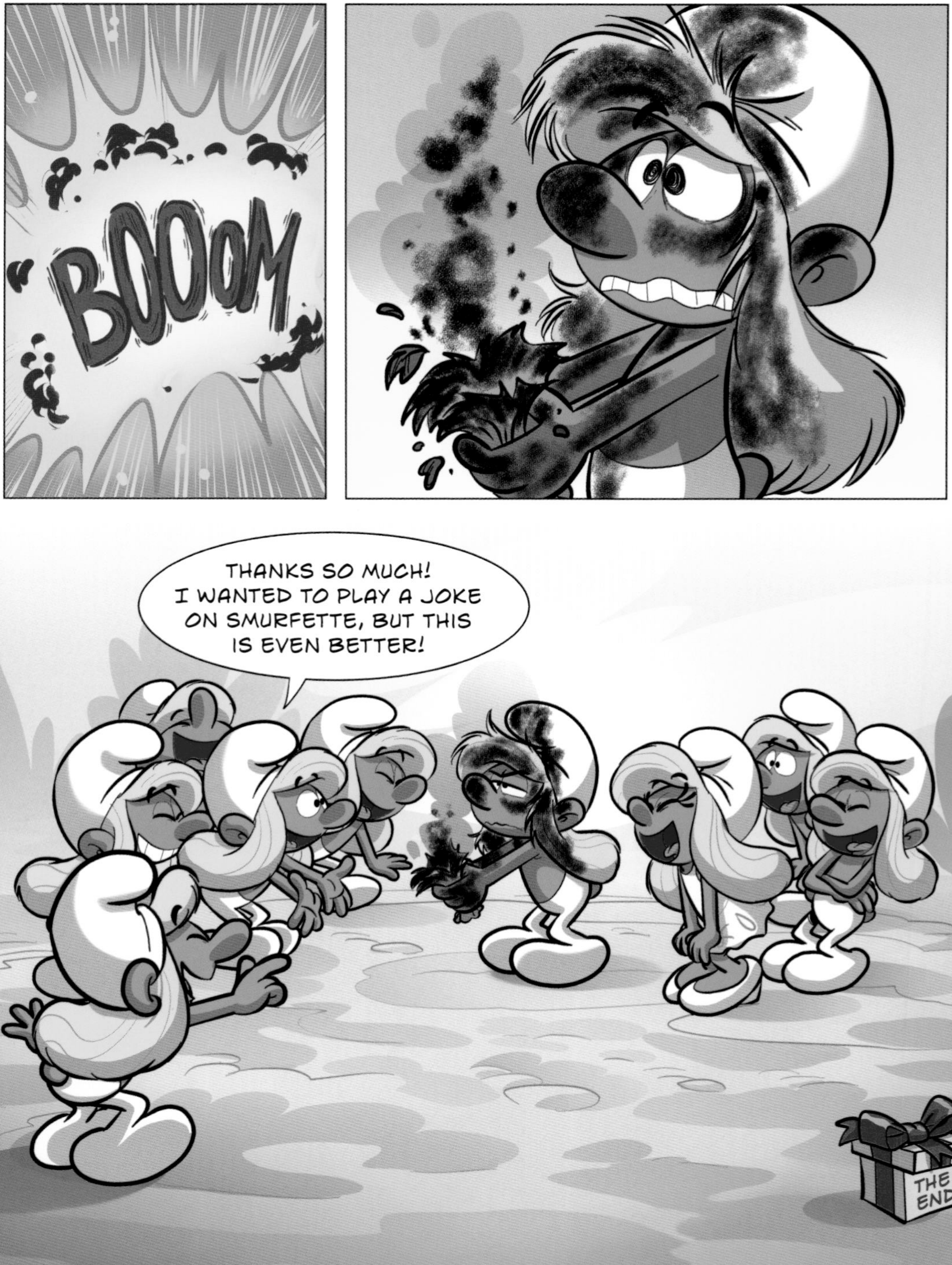
BOOOM
THANKS SO MUCH! I WANTED TO PLAY A JOKE ON SMURFETTE, BUT THIS IS EVEN BETTER!
THE END

THE SMURF WHO THOUGHT EVERYTHING WAS UNFAIR

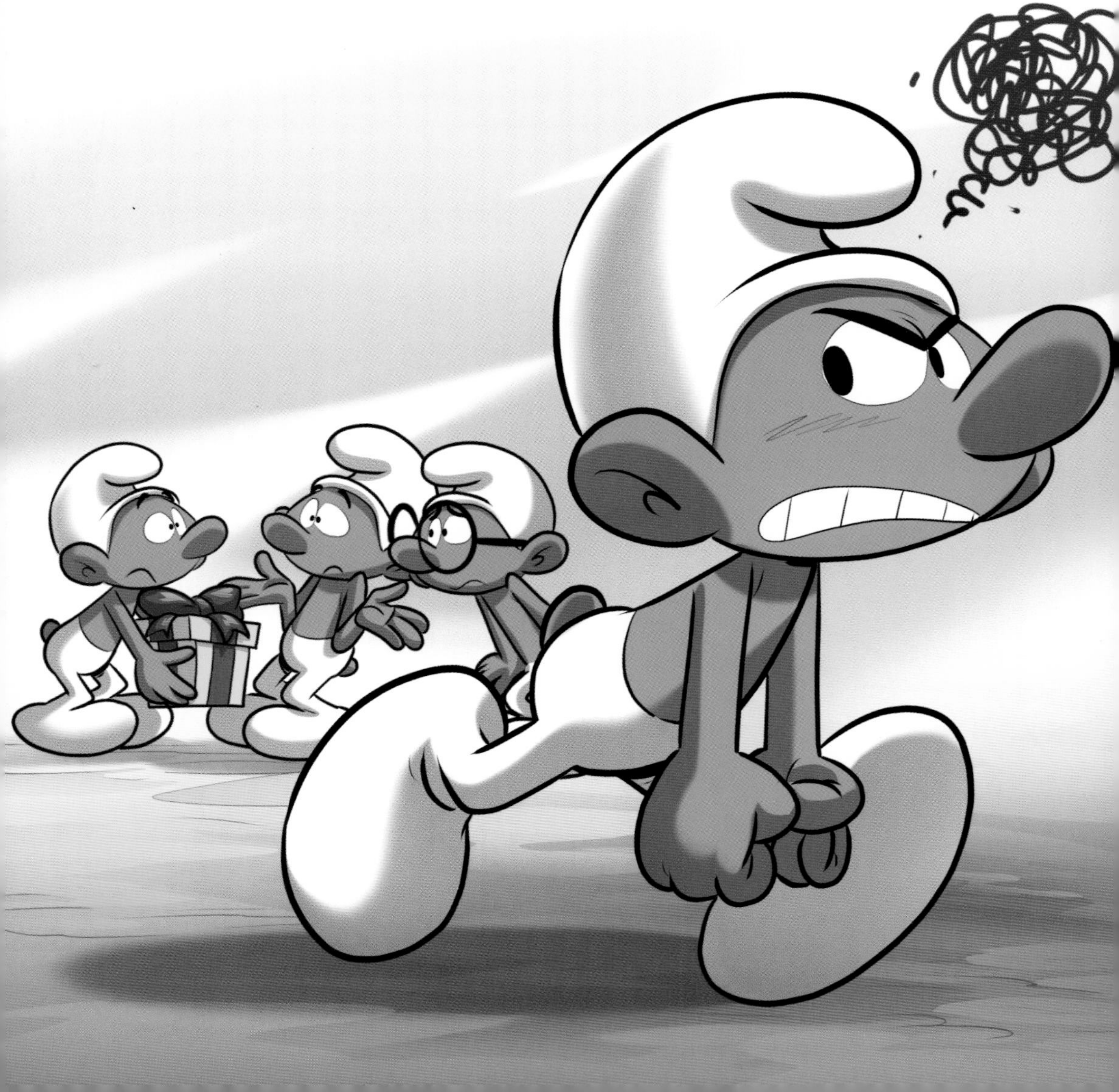

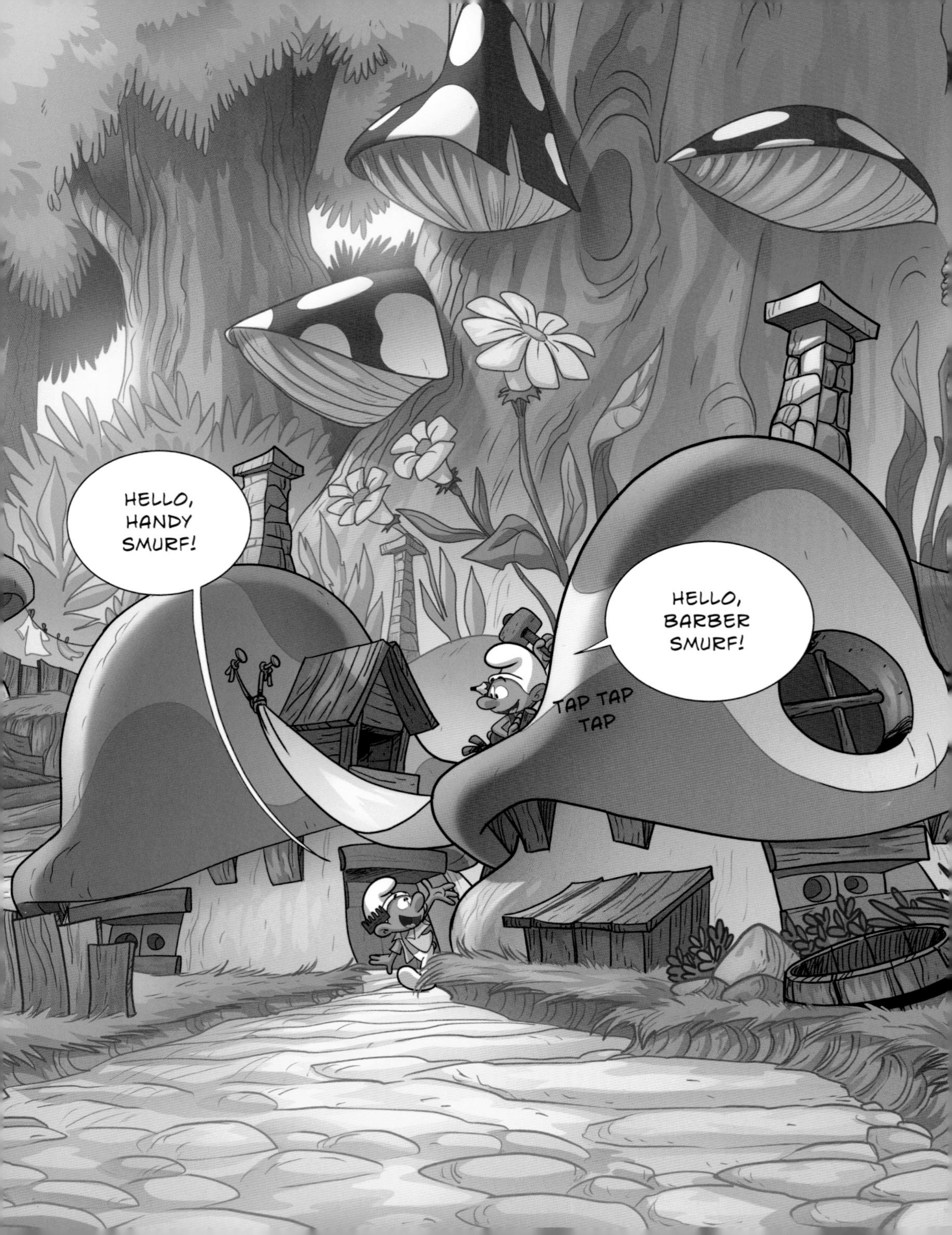
HELLO, HANDY SMURF!
HELLO, BARBER SMURF!
TAP TAP TAP

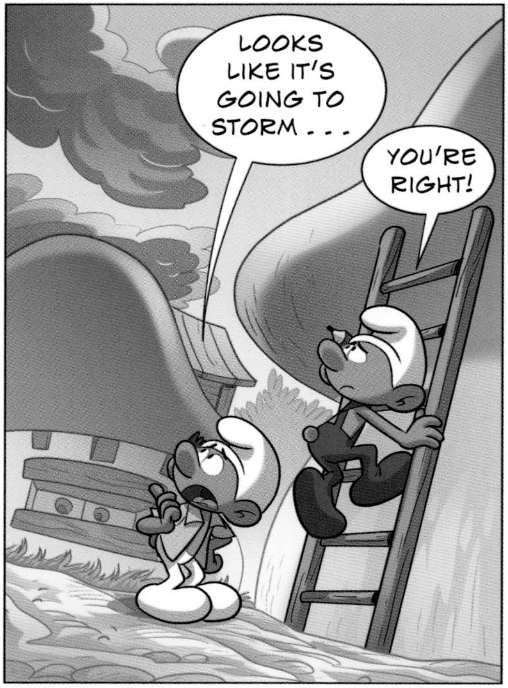
LOOKS LIKE IT'S GOING TO STORM . . .
YOU'RE RIGHT!

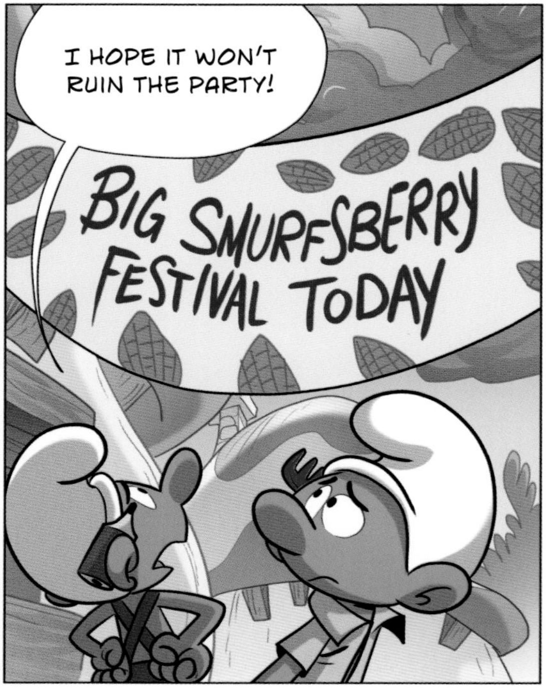
I HOPE IT WON'T RUIN THE PARTY!
BIG SMURFSBERRY FESTIVAL TODAY

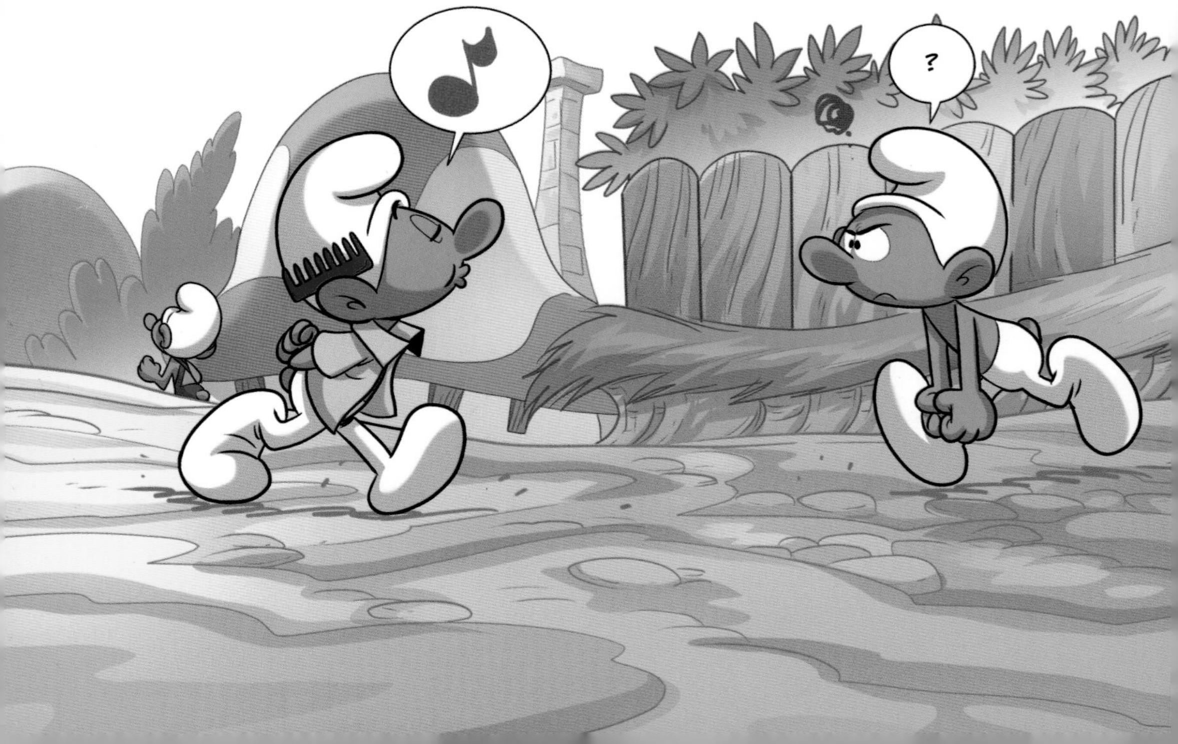
?

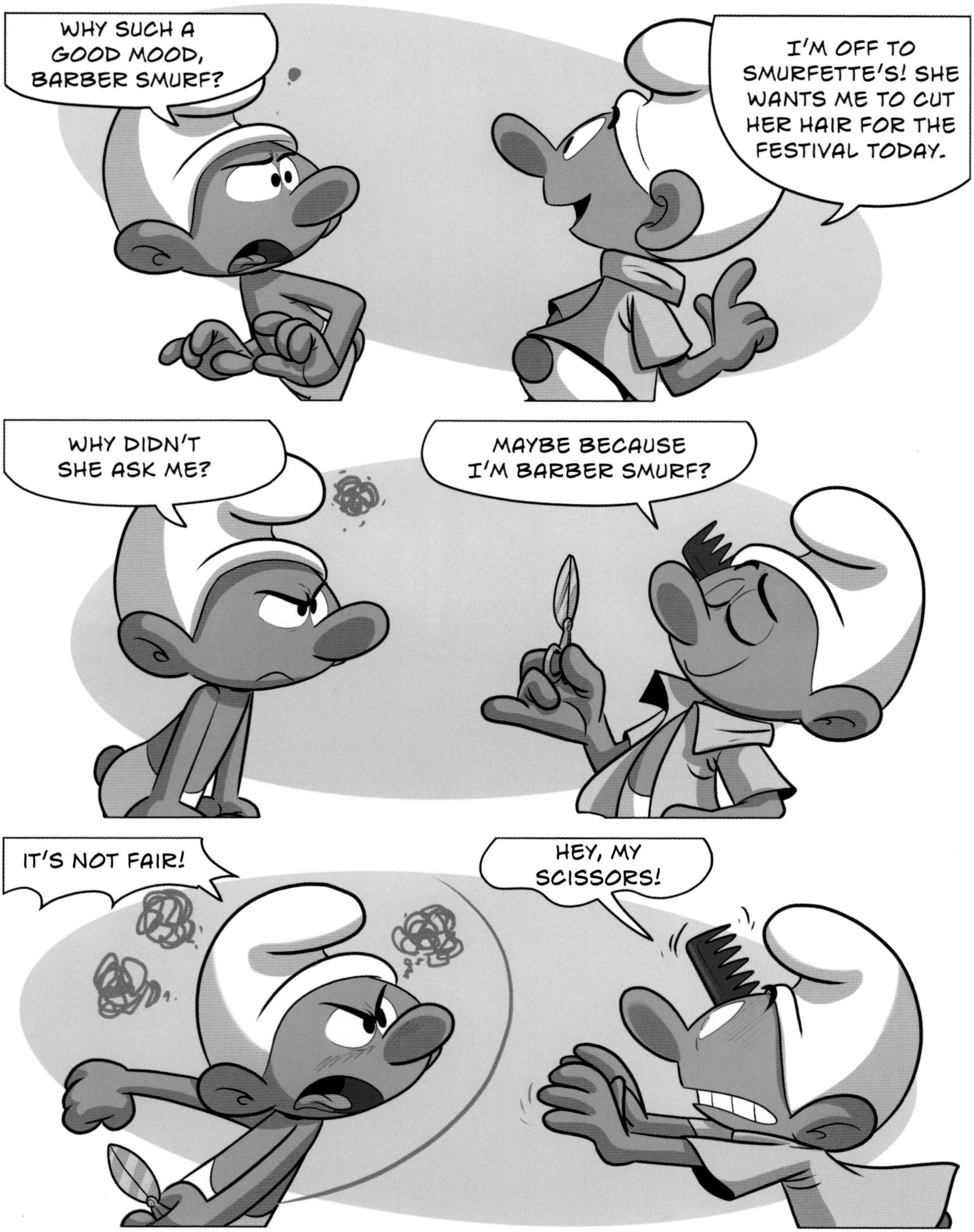
WHY SUCH A GOOD MOOD, BARBER SMURF?
I'M OFF TO SMURFETTE'S! SHE WANTS ME TO CUT HER HAIR FOR THE FESTIVAL TODAY.
WHY DIDN'T SHE ASK ME?
MAYBE BECAUSE I'M BARBER SMURF?
IT'S NOT FAIR!
HEY, MY SCISSORS!

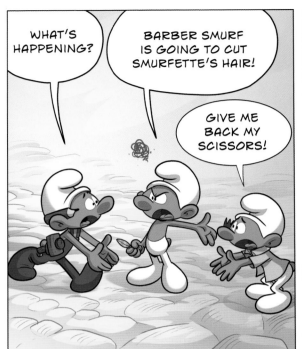

WHAT'S HAPPENING?

BARBER SMURF IS GOING TO CUT SMURFETTE'S HAIR!

GIVE ME BACK MY SCISSORS!

LUCKY HIM . . .

I COULD DO IT TOO! CUTTING HAIR ISN'T *THAT* HARD!

IT'S NOT GOOD TO ARGUE. DON'T MAKE ME TELL PAPA SMURF, BECAUSE HE ALWAYS SAYS THAT--

HEY, WE DIDN'T ASK FOR YOUR HELP!
OH?
WHAT'S GOING ON HERE?
IT'S NOT FAIR! BARBER SMURF CAN CUT SMURFETTE'S HAIR AND I CAN'T!
THIS IS NORMAL! EACH SMURF HAS THEIR SPECIALTY. FOR EXAMPLE, HANDY SMURF IS GOOD AT FIXING THINGS . . .

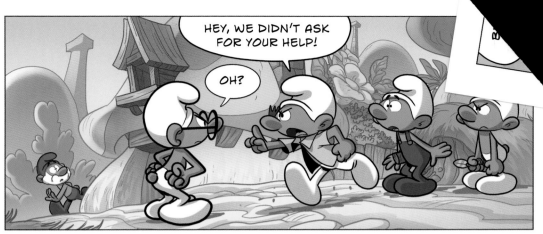

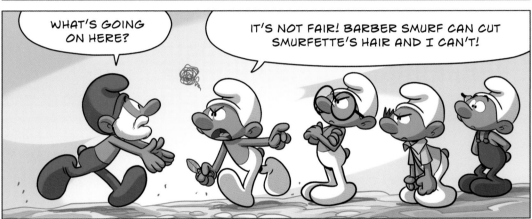

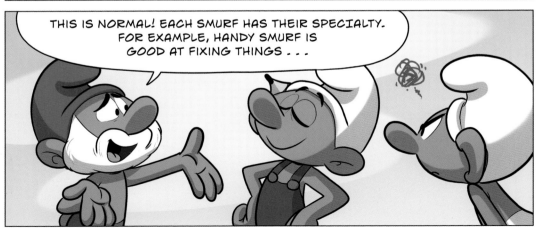

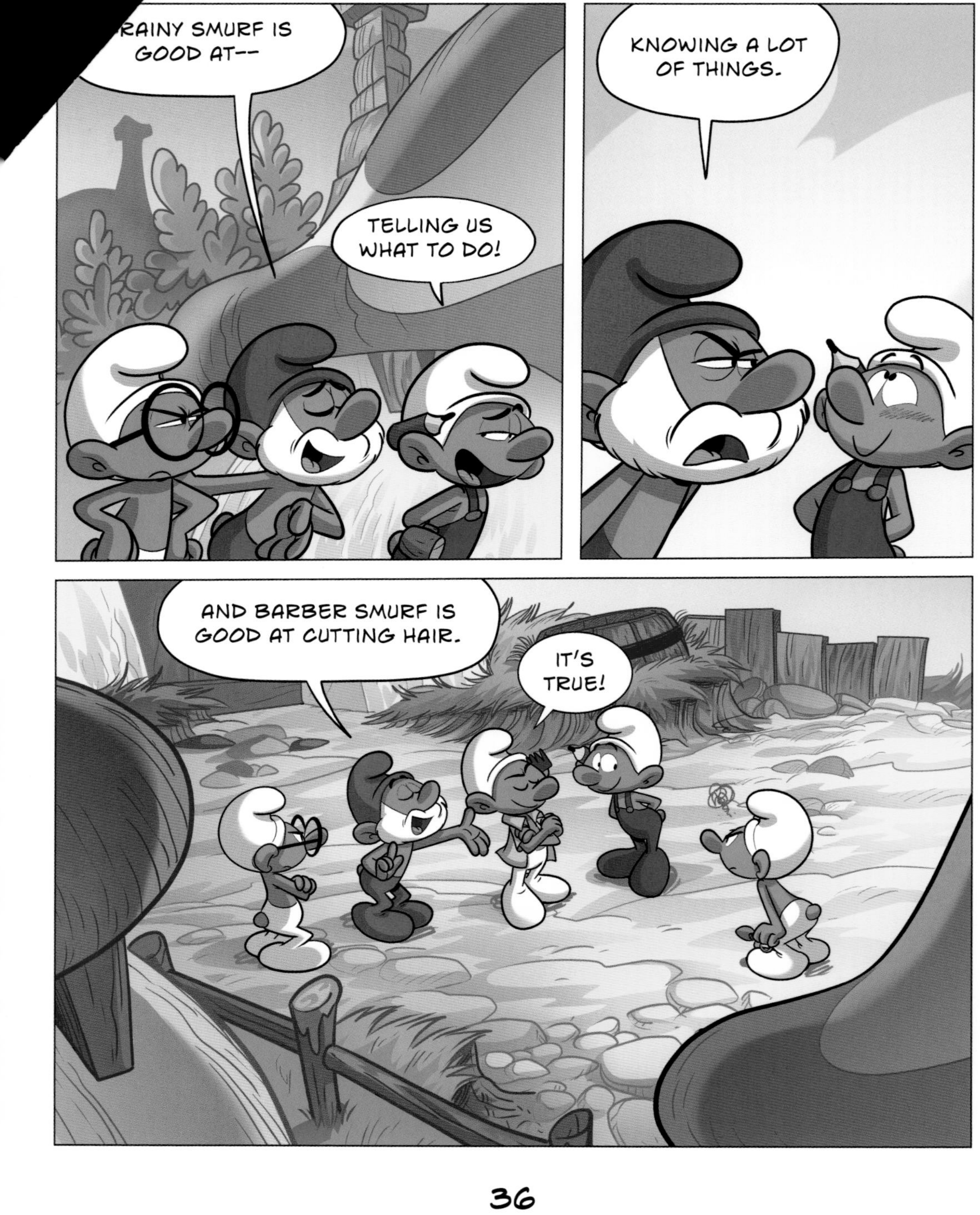
RAINY SMURF IS GOOD AT--
TELLING US WHAT TO DO!
KNOWING A LOT OF THINGS.
AND BARBER SMURF IS GOOD AT CUTTING HAIR.
IT'S TRUE!

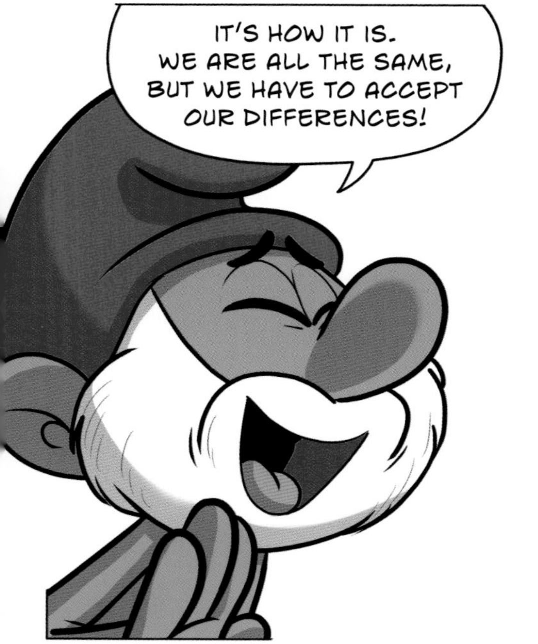
IT'S HOW IT IS.
WE ARE ALL THE SAME, BUT WE HAVE TO ACCEPT OUR DIFFERENCES!

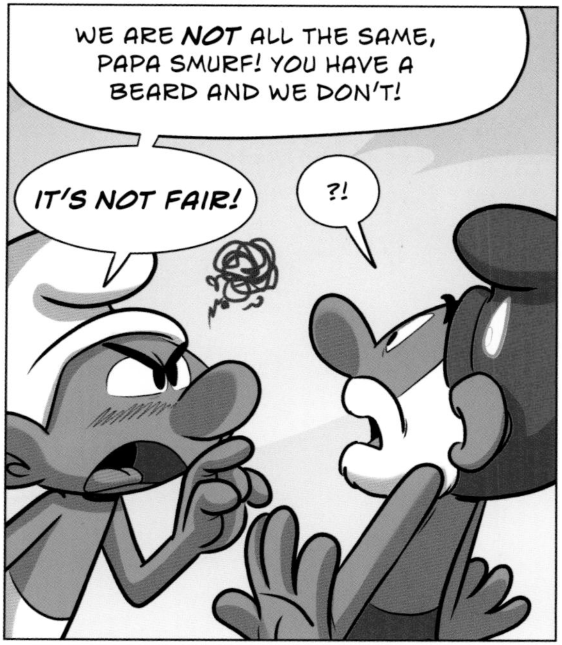
WE ARE **NOT** ALL THE SAME, PAPA SMURF! YOU HAVE A BEARD AND WE DON'T!
IT'S NOT FAIR!
?!

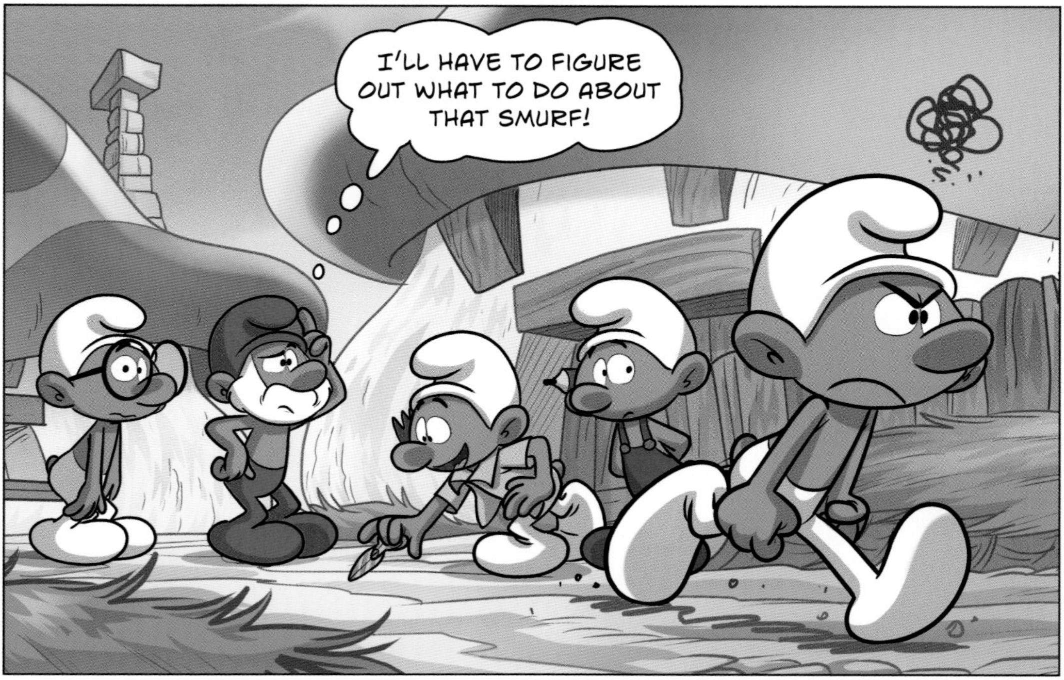
I'LL HAVE TO FIGURE OUT WHAT TO DO ABOUT THAT SMURF!

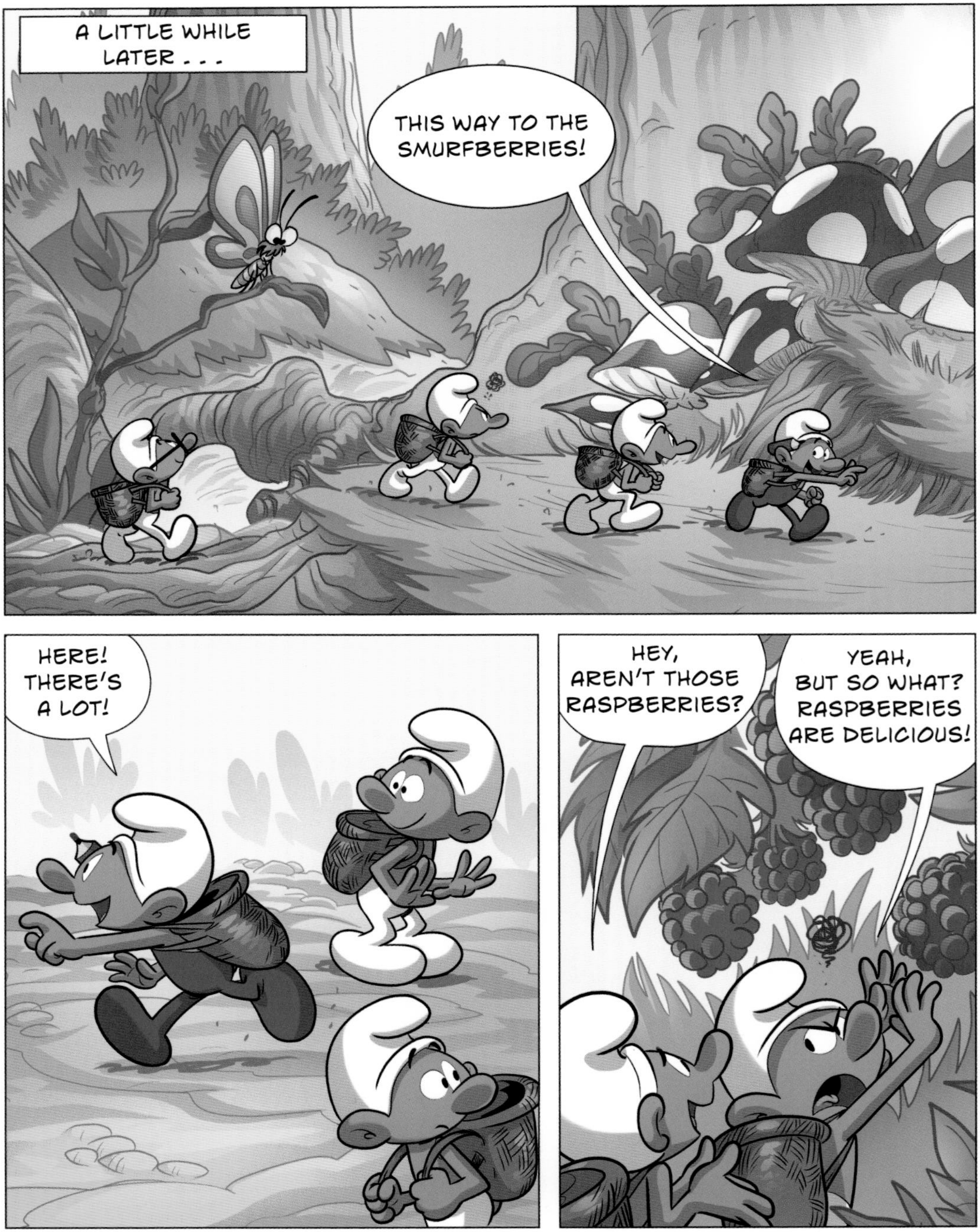
A LITTLE WHILE LATER . . .
THIS WAY TO THE SMURFBERRIES!
HERE! THERE'S A LOT!
HEY, AREN'T THOSE RASPBERRIES?
YEAH, BUT SO WHAT? RASPBERRIES ARE DELICIOUS!

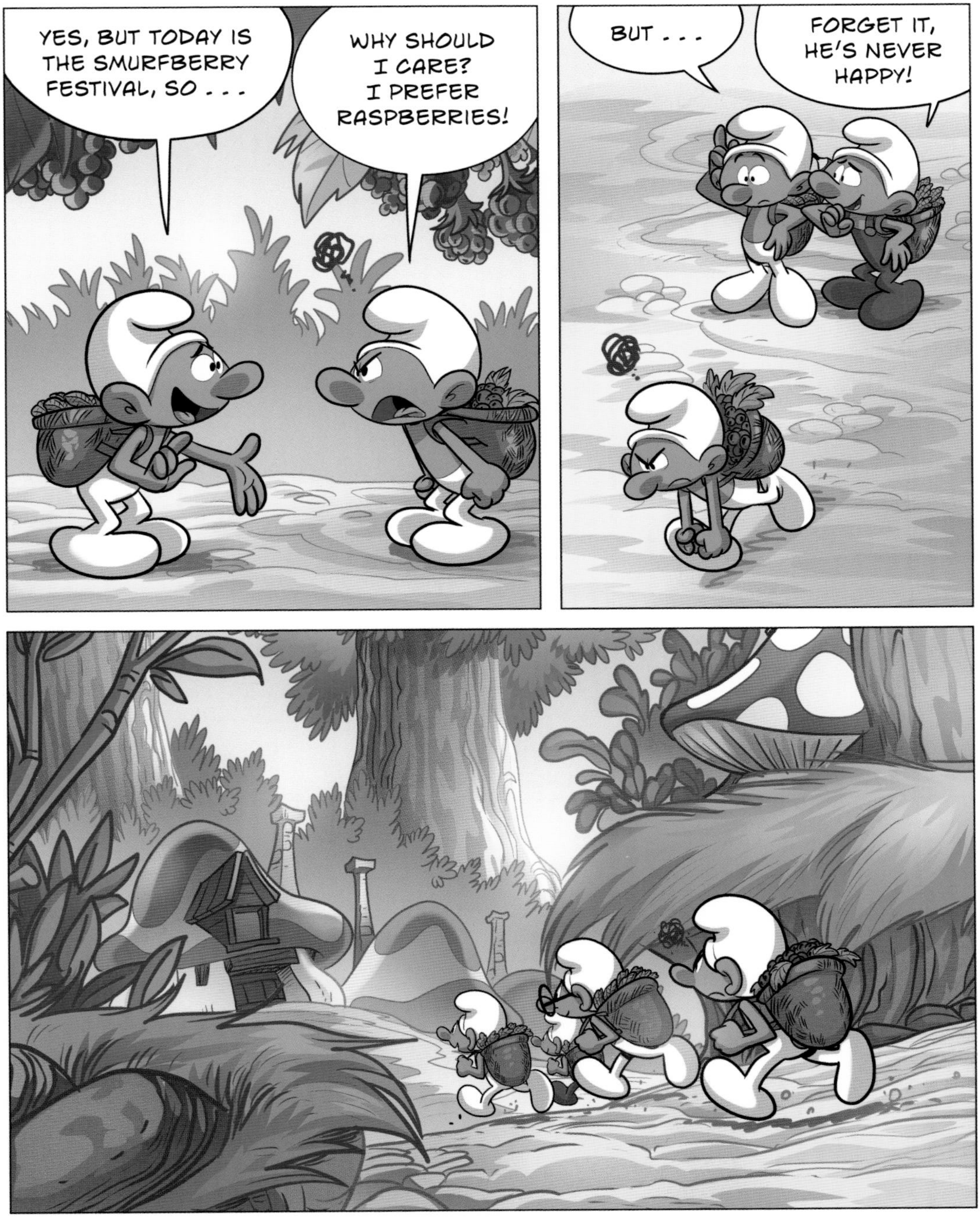
YES, BUT TODAY IS THE SMURFBERRY FESTIVAL, SO . . .
WHY SHOULD I CARE? I PREFER RASPBERRIES!
BUT . . .
FORGET IT, HE'S NEVER HAPPY!

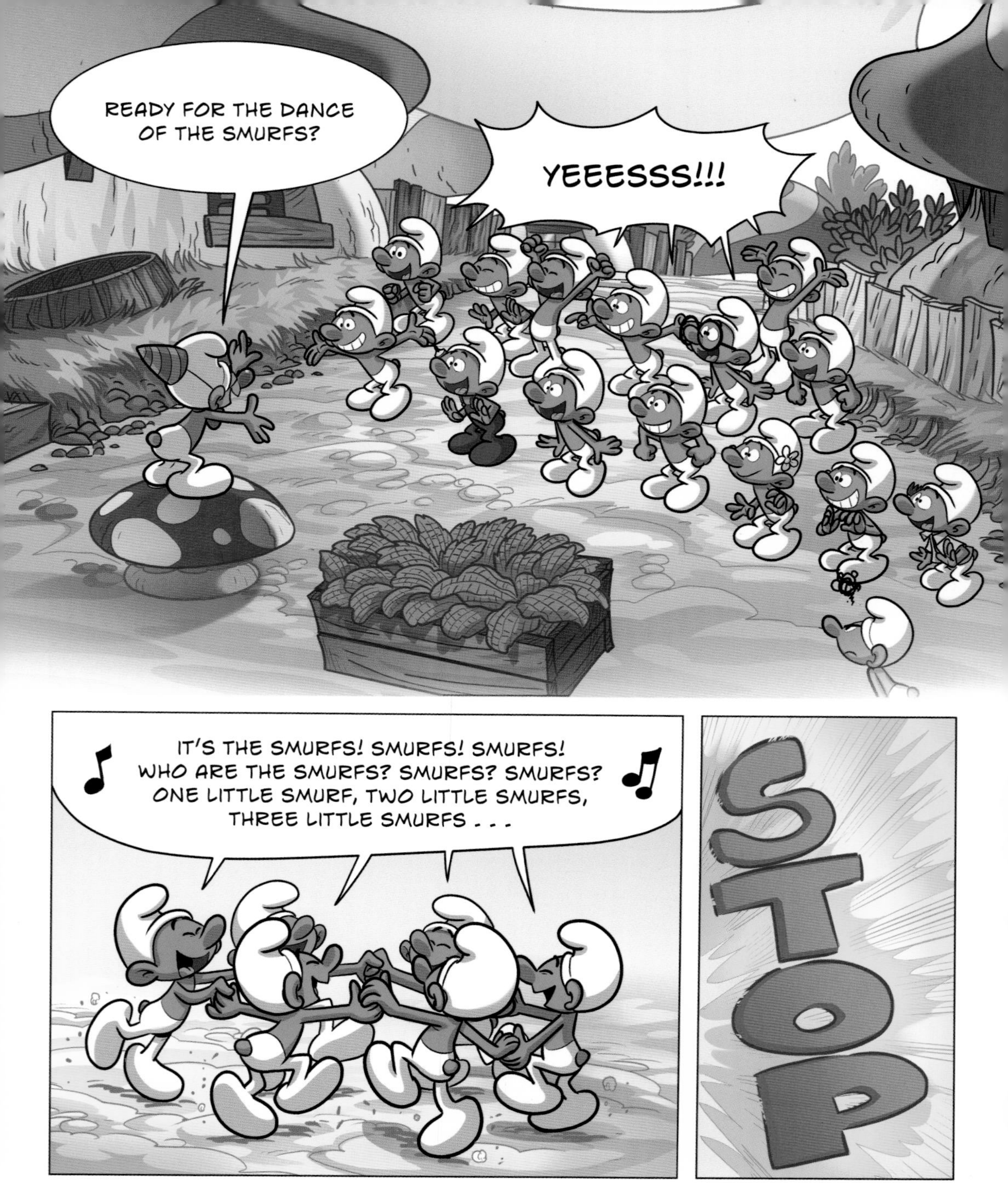
READY FOR THE DANCE OF THE SMURFS?
YEEESSS!!!
IT'S THE SMURFS! SMURFS! SMURFS! WHO ARE THE SMURFS? SMURFS? SMURFS? ONE LITTLE SMURF, TWO LITTLE SMURFS, THREE LITTLE SMURFS . . .
STOP

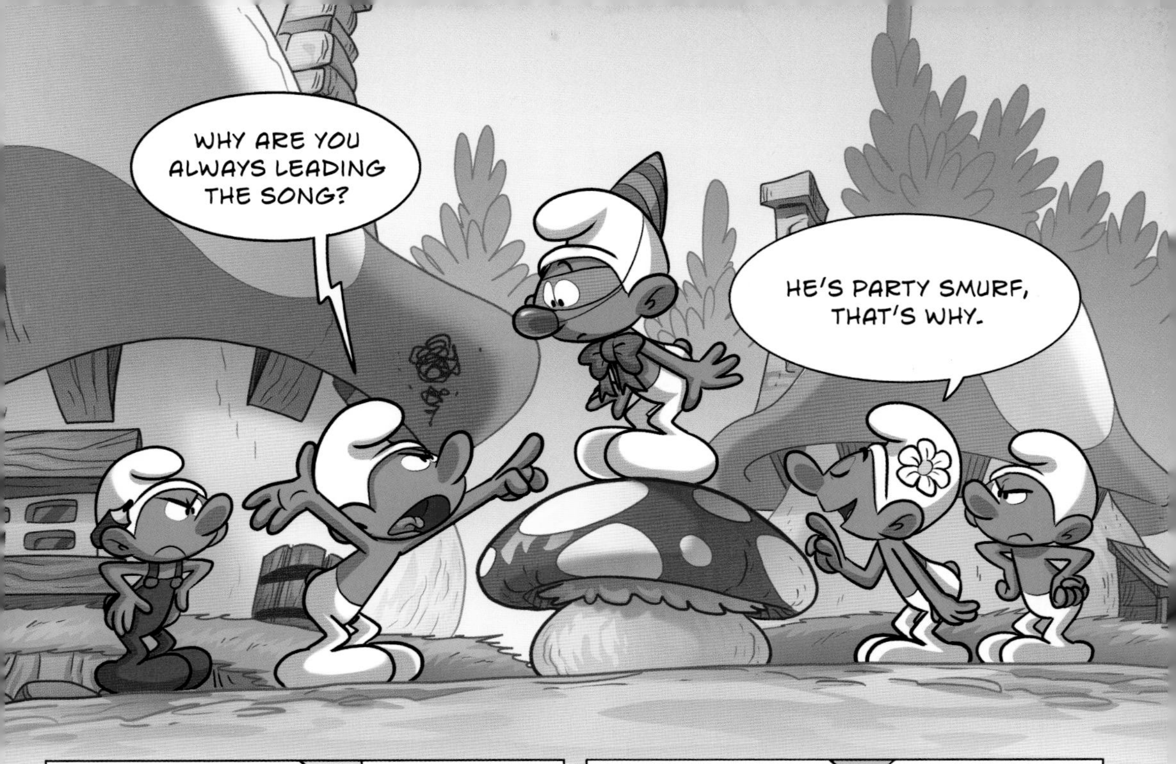
WHY ARE YOU ALWAYS LEADING THE SONG?
HE'S PARTY SMURF, THAT'S WHY.

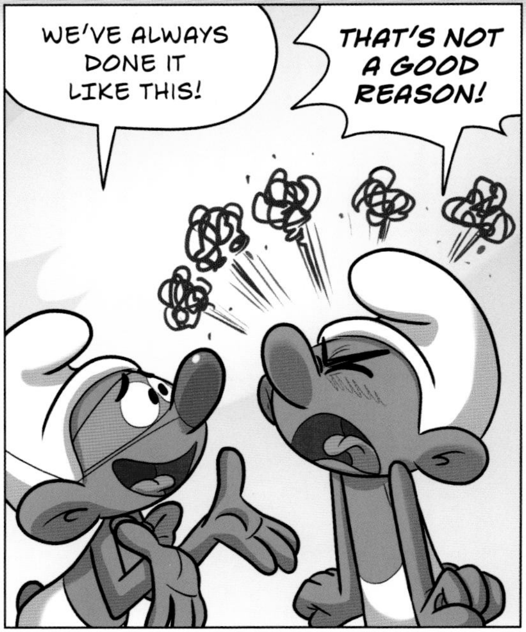
WE'VE ALWAYS DONE IT LIKE THIS!
THAT'S NOT A GOOD REASON!

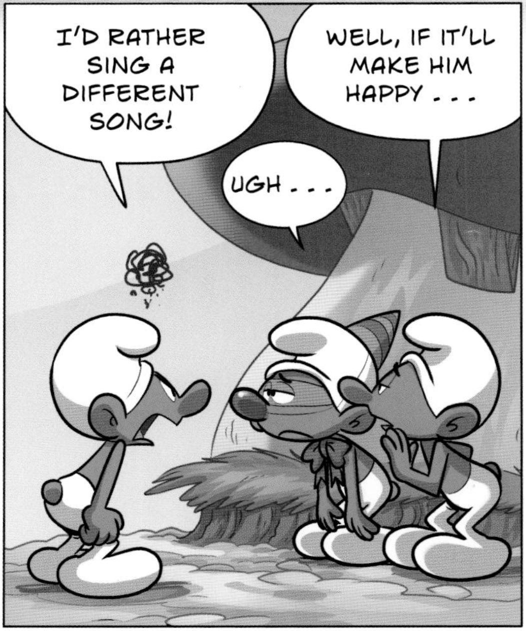
I'D RATHER SING A DIFFERENT SONG!
WELL, IF IT'LL MAKE HIM HAPPY . . .
UGH . . .

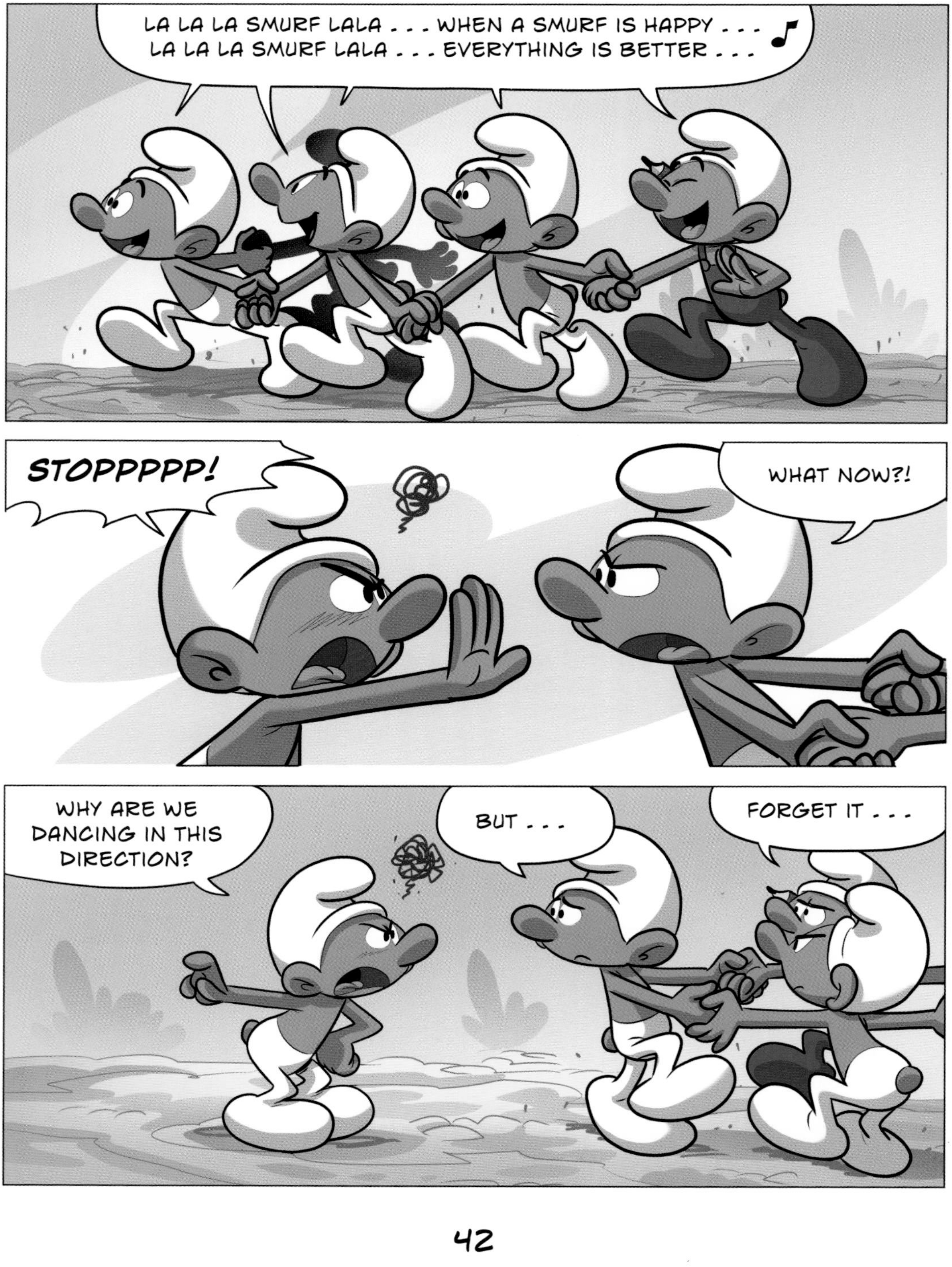
LA LA LA SMURF LALA . . . WHEN A SMURF IS HAPPY . . .
LA LA LA SMURF LALA . . . EVERYTHING IS BETTER . . .
STOPPPPP!
WHAT NOW?!
WHY ARE WE DANCING IN THIS DIRECTION?
BUT . . .
FORGET IT . . .

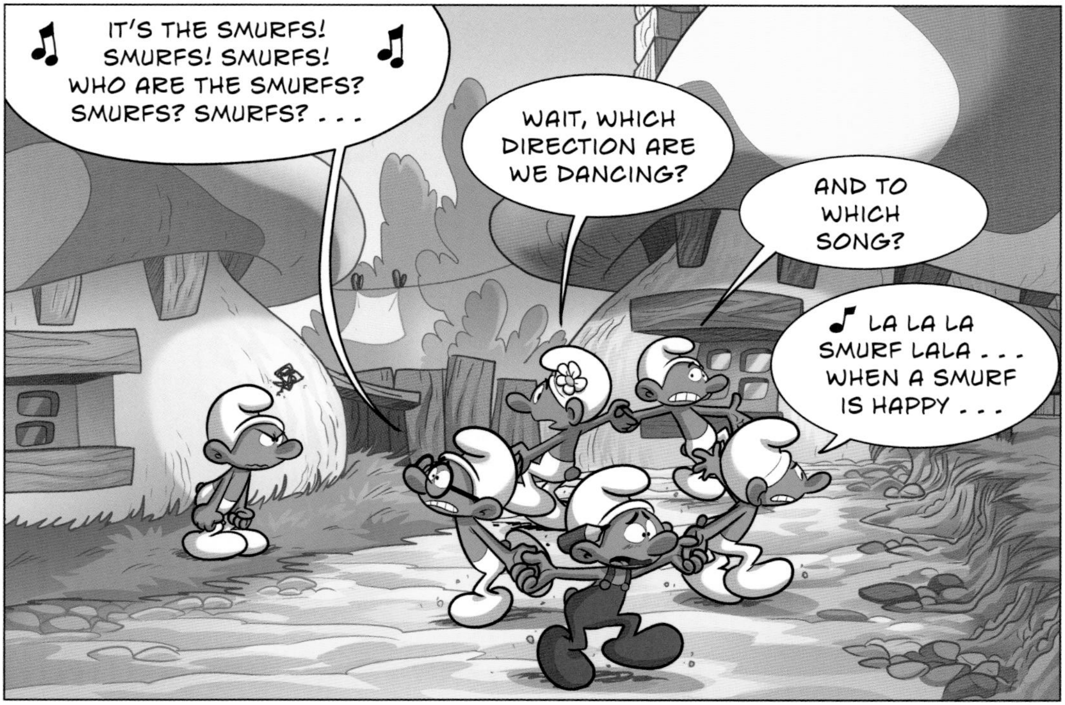
IT'S THE SMURFS! SMURFS! SMURFS! WHO ARE THE SMURFS? SMURFS? SMURFS? . . .
WAIT, WHICH DIRECTION ARE WE DANCING?
AND TO WHICH SONG?
LA LA LA SMURF LALA . . . WHEN A SMURF IS HAPPY . . .

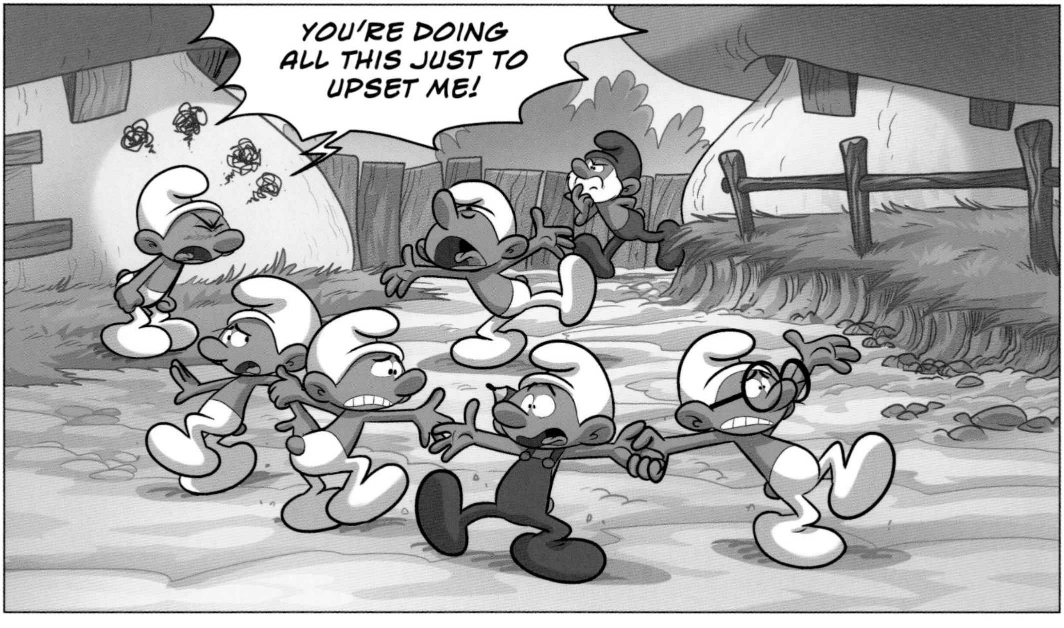
YOU'RE DOING ALL THIS JUST TO UPSET ME!

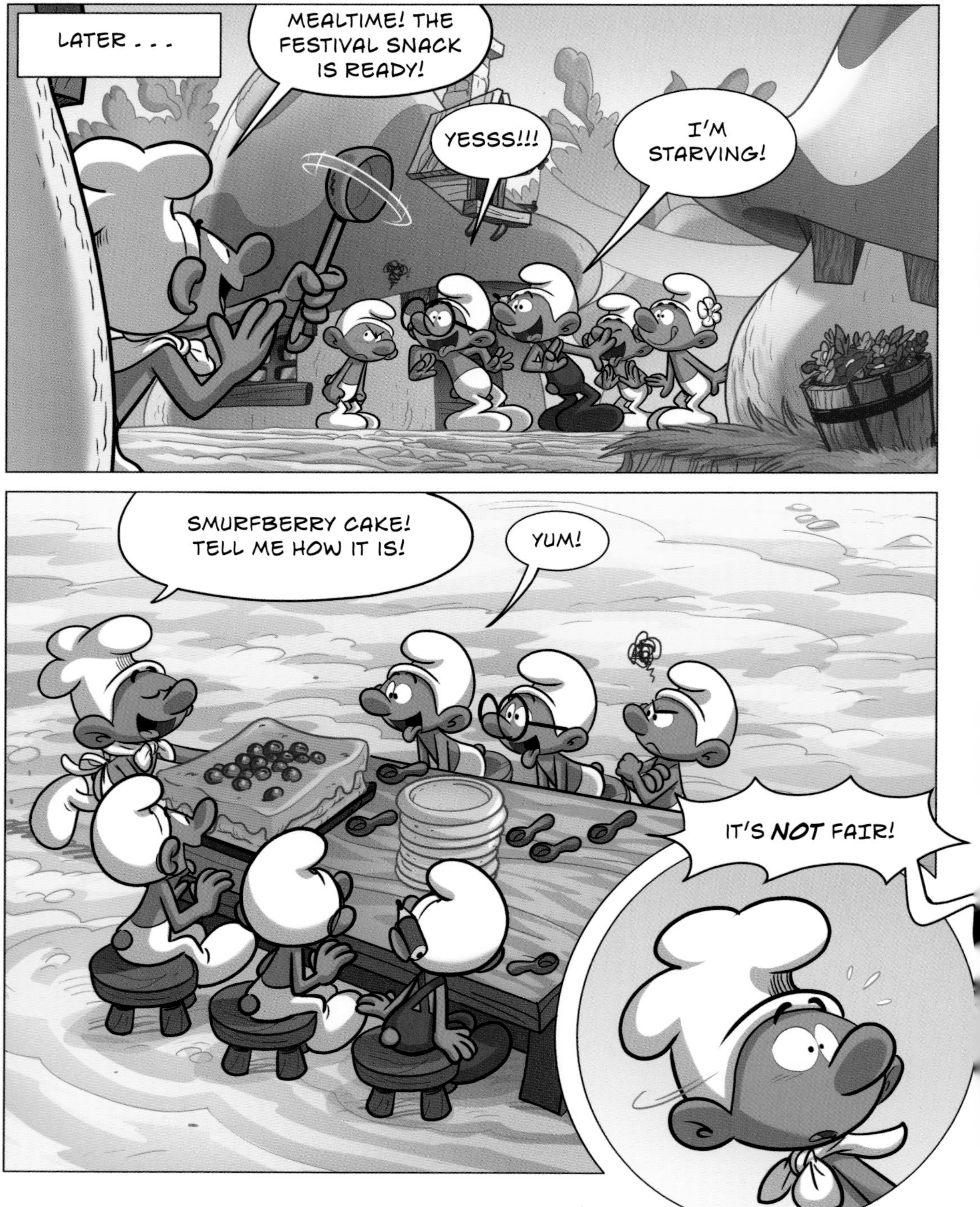
LATER . . .
MEALTIME! THE FESTIVAL SNACK IS READY!
YESSS!!!
I'M STARVING!
SMURFBERRY CAKE! TELL ME HOW IT IS!
YUM!
IT'S **NOT** FAIR!

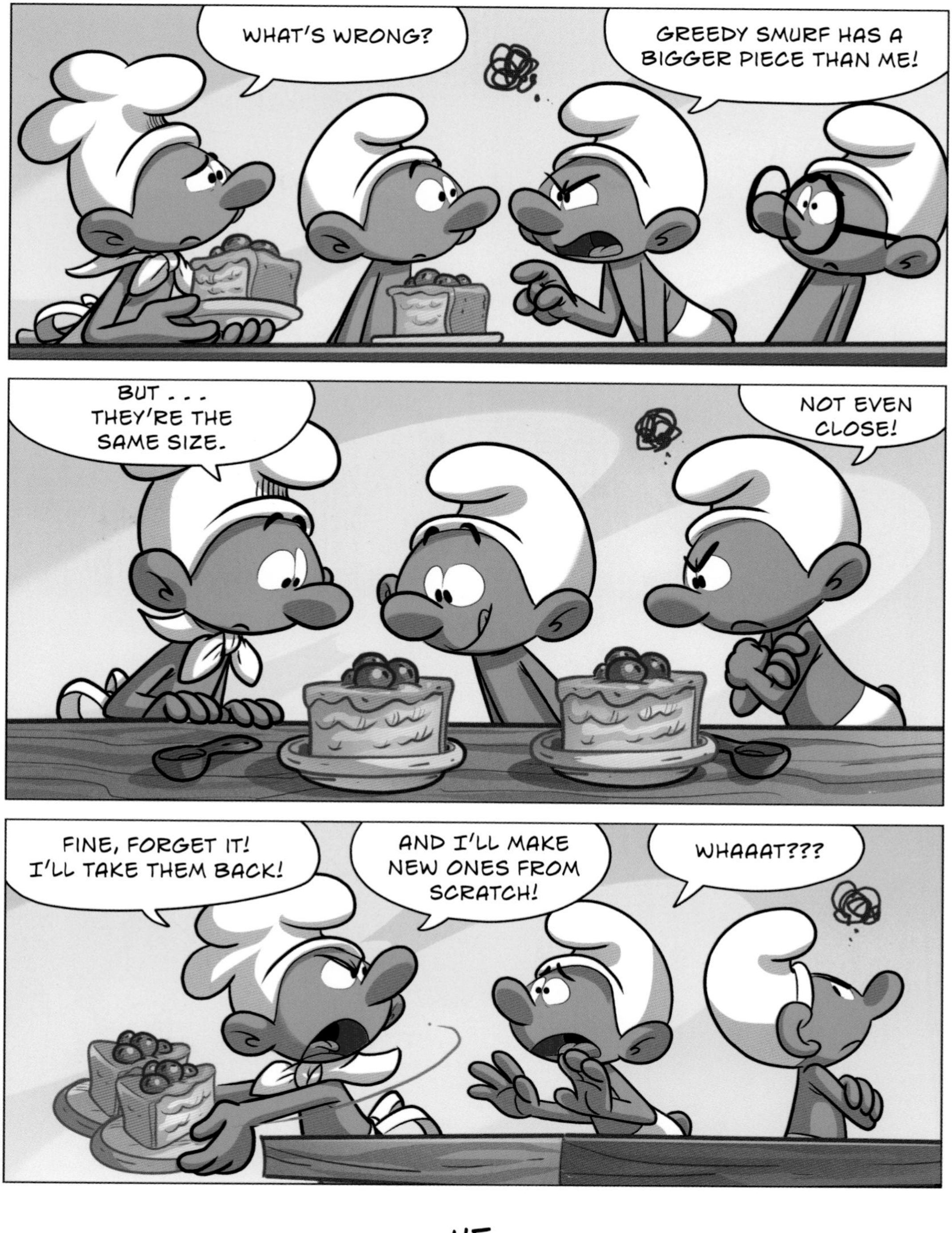
WHAT'S WRONG?
GREEDY SMURF HAS A BIGGER PIECE THAN ME!
BUT . . . THEY'RE THE SAME SIZE.
NOT EVEN CLOSE!
FINE, FORGET IT! I'LL TAKE THEM BACK!
AND I'LL MAKE NEW ONES FROM SCRATCH!
WHAAAT???

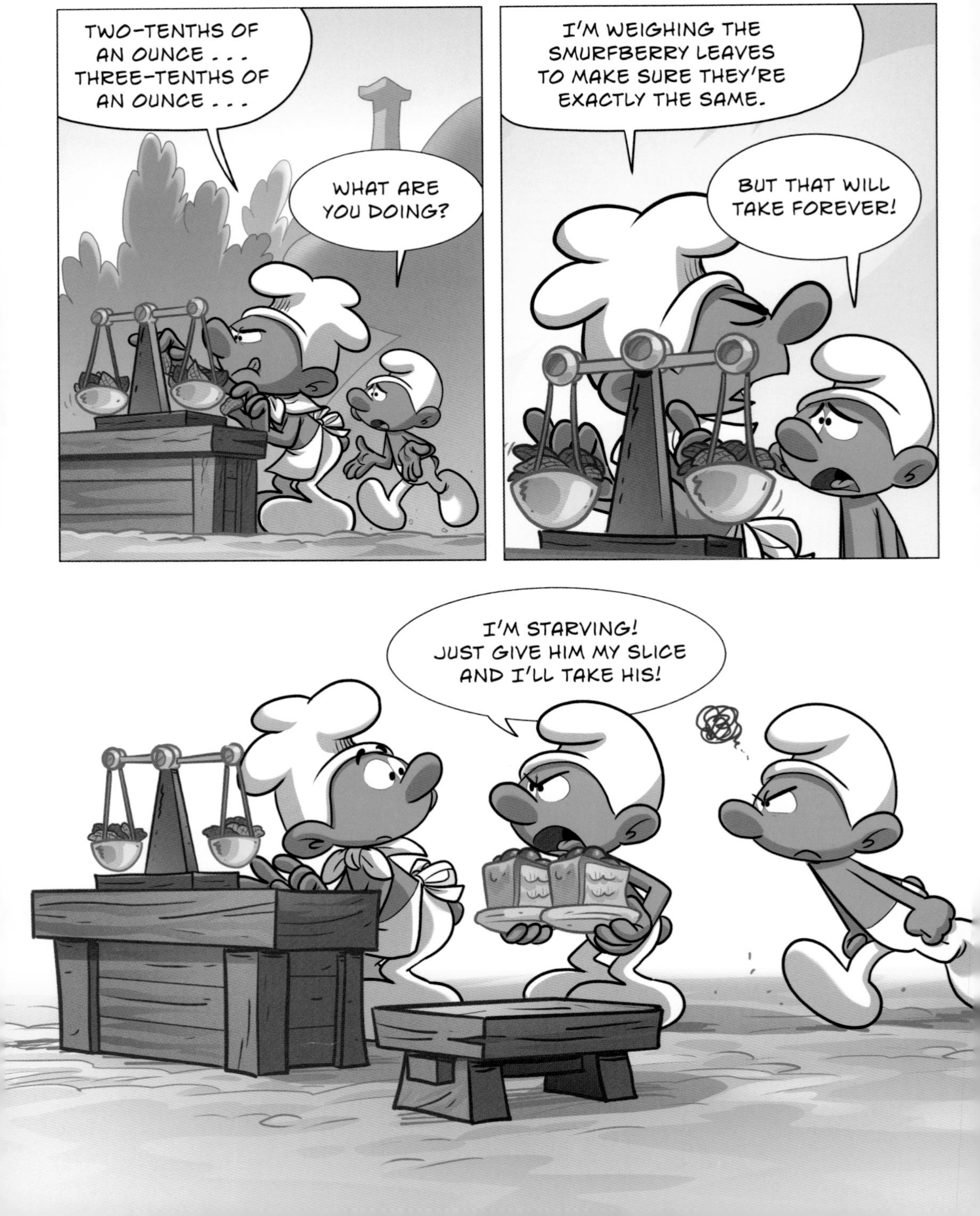
TWO-TENTHS OF AN OUNCE . . . THREE-TENTHS OF AN OUNCE . . .
WHAT ARE YOU DOING?
I'M WEIGHING THE SMURFBERRY LEAVES TO MAKE SURE THEY'RE EXACTLY THE SAME.
BUT THAT WILL TAKE FOREVER!
I'M STARVING! JUST GIVE HIM MY SLICE AND I'LL TAKE HIS!

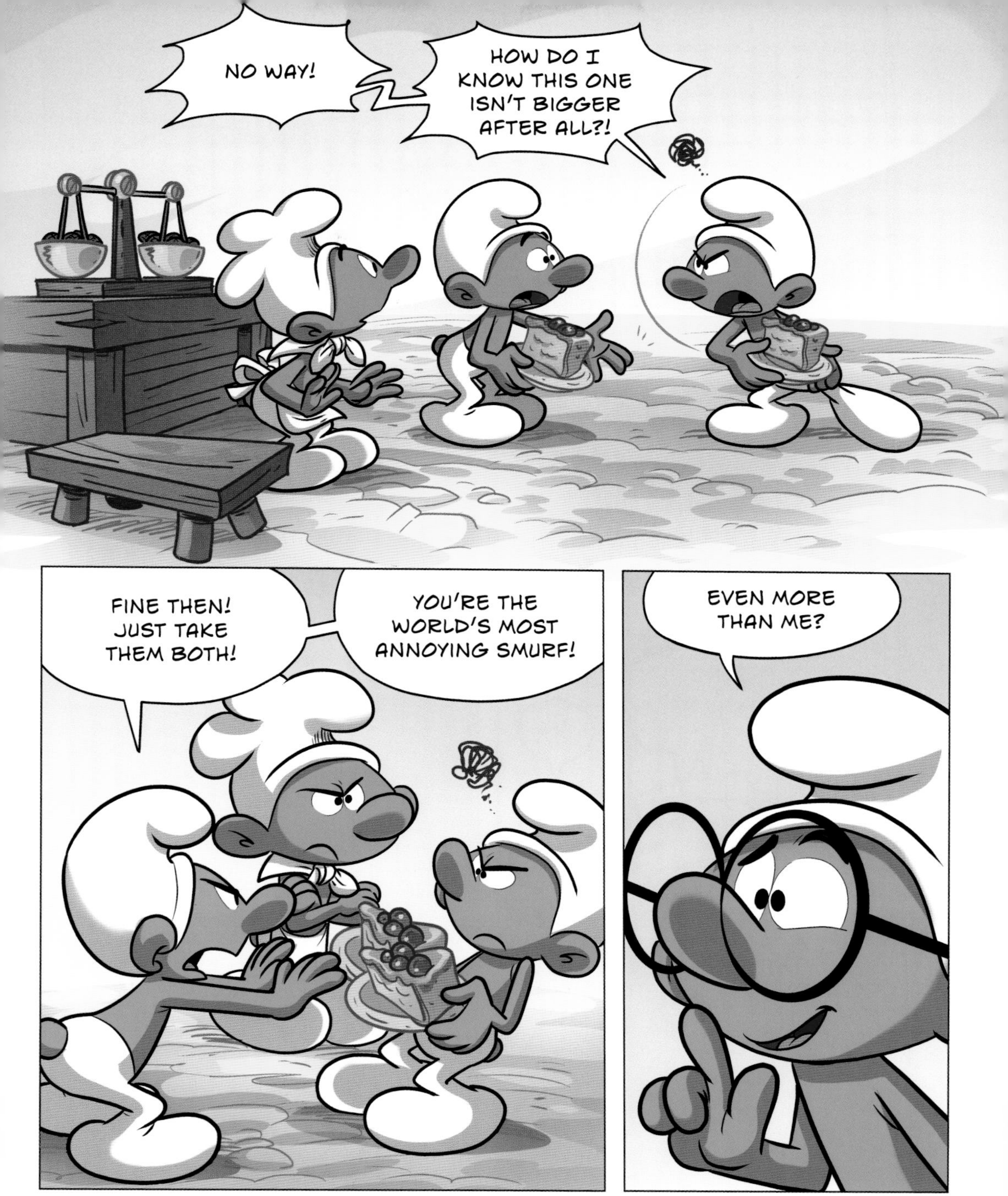
NO WAY!
HOW DO I KNOW THIS ONE ISN'T BIGGER AFTER ALL?!
FINE THEN! JUST TAKE THEM BOTH!
YOU'RE THE WORLD'S MOST ANNOYING SMURF!
EVEN MORE THAN ME?

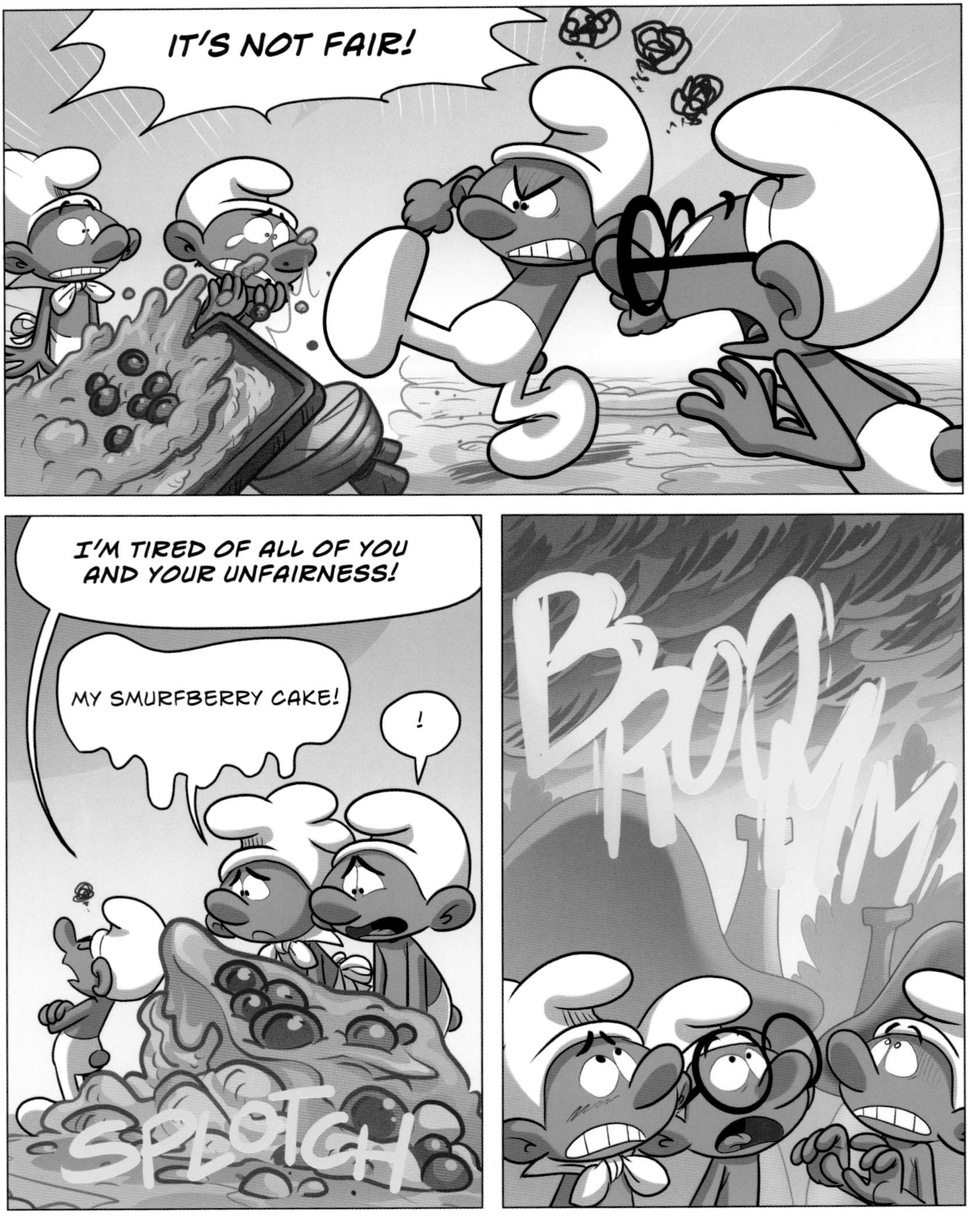
IT'S NOT FAIR!
I'M TIRED OF ALL OF YOU AND YOUR UNFAIRNESS!
MY SMURFBERRY CAKE!
!
SPLOTCH
BROOM

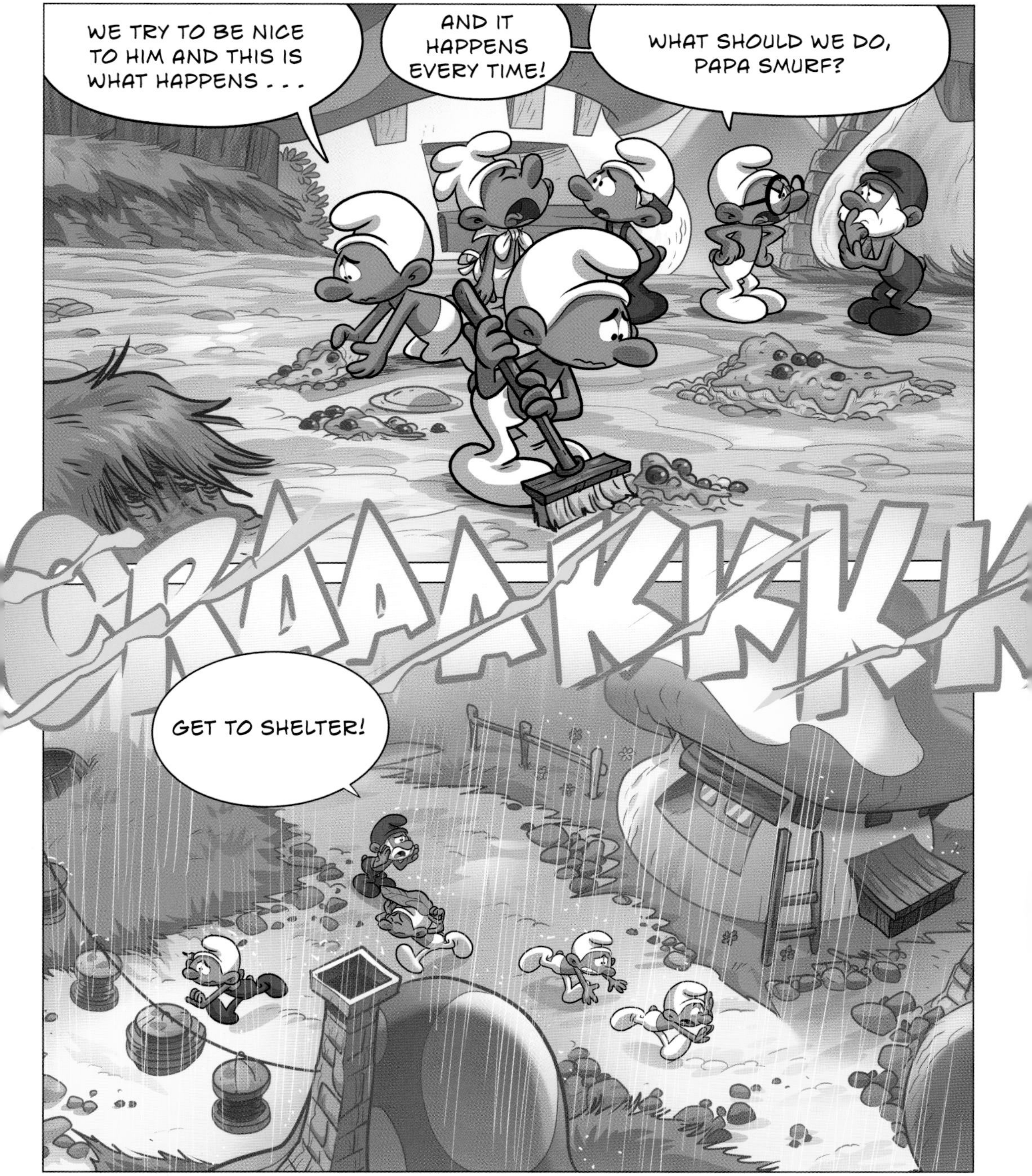
WE TRY TO BE NICE TO HIM AND THIS IS WHAT HAPPENS . . .
AND IT HAPPENS EVERY TIME!
WHAT SHOULD WE DO, PAPA SMURF?
CRAAAKKKK
GET TO SHELTER!

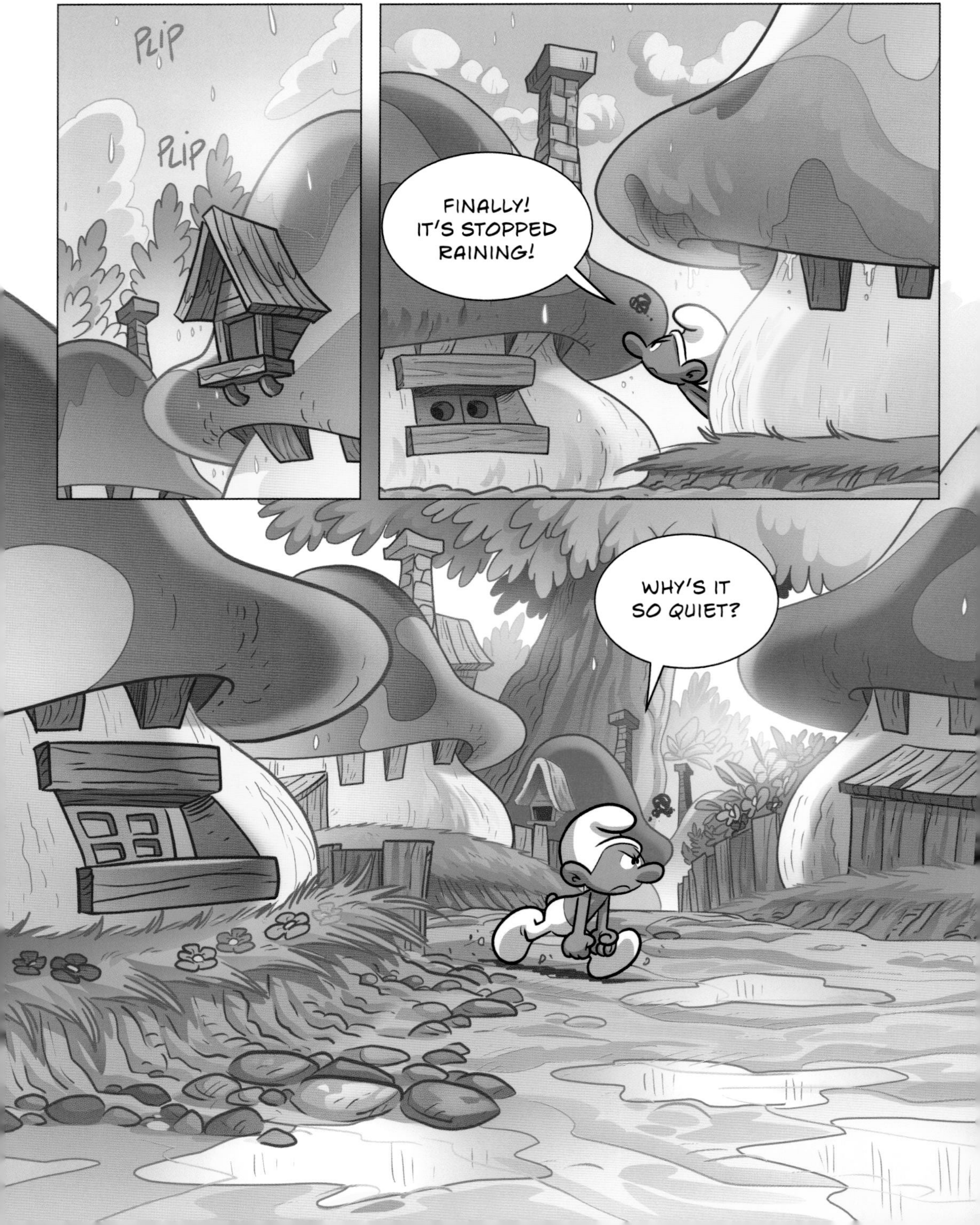
PLIP
PLIP
FINALLY! IT'S STOPPED RAINING!
WHY'S IT SO QUIET?

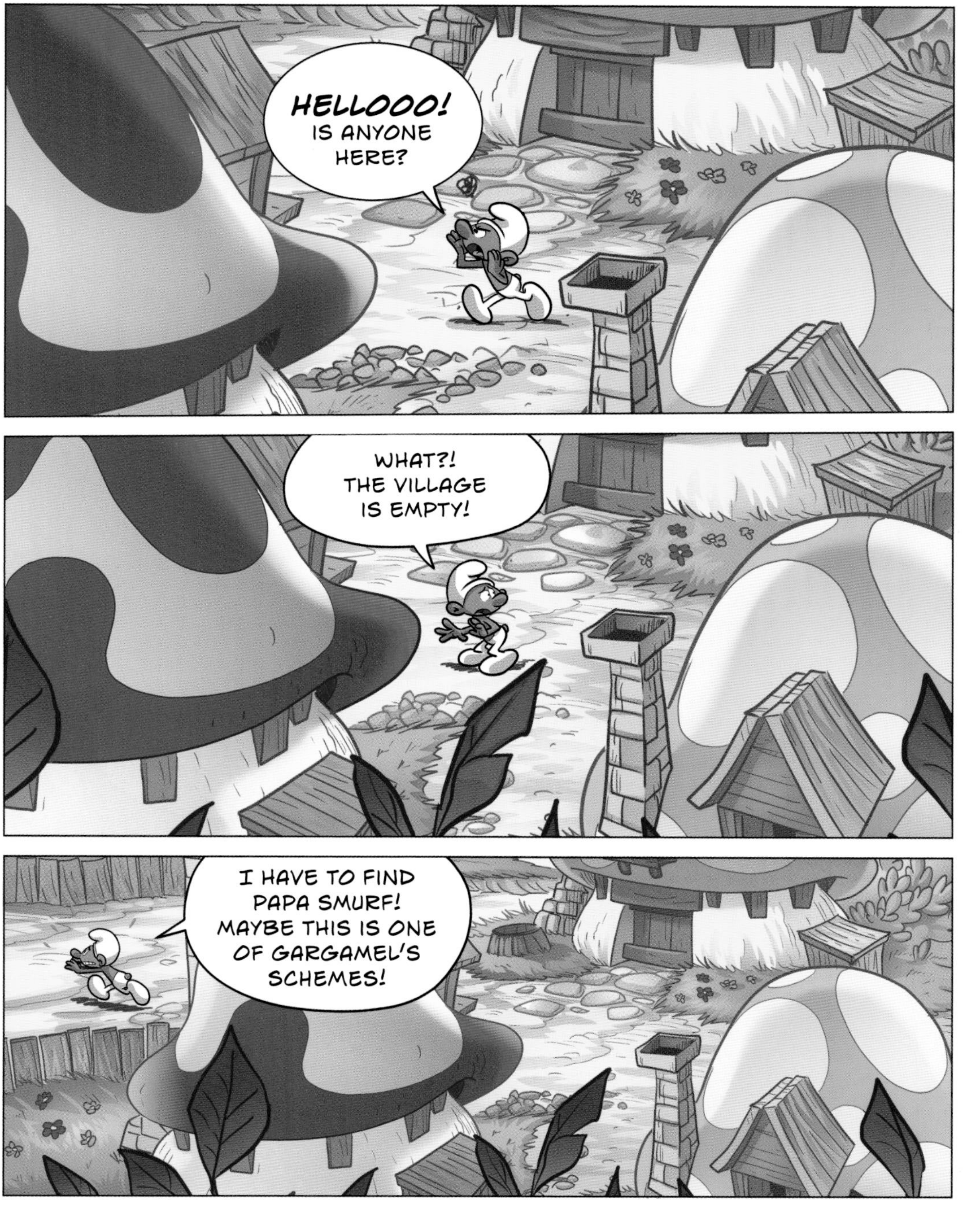
HELLOOO! IS ANYONE HERE?
WHAT?! THE VILLAGE IS EMPTY!
I HAVE TO FIND PAPA SMURF! MAYBE THIS IS ONE OF GARGAMEL'S SCHEMES!

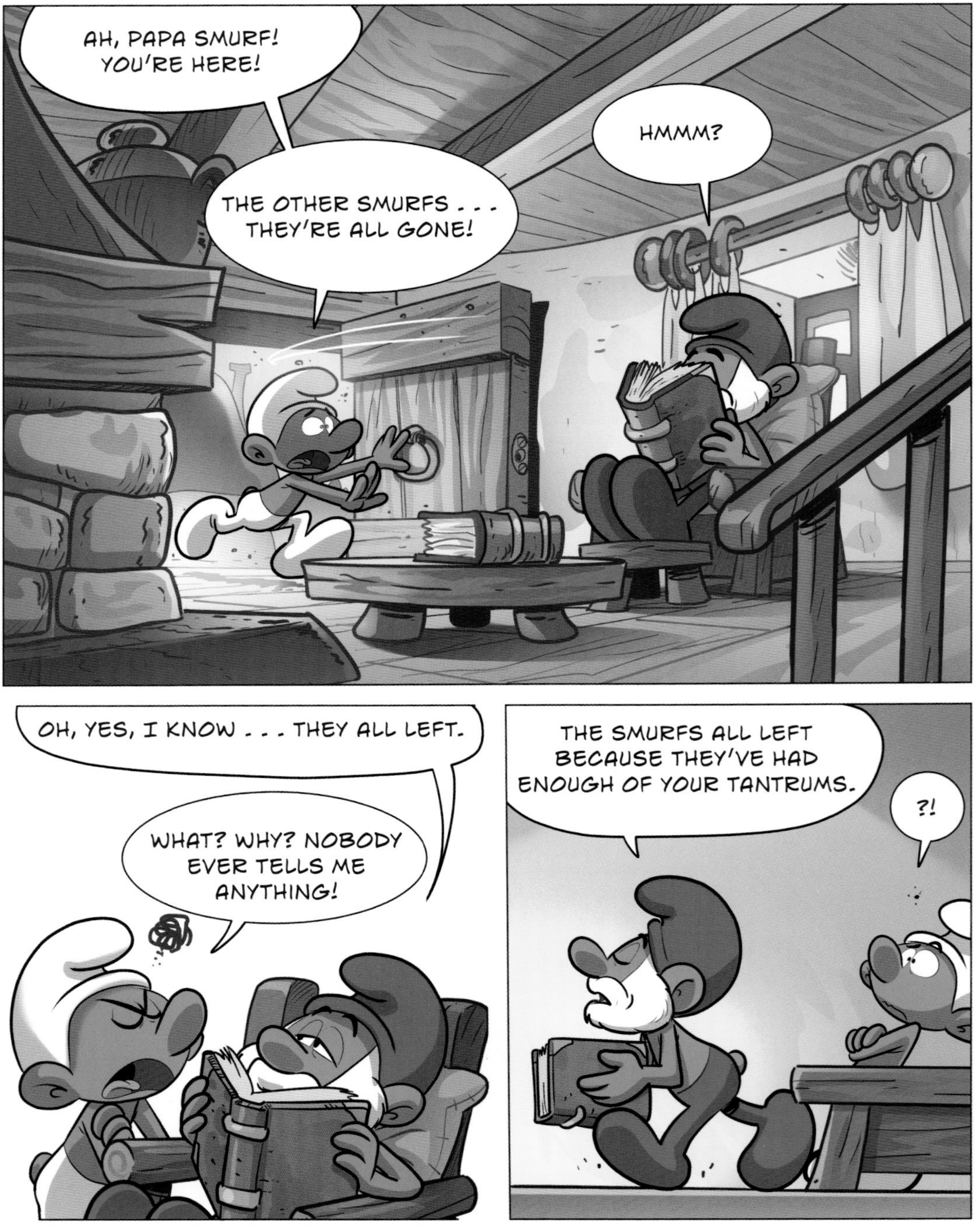
AH, PAPA SMURF! YOU'RE HERE!
THE OTHER SMURFS . . . THEY'RE ALL GONE!
HMMM?
OH, YES, I KNOW . . . THEY ALL LEFT.
WHAT? WHY? NOBODY EVER TELLS ME ANYTHING!
THE SMURFS ALL LEFT BECAUSE THEY'VE HAD ENOUGH OF YOUR TANTRUMS.
?!

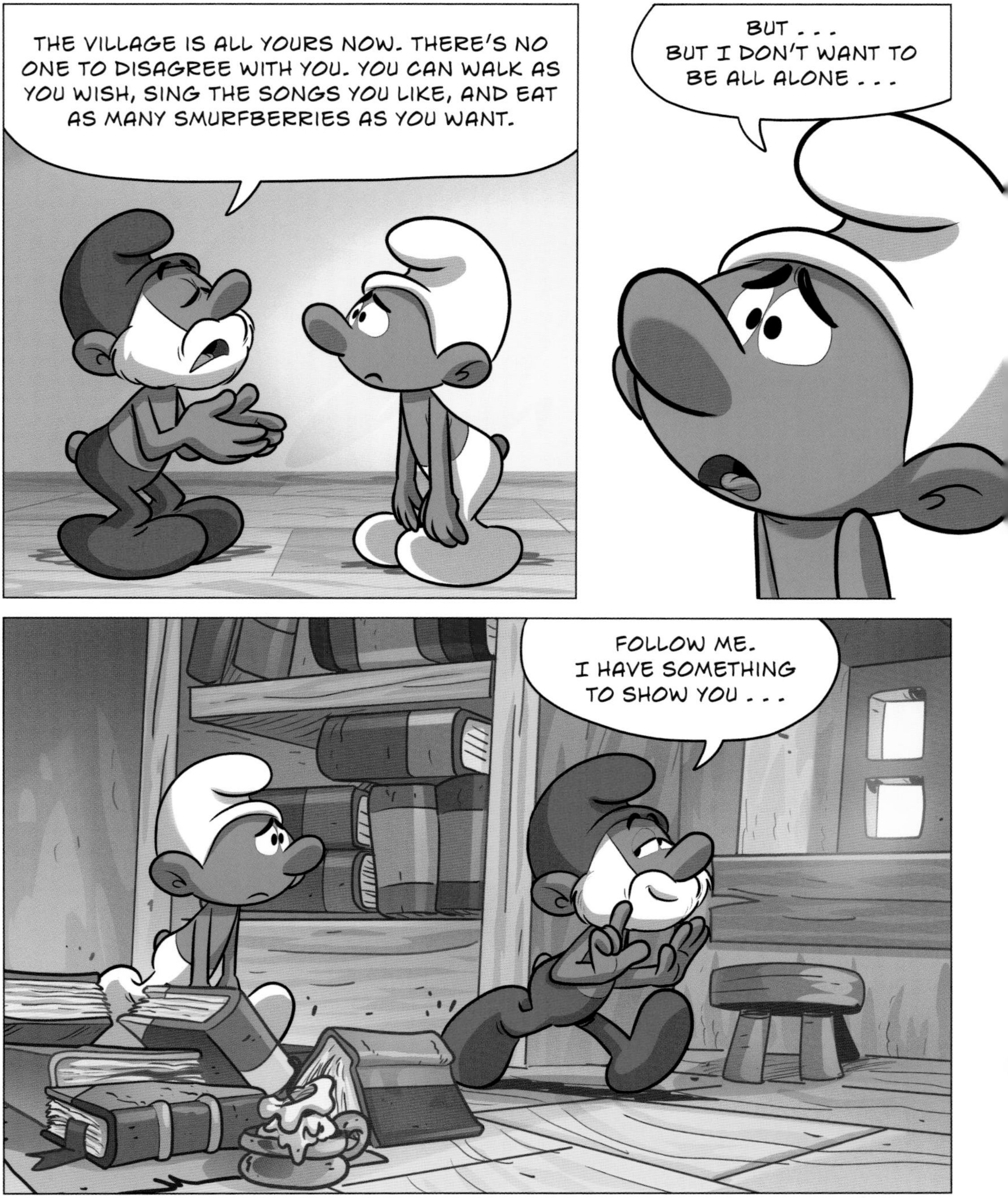
THE VILLAGE IS ALL YOURS NOW. THERE'S NO ONE TO DISAGREE WITH YOU. YOU CAN WALK AS YOU WISH, SING THE SONGS YOU LIKE, AND EAT AS MANY SMURFBERRIES AS YOU WANT.
BUT . . . BUT I DON'T WANT TO BE ALL ALONE . . .
FOLLOW ME. I HAVE SOMETHING TO SHOW YOU . . .

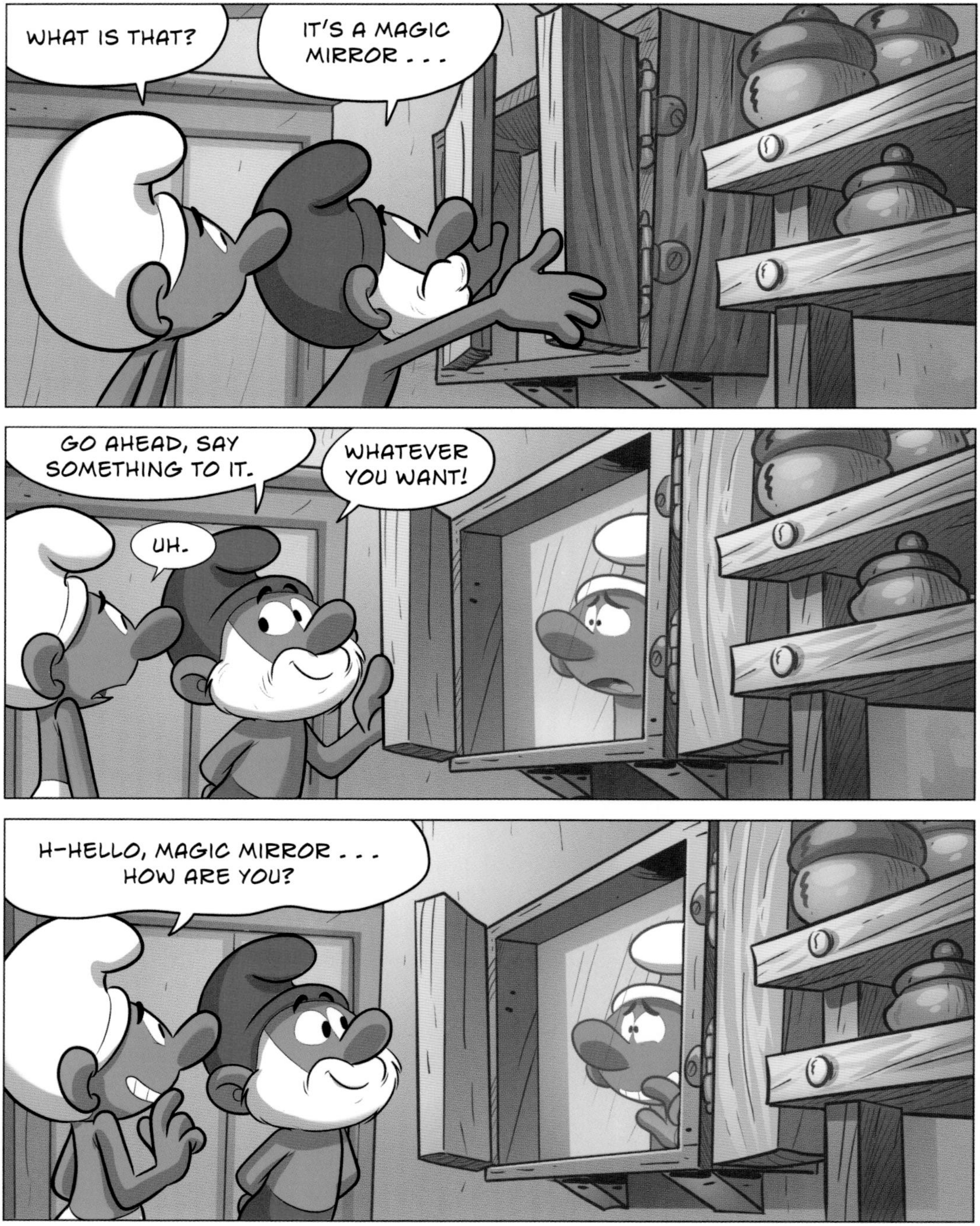
WHAT IS THAT?
IT'S A MAGIC MIRROR . . .
GO AHEAD, SAY SOMETHING TO IT.
WHATEVER YOU WANT!
UH.
H-HELLO, MAGIC MIRROR . . . HOW ARE YOU?

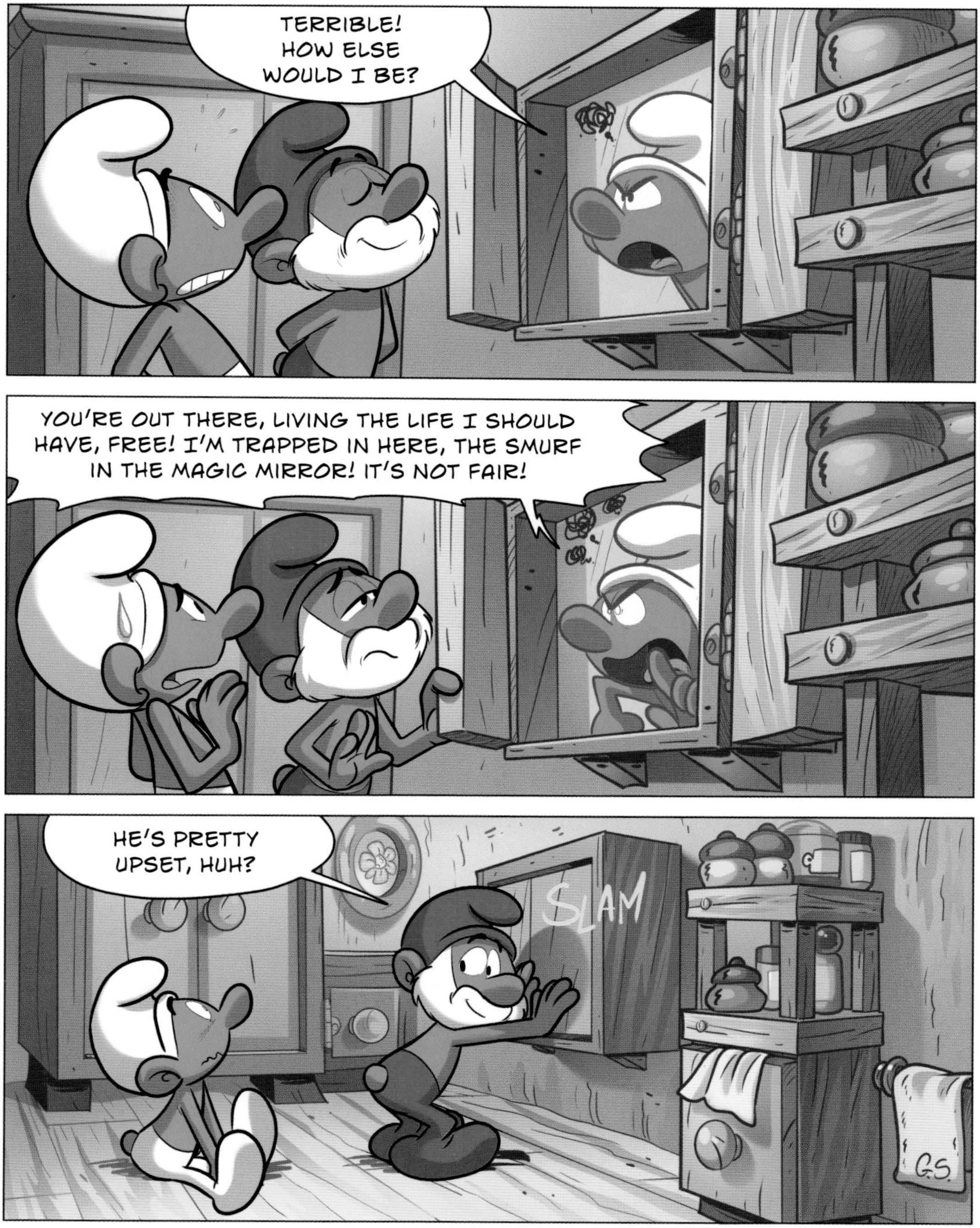
TERRIBLE! HOW ELSE WOULD I BE?
YOU'RE OUT THERE, LIVING THE LIFE I SHOULD HAVE, FREE! I'M TRAPPED IN HERE, THE SMURF IN THE MAGIC MIRROR! IT'S NOT FAIR!
HE'S PRETTY UPSET, HUH?
SLAM

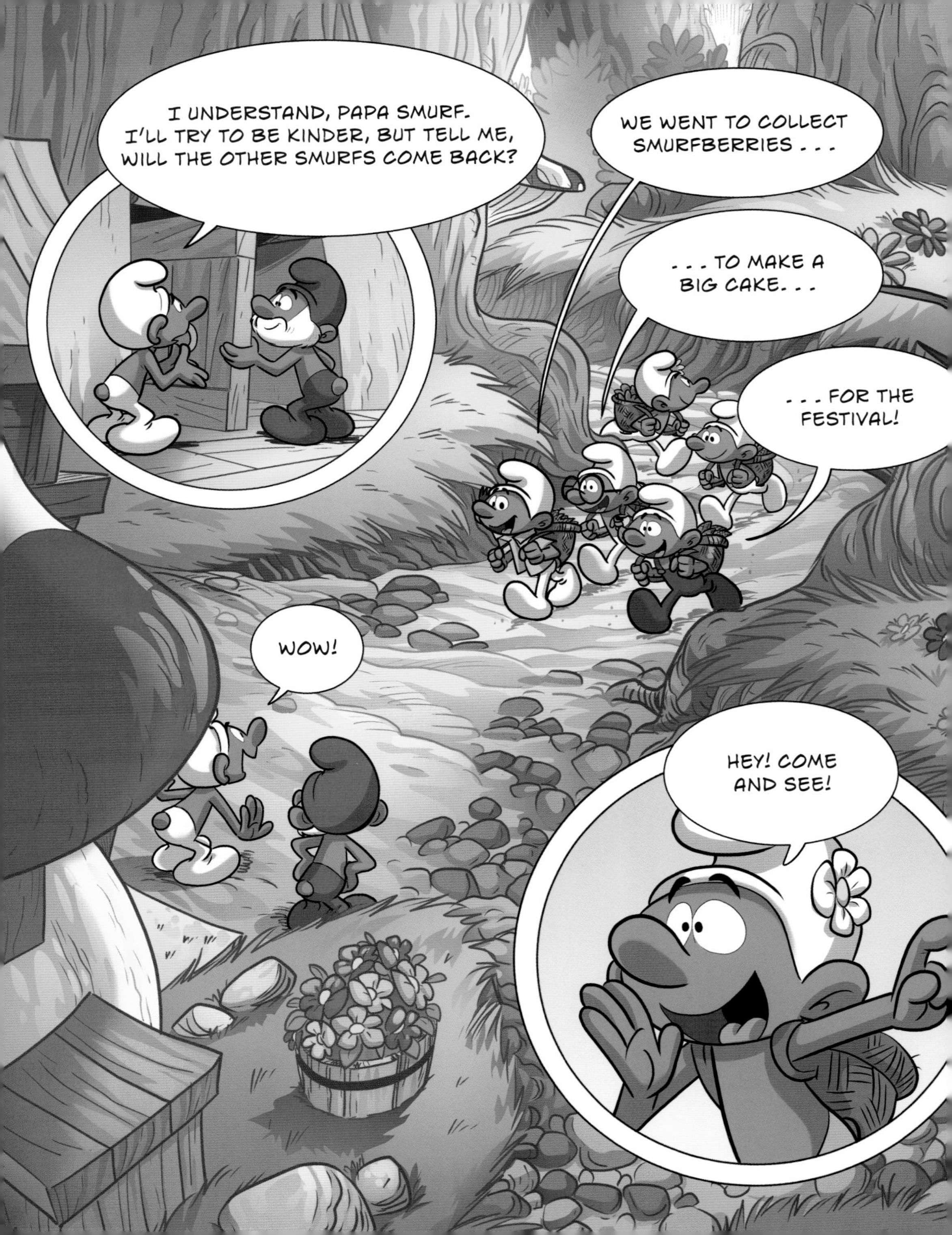
I UNDERSTAND, PAPA SMURF. I'LL TRY TO BE KINDER, BUT TELL ME, WILL THE OTHER SMURFS COME BACK?
WE WENT TO COLLECT SMURFBERRIES . . .
. . . TO MAKE A BIG CAKE. . .
. . . FOR THE FESTIVAL!
WOW!
HEY! COME AND SEE!

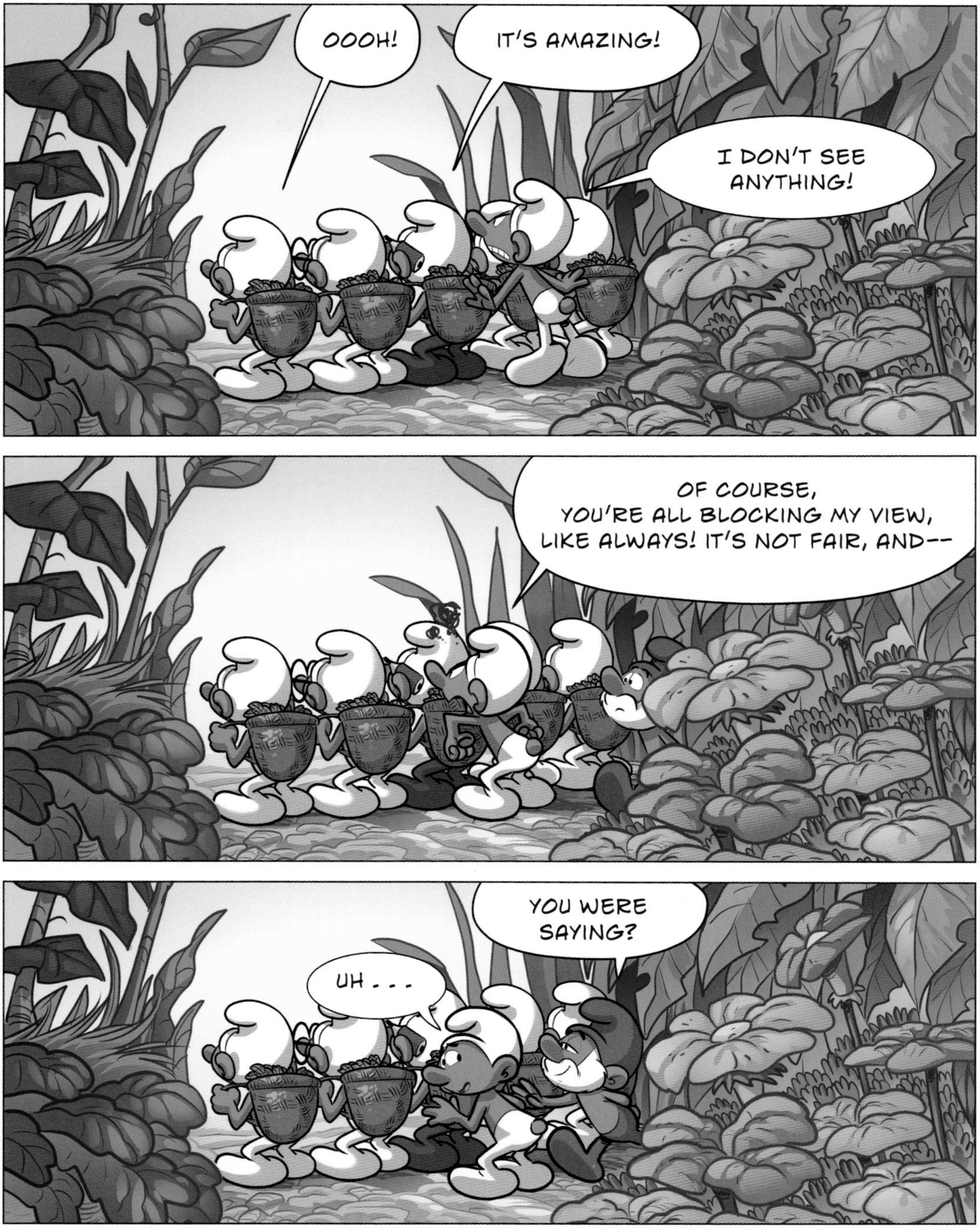
OOOH!
IT'S AMAZING!
I DON'T SEE ANYTHING!
OF COURSE, YOU'RE ALL BLOCKING MY VIEW, LIKE ALWAYS! IT'S NOT FAIR, AND--
YOU WERE SAYING?
UH . . .

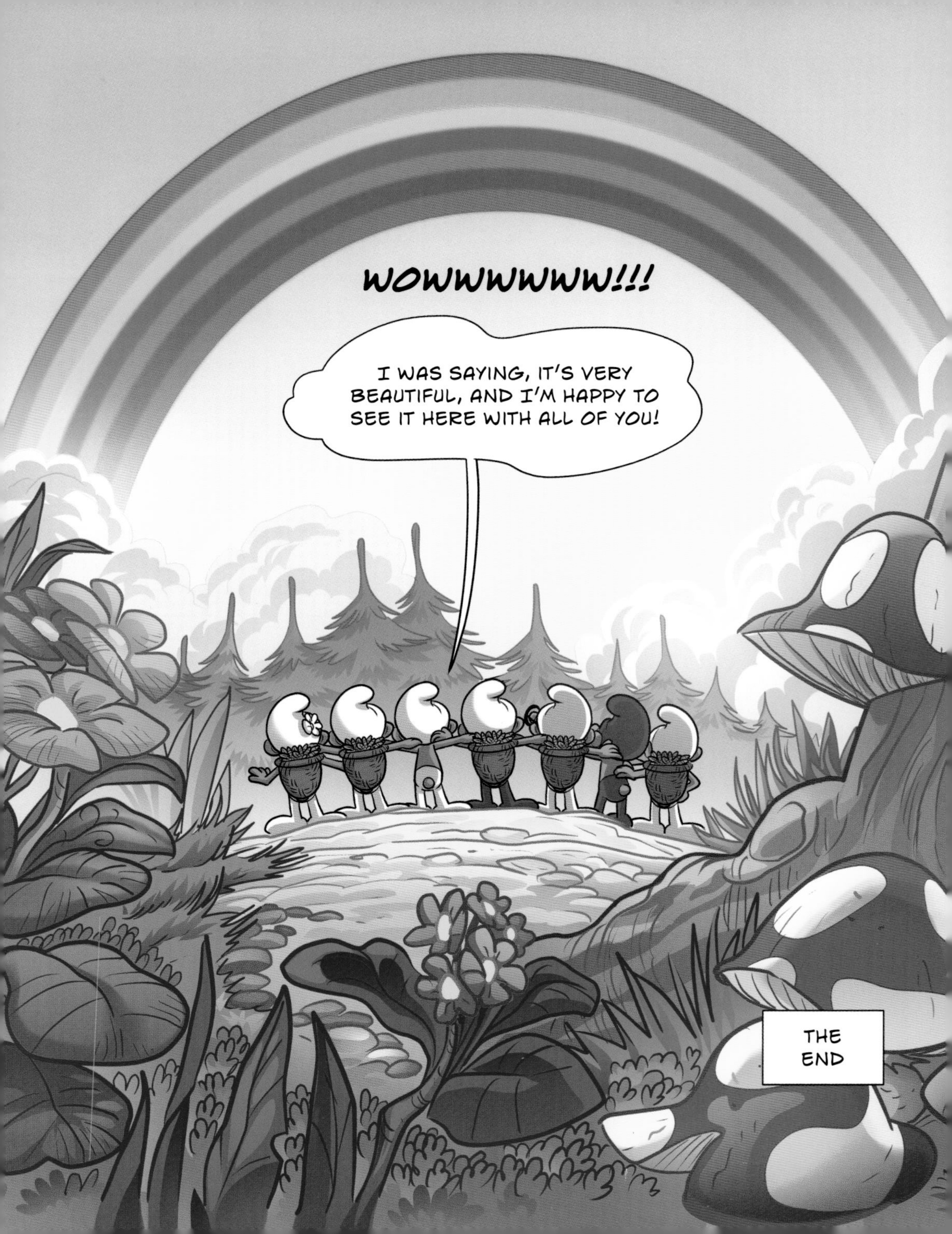
WOWWWWWW!!!
I WAS SAYING, IT'S VERY BEAUTIFUL, AND I'M HAPPY TO SEE IT HERE WITH ALL OF YOU!
THE END

THE SMURF WHO TOLD LIES

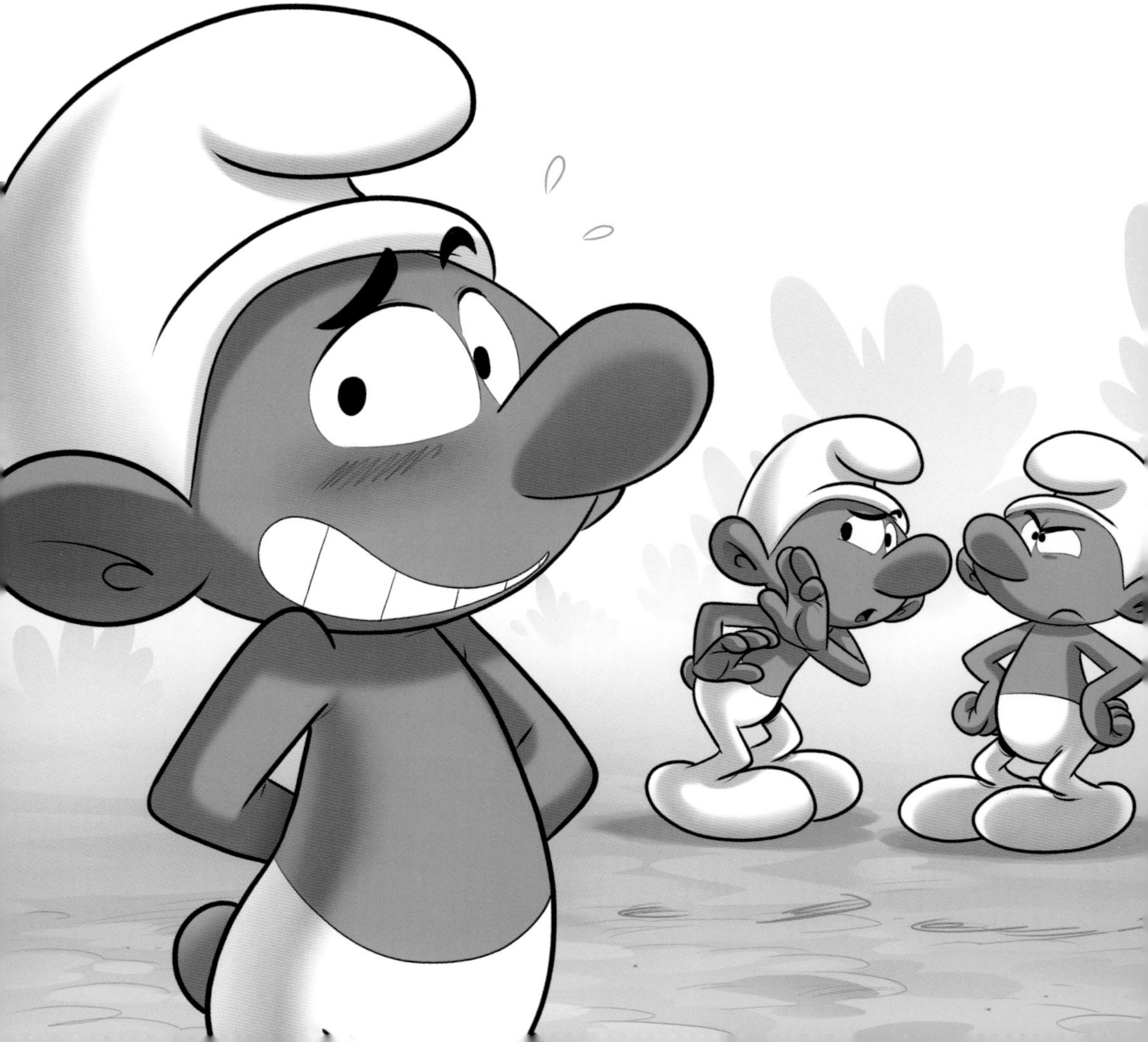

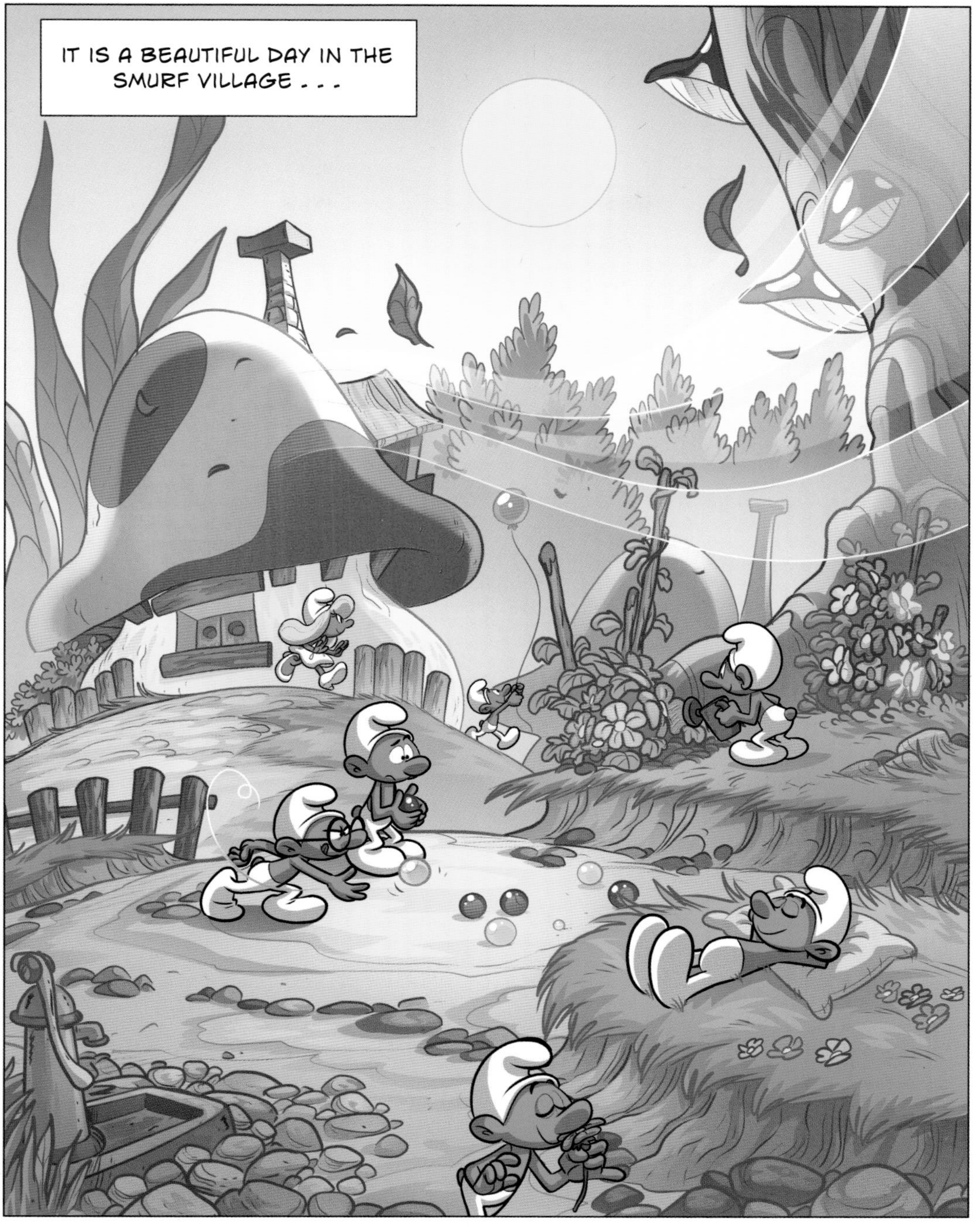
IT IS A BEAUTIFUL DAY IN THE SMURF VILLAGE . . .

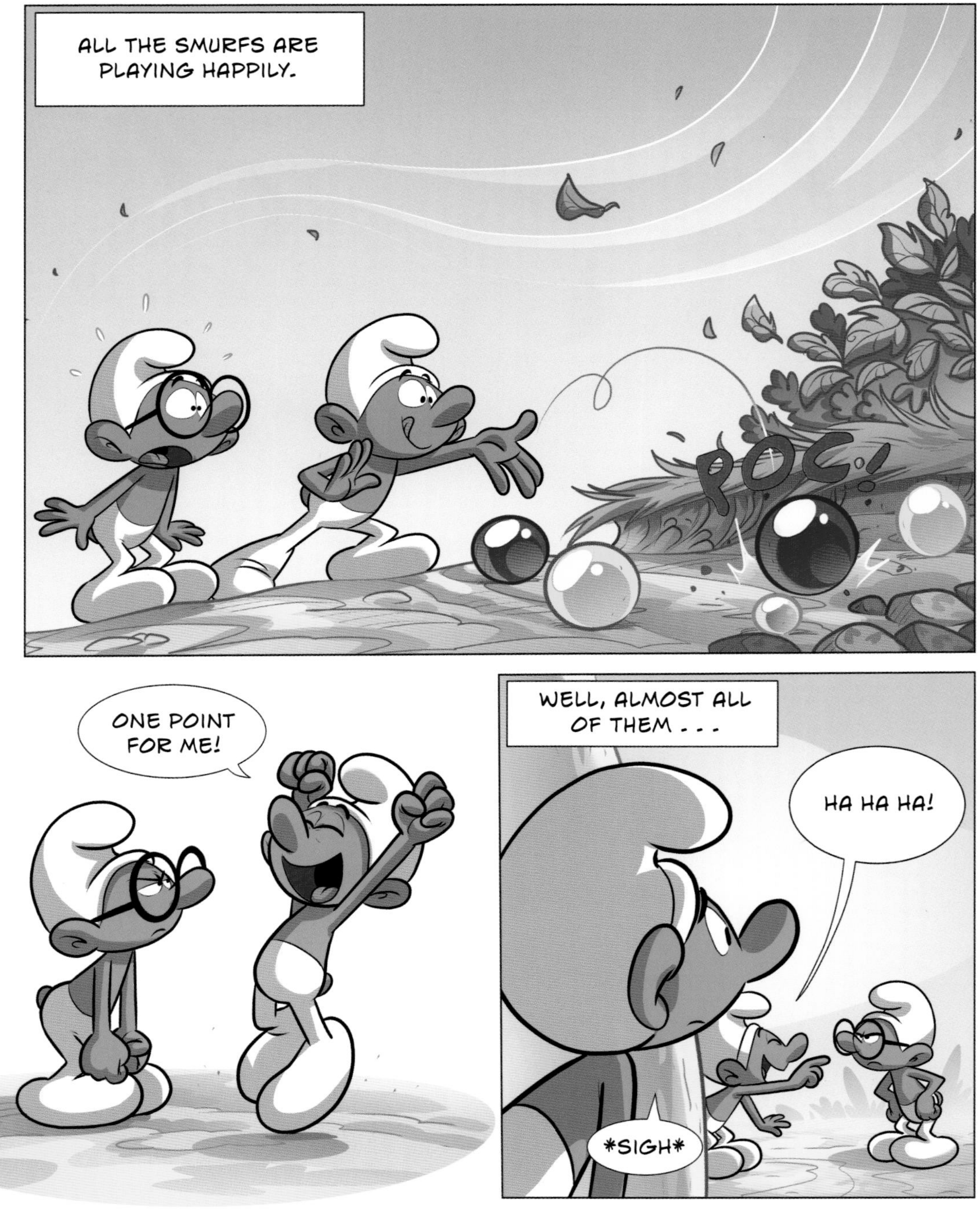

ALL THE SMURFS ARE PLAYING HAPPILY.
POC!
ONE POINT FOR ME!
WELL, ALMOST ALL OF THEM . . .
HA HA HA!
SIGH

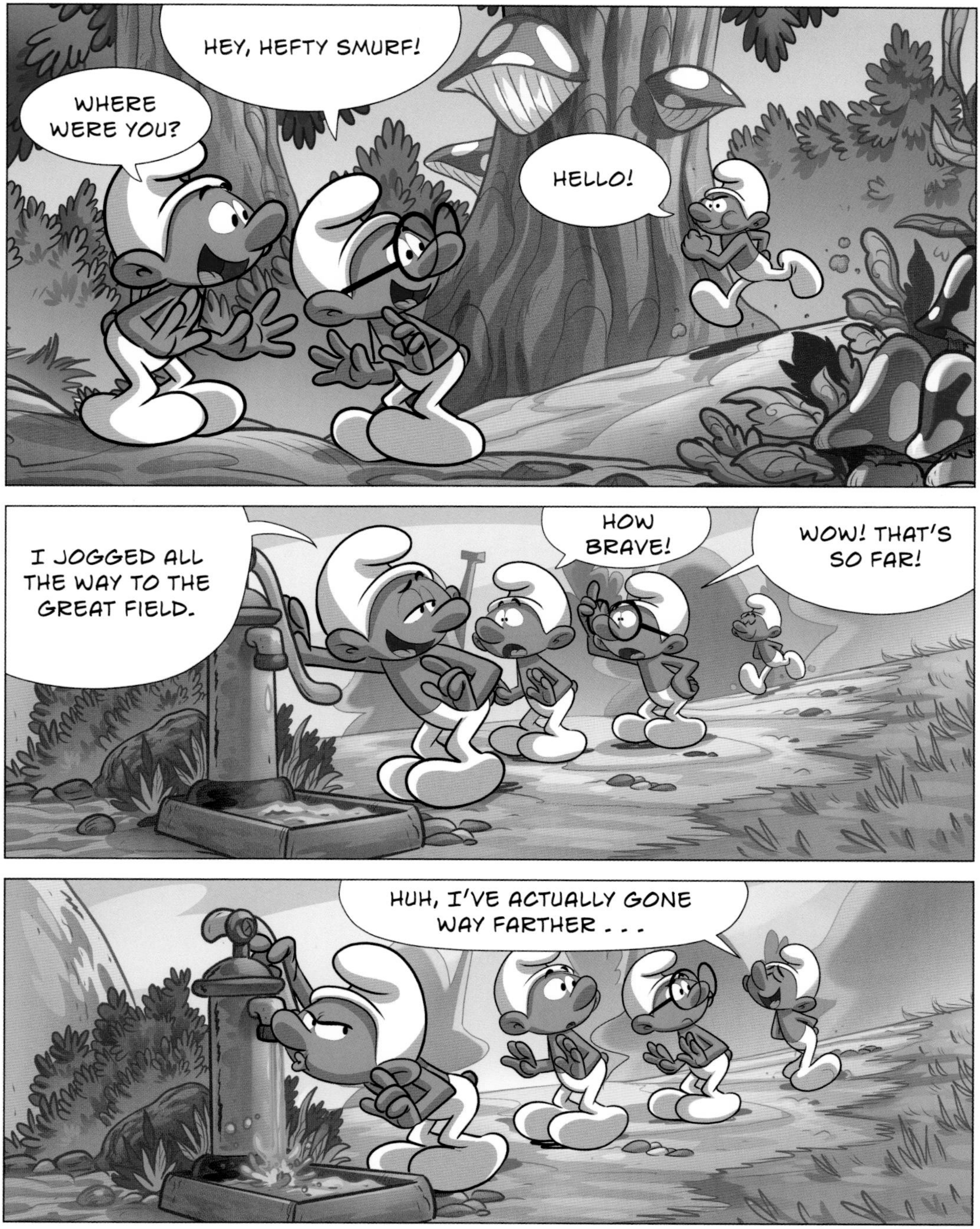
HEY, HEFTY SMURF!
WHERE WERE YOU?
HELLO!
I JOGGED ALL THE WAY TO THE GREAT FIELD.
HOW BRAVE!
WOW! THAT'S SO FAR!
HUH, I'VE ACTUALLY GONE WAY FARTHER . . .

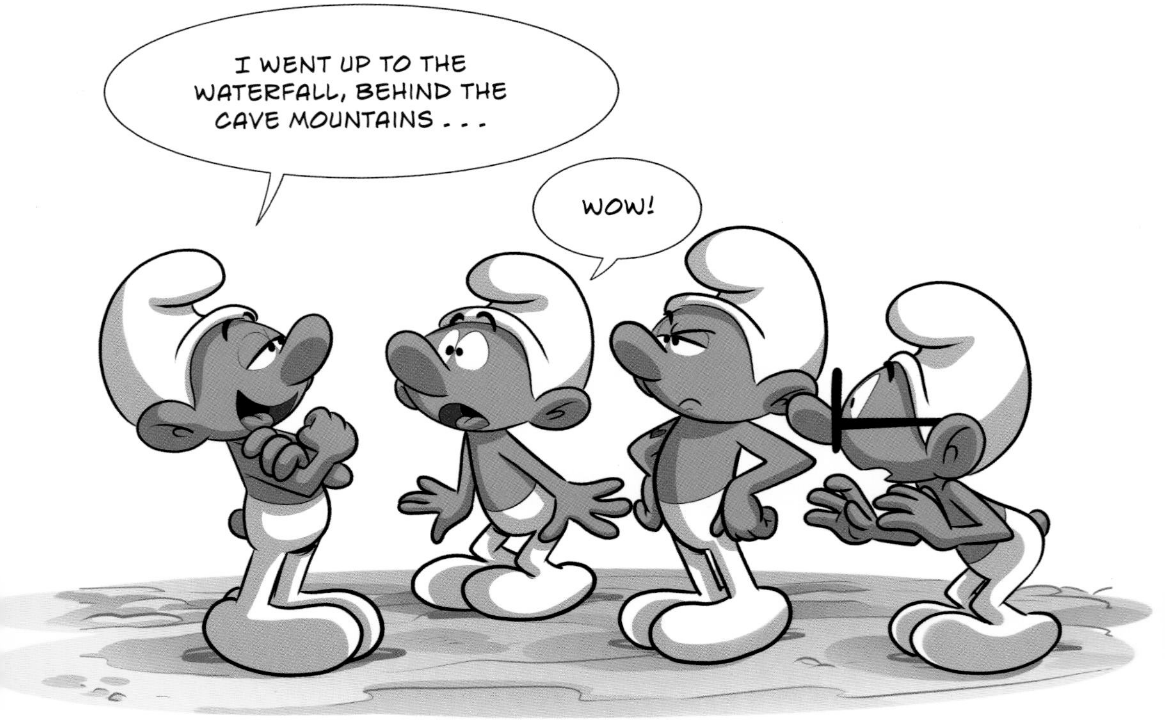
I WENT UP TO THE WATERFALL, BEHIND THE CAVE MOUNTAINS . . .
WOW!

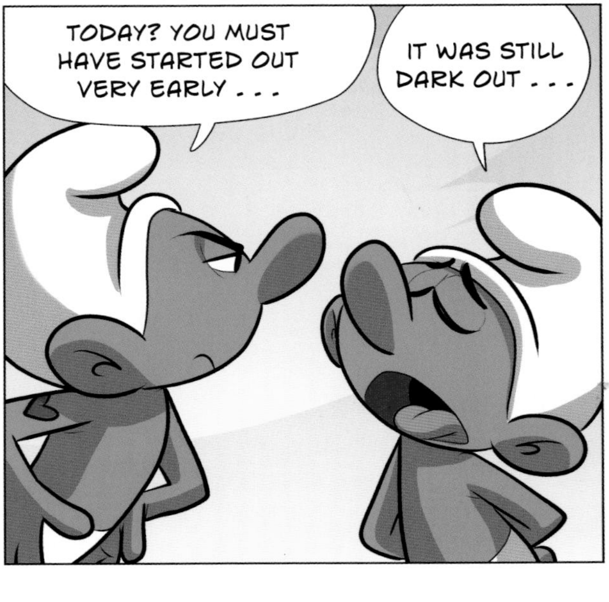
TODAY? YOU MUST HAVE STARTED OUT VERY EARLY . . .
IT WAS STILL DARK OUT . . .

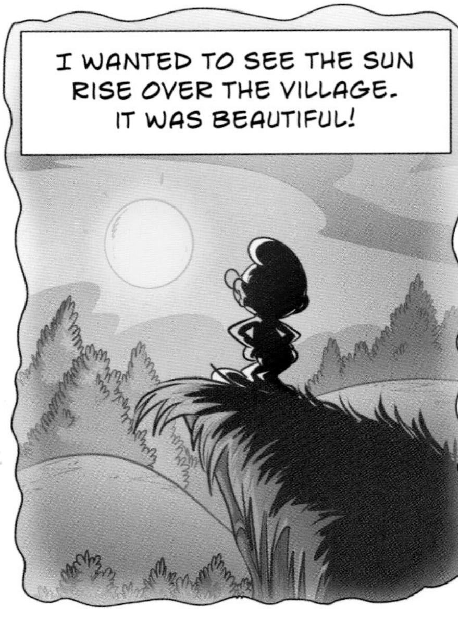
I WANTED TO SEE THE SUN RISE OVER THE VILLAGE. IT WAS BEAUTIFUL!

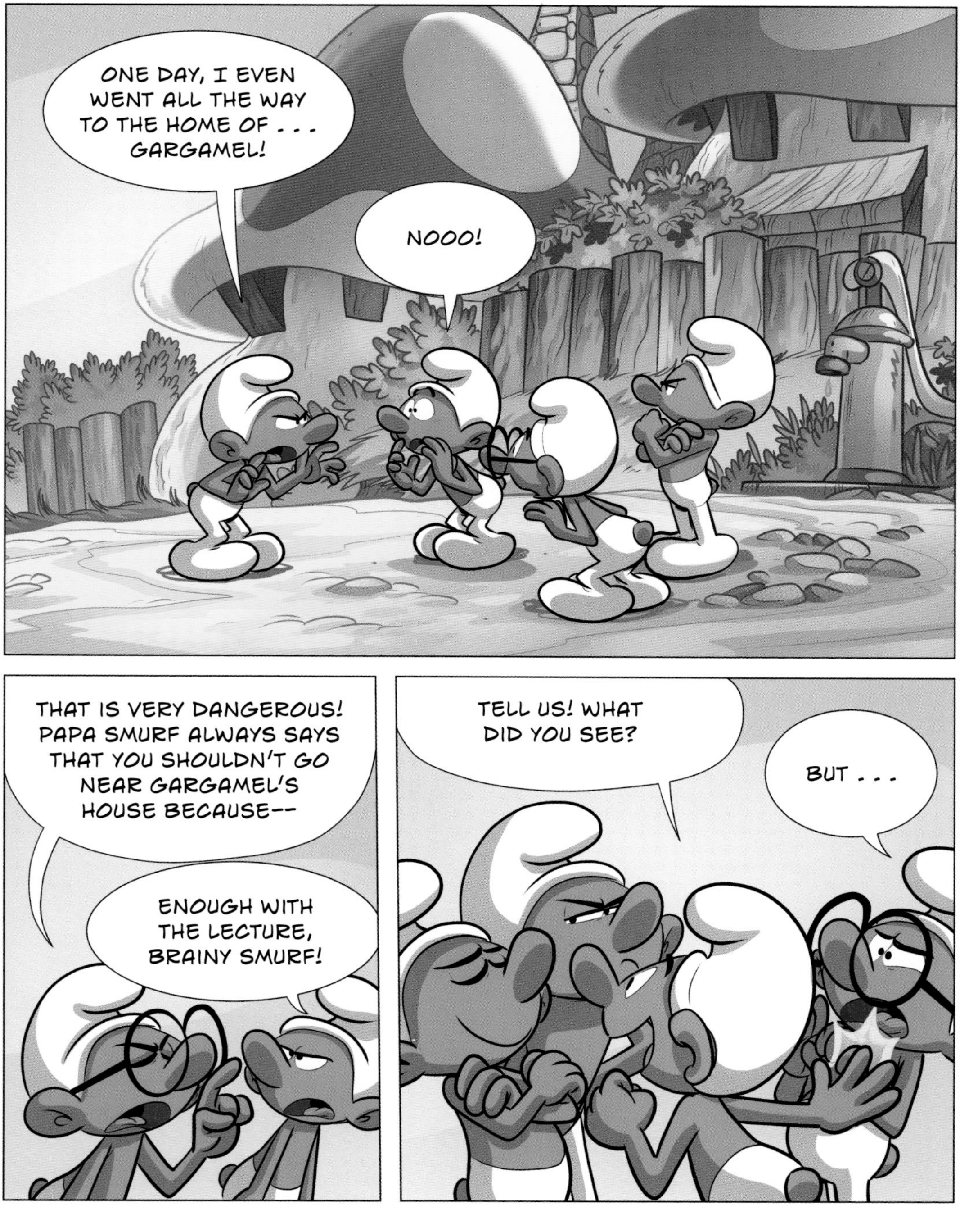
ONE DAY, I EVEN WENT ALL THE WAY TO THE HOME OF . . . GARGAMEL!
NOOO!
THAT IS VERY DANGEROUS! PAPA SMURF ALWAYS SAYS THAT YOU SHOULDN'T GO NEAR GARGAMEL'S HOUSE BECAUSE--
ENOUGH WITH THE LECTURE, BRAINY SMURF!
TELL US! WHAT DID YOU SEE?
BUT . . .

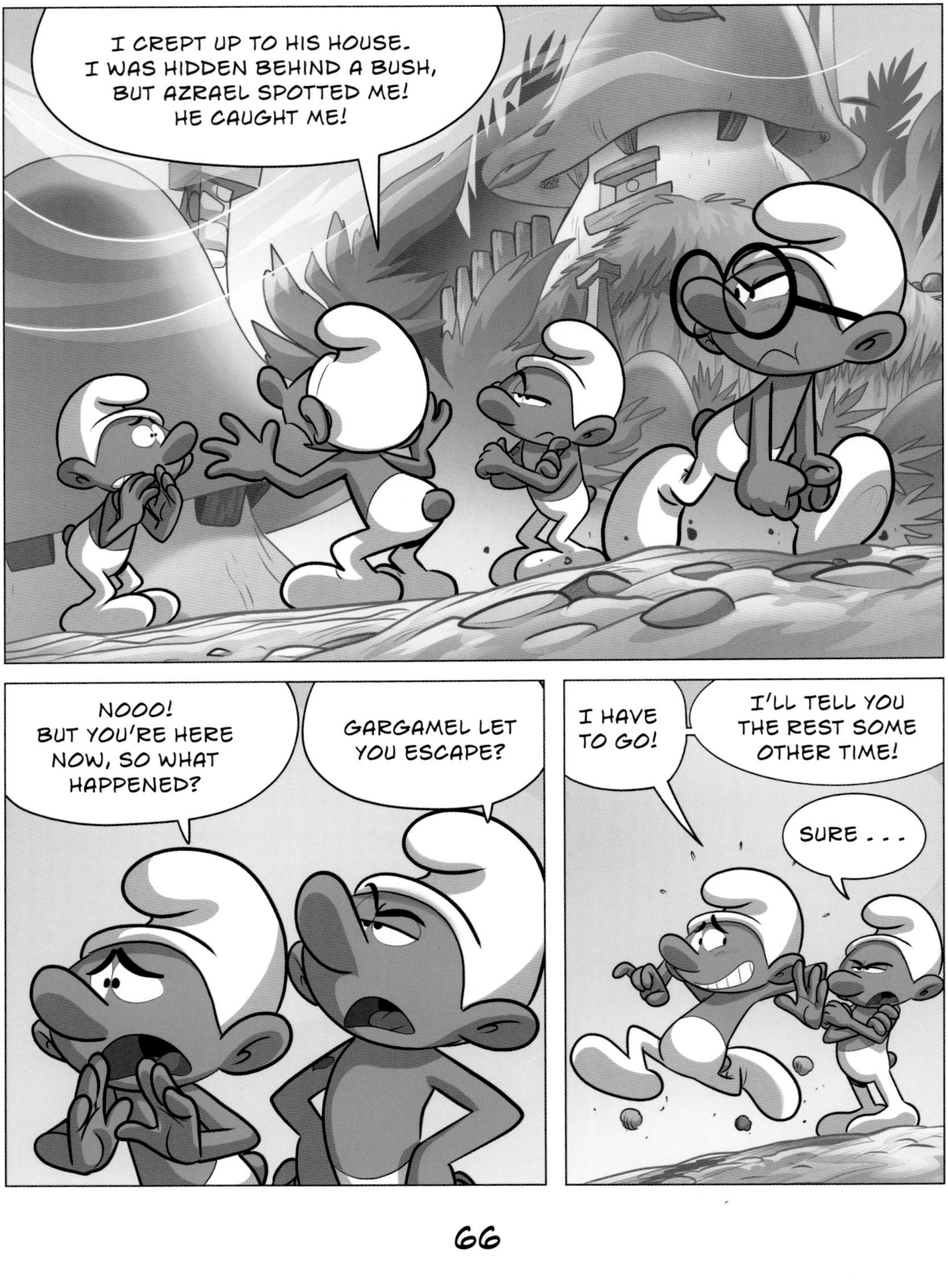
I CREPT UP TO HIS HOUSE. I WAS HIDDEN BEHIND A BUSH, BUT AZRAEL SPOTTED ME! HE CAUGHT ME!
NOOO! BUT YOU'RE HERE NOW, SO WHAT HAPPENED?
GARGAMEL LET YOU ESCAPE?
I HAVE TO GO!
I'LL TELL YOU THE REST SOME OTHER TIME!
SURE . . .

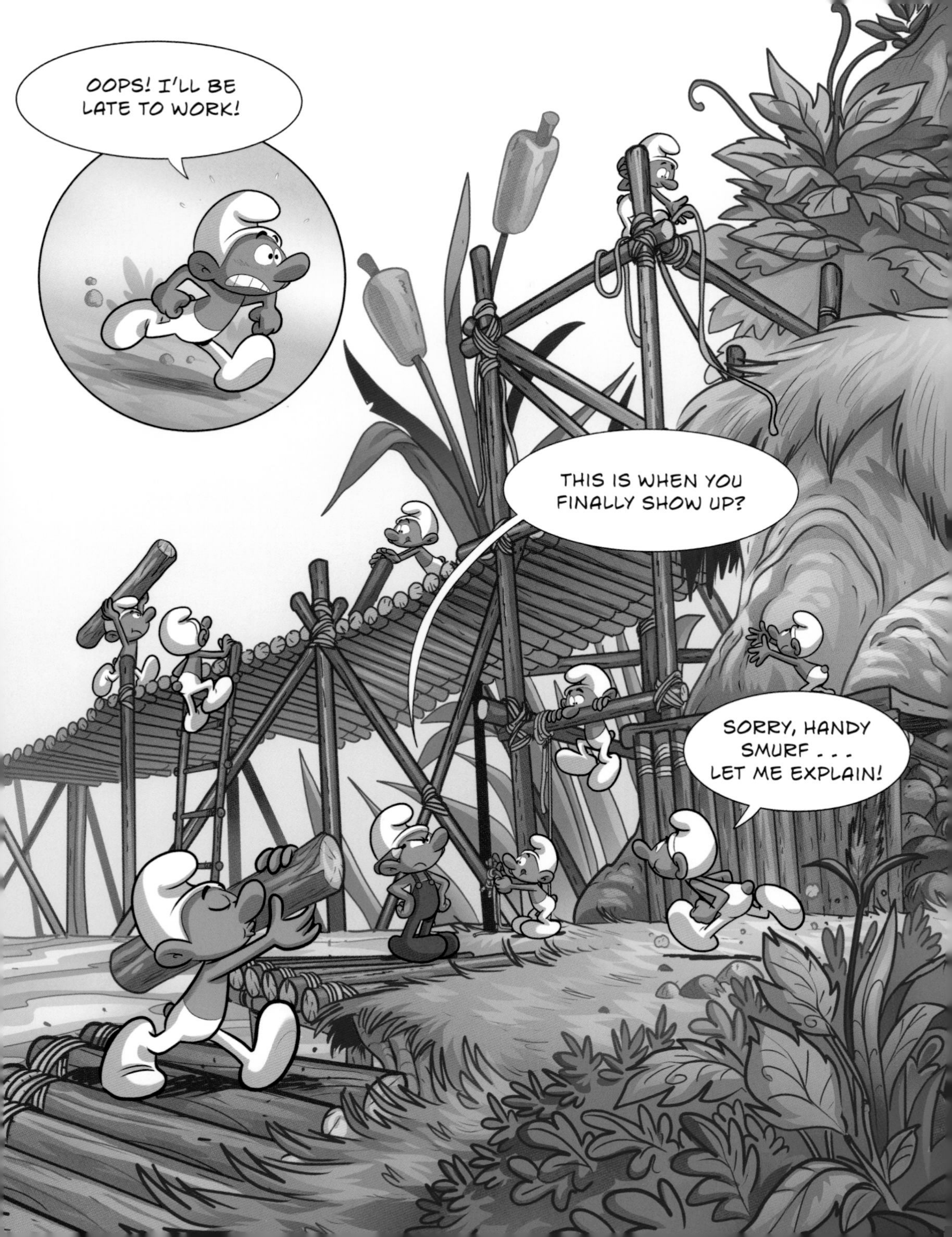
OOPS! I'LL BE LATE TO WORK!
THIS IS WHEN YOU FINALLY SHOW UP?
SORRY, HANDY SMURF . . . LET ME EXPLAIN!

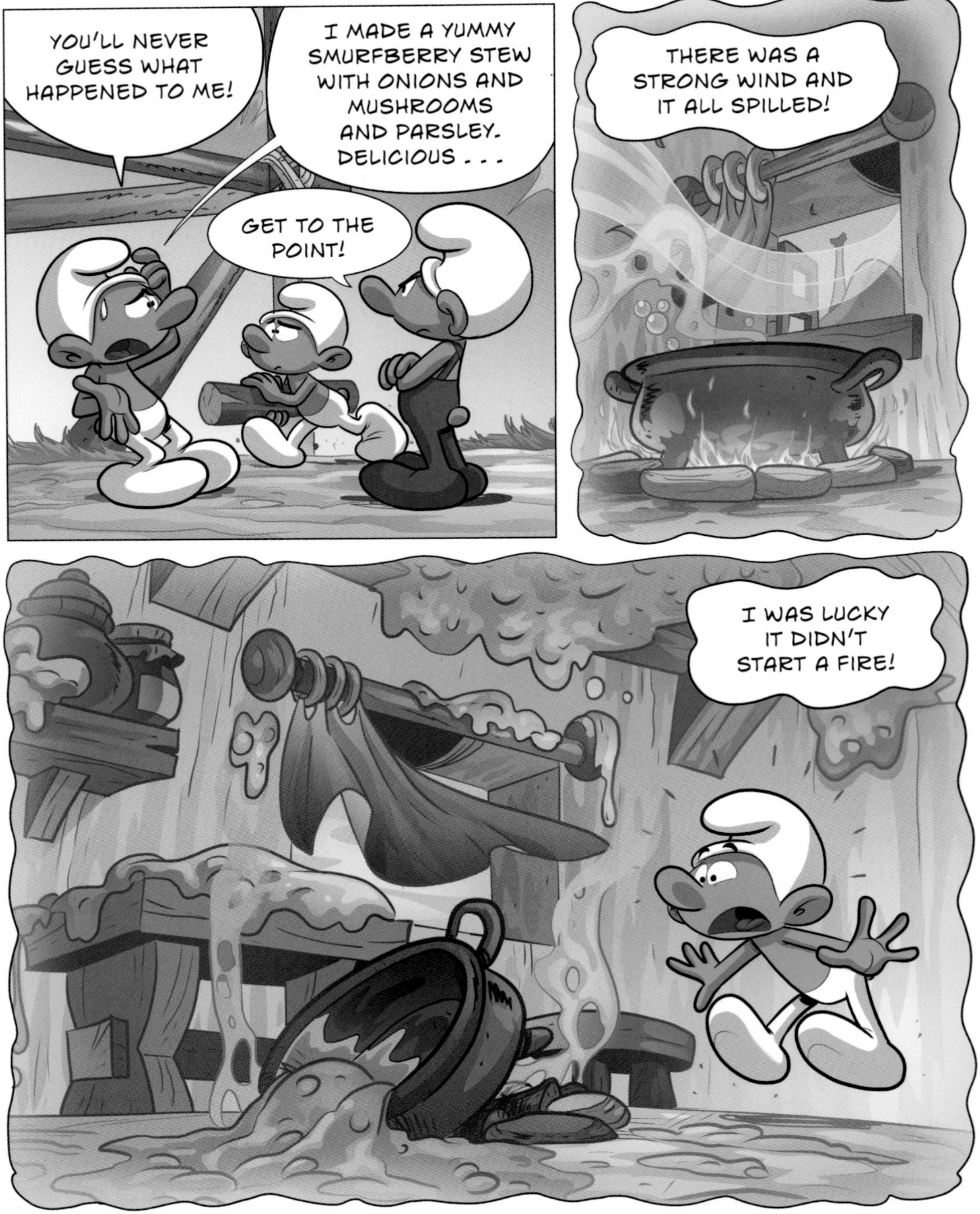
YOU'LL NEVER GUESS WHAT HAPPENED TO ME!
I MADE A YUMMY SMURFBERRY STEW WITH ONIONS AND MUSHROOMS AND PARSLEY. DELICIOUS . . .
GET TO THE POINT!
THERE WAS A STRONG WIND AND IT ALL SPILLED!
I WAS LUCKY IT DIDN'T START A FIRE!

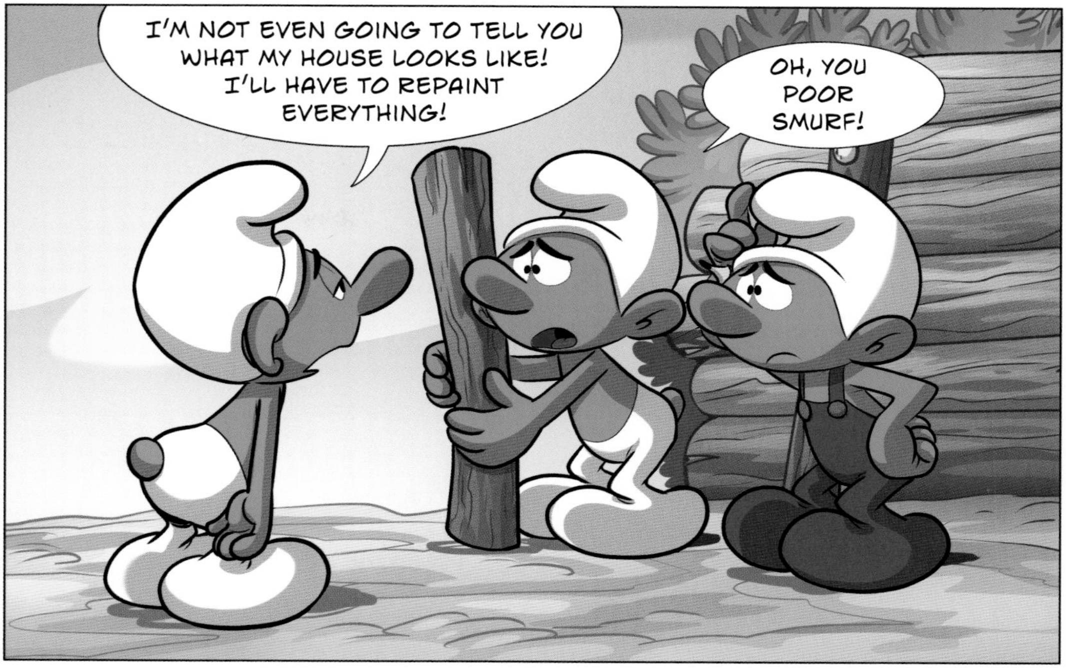
I'M NOT EVEN GOING TO TELL YOU WHAT MY HOUSE LOOKS LIKE! I'LL HAVE TO REPAINT EVERYTHING!
OH, YOU POOR SMURF!

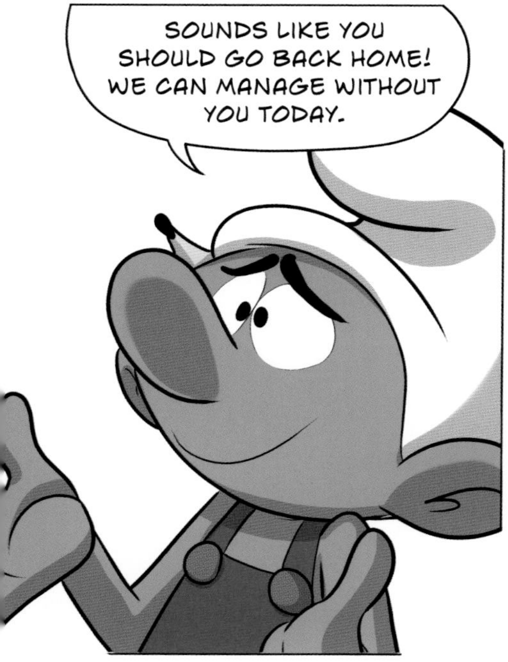
SOUNDS LIKE YOU SHOULD GO BACK HOME! WE CAN MANAGE WITHOUT YOU TODAY.

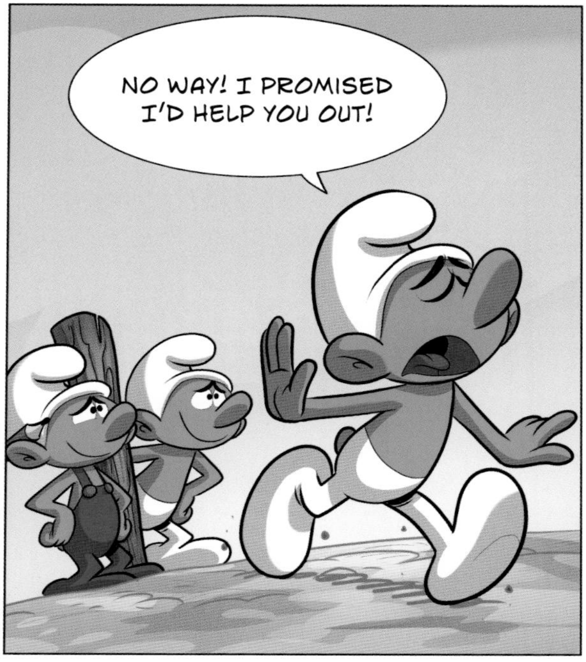
NO WAY! I PROMISED I'D HELP YOU OUT!

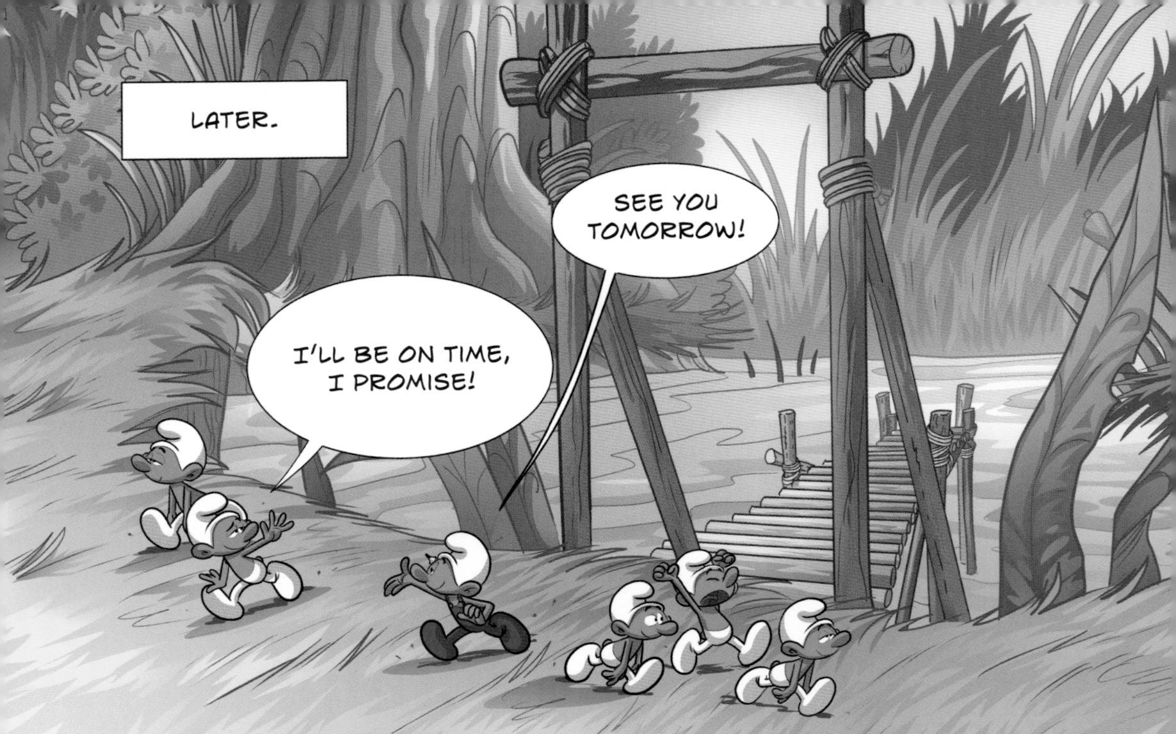
LATER.
I'LL BE ON TIME, I PROMISE!
SEE YOU TOMORROW!

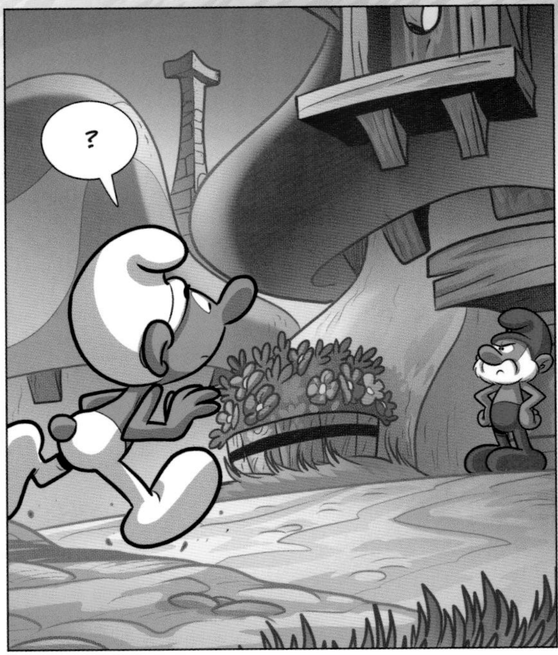
?

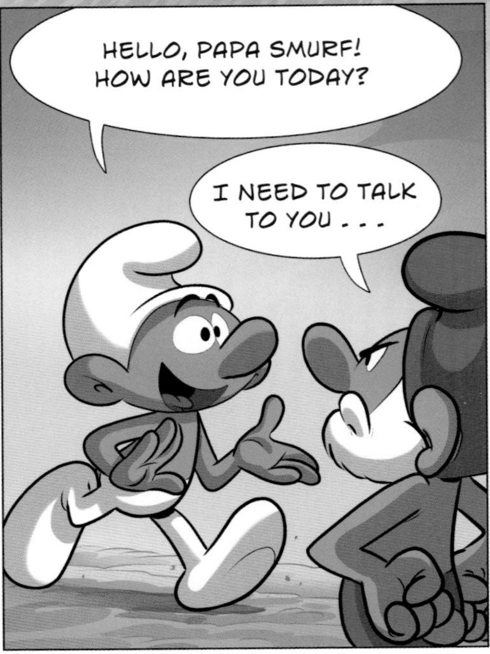
HELLO, PAPA SMURF! HOW ARE YOU TODAY?
I NEED TO TALK TO YOU . . .

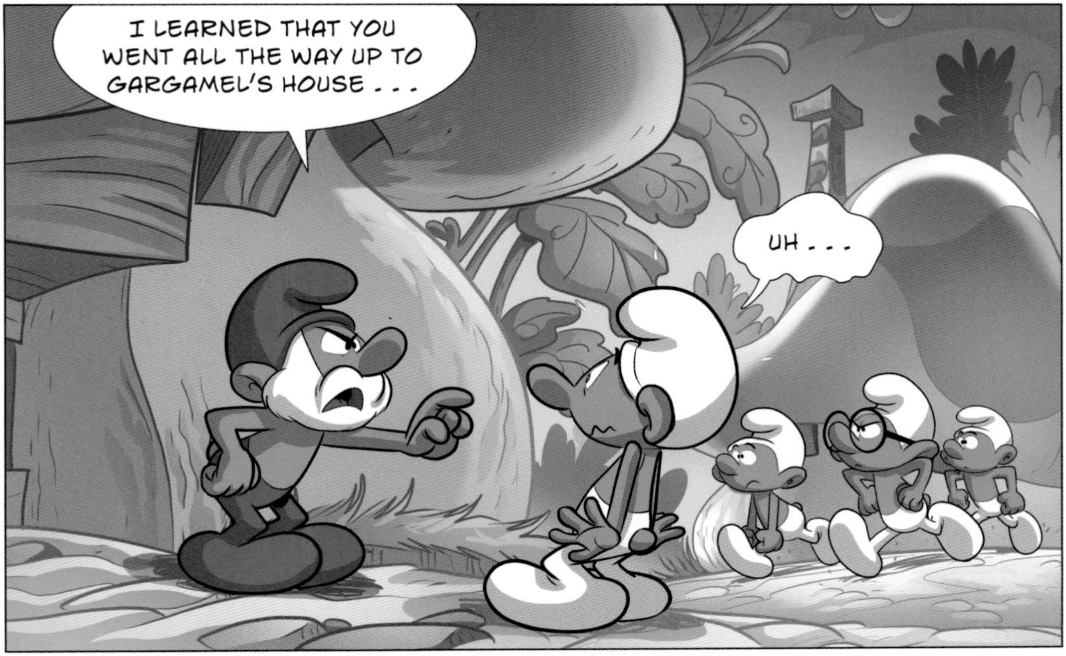
I LEARNED THAT YOU WENT ALL THE WAY UP TO GARGAMEL'S HOUSE . . .
UH . . .

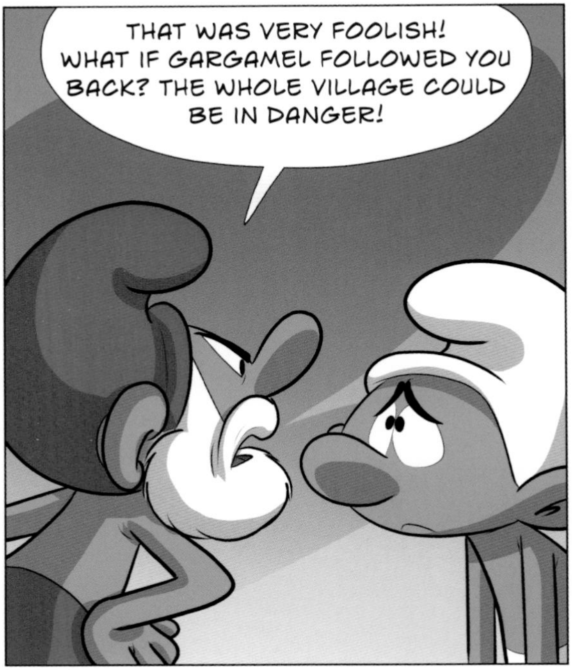
THAT WAS VERY FOOLISH! WHAT IF GARGAMEL FOLLOWED YOU BACK? THE WHOLE VILLAGE COULD BE IN DANGER!

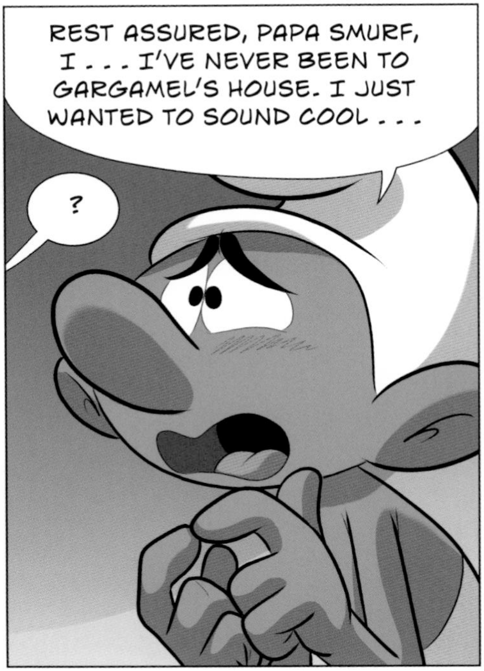
REST ASSURED, PAPA SMURF, I . . . I'VE NEVER BEEN TO GARGAMEL'S HOUSE. I JUST WANTED TO SOUND COOL . . .
?

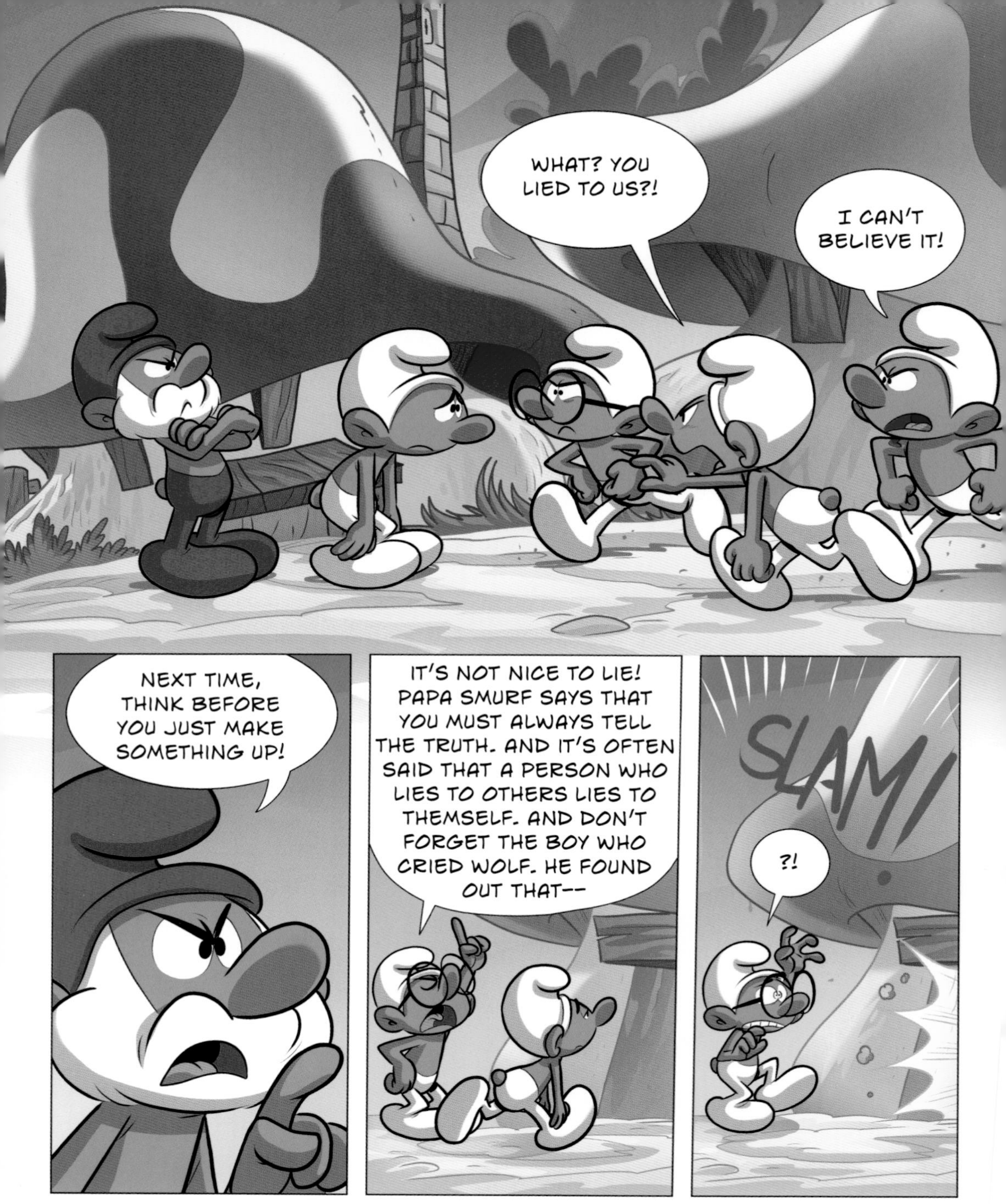

WHAT? YOU LIED TO US?!
I CAN'T BELIEVE IT!
NEXT TIME, THINK BEFORE YOU JUST MAKE SOMETHING UP!
IT'S NOT NICE TO LIE! PAPA SMURF SAYS THAT YOU MUST ALWAYS TELL THE TRUTH. AND IT'S OFTEN SAID THAT A PERSON WHO LIES TO OTHERS LIES TO THEMSELF. AND DON'T FORGET THE BOY WHO CRIED WOLF. HE FOUND OUT THAT--
SLAM!
?!

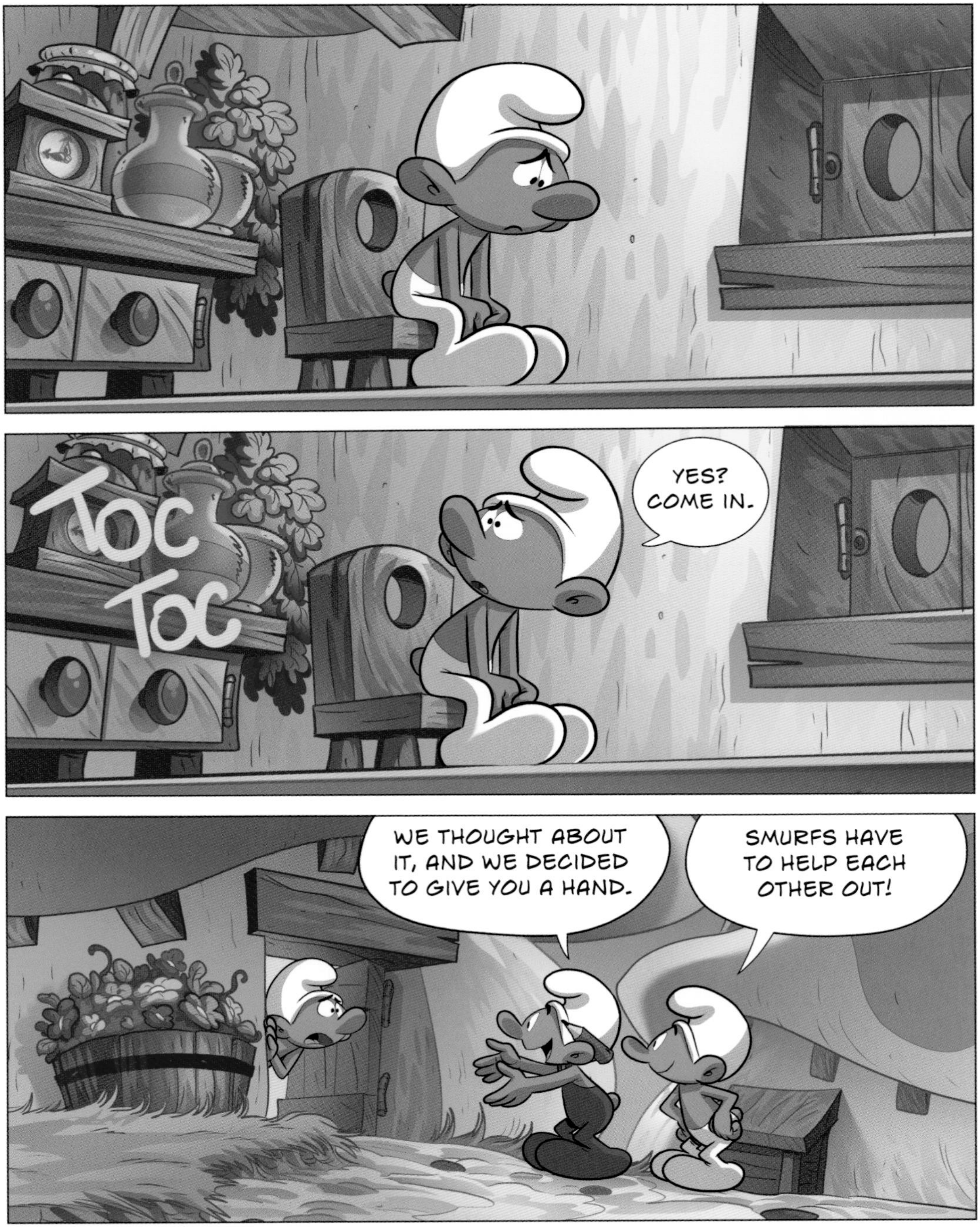
TOC TOC
YES? COME IN.
WE THOUGHT ABOUT IT, AND WE DECIDED TO GIVE YOU A HAND.
SMURFS HAVE TO HELP EACH OTHER OUT!

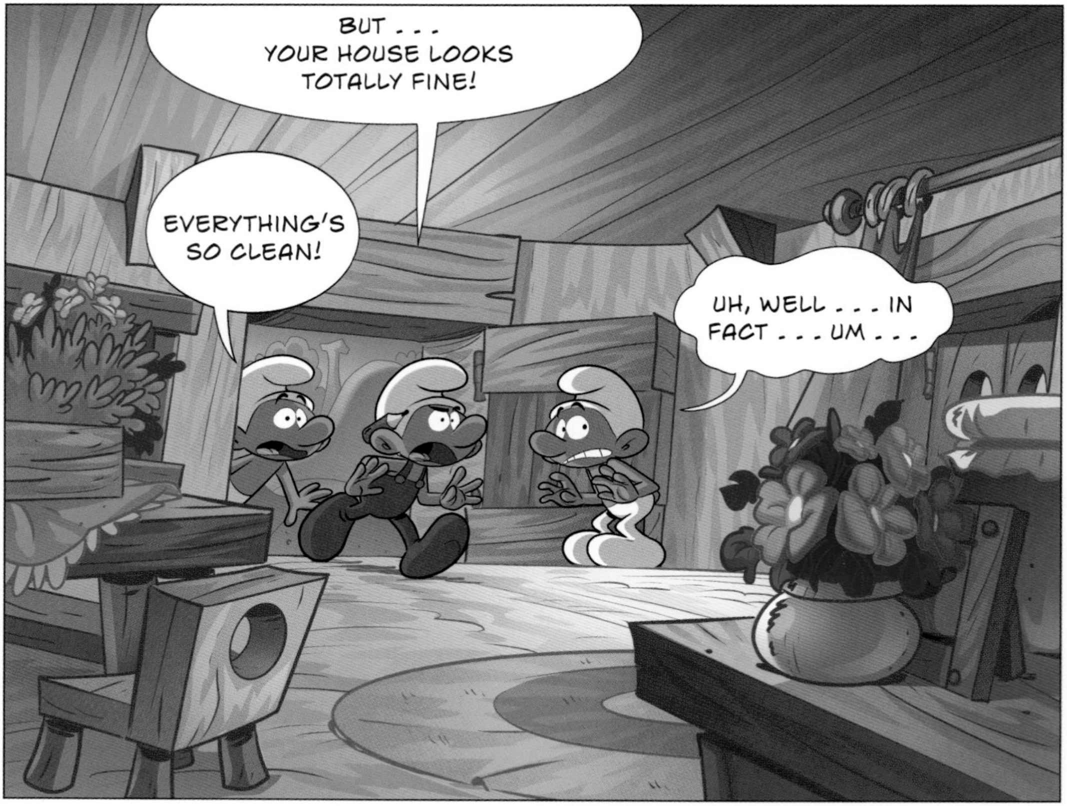
BUT . . .
YOUR HOUSE LOOKS TOTALLY FINE!
EVERYTHING'S SO CLEAN!
UH, WELL . . . IN FACT . . . UM . . .

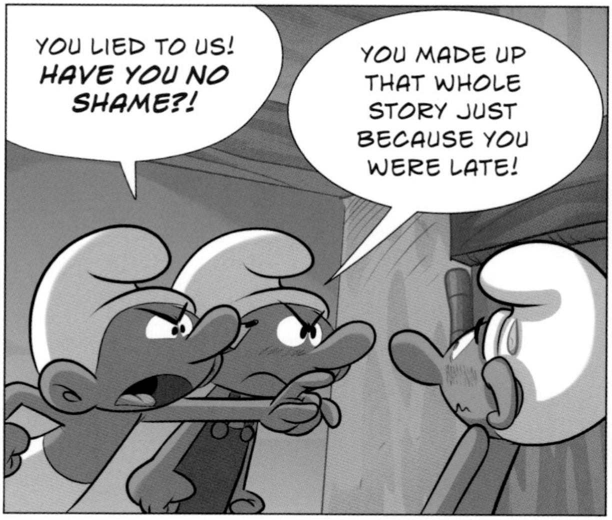
YOU LIED TO US! HAVE YOU NO SHAME?!
YOU MADE UP THAT WHOLE STORY JUST BECAUSE YOU WERE LATE!

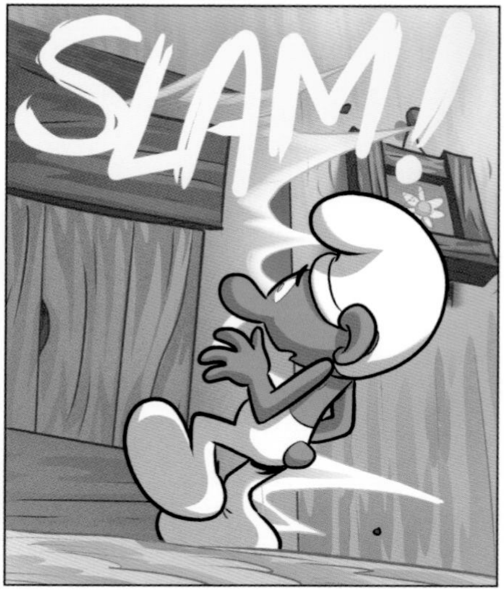
SLAM!

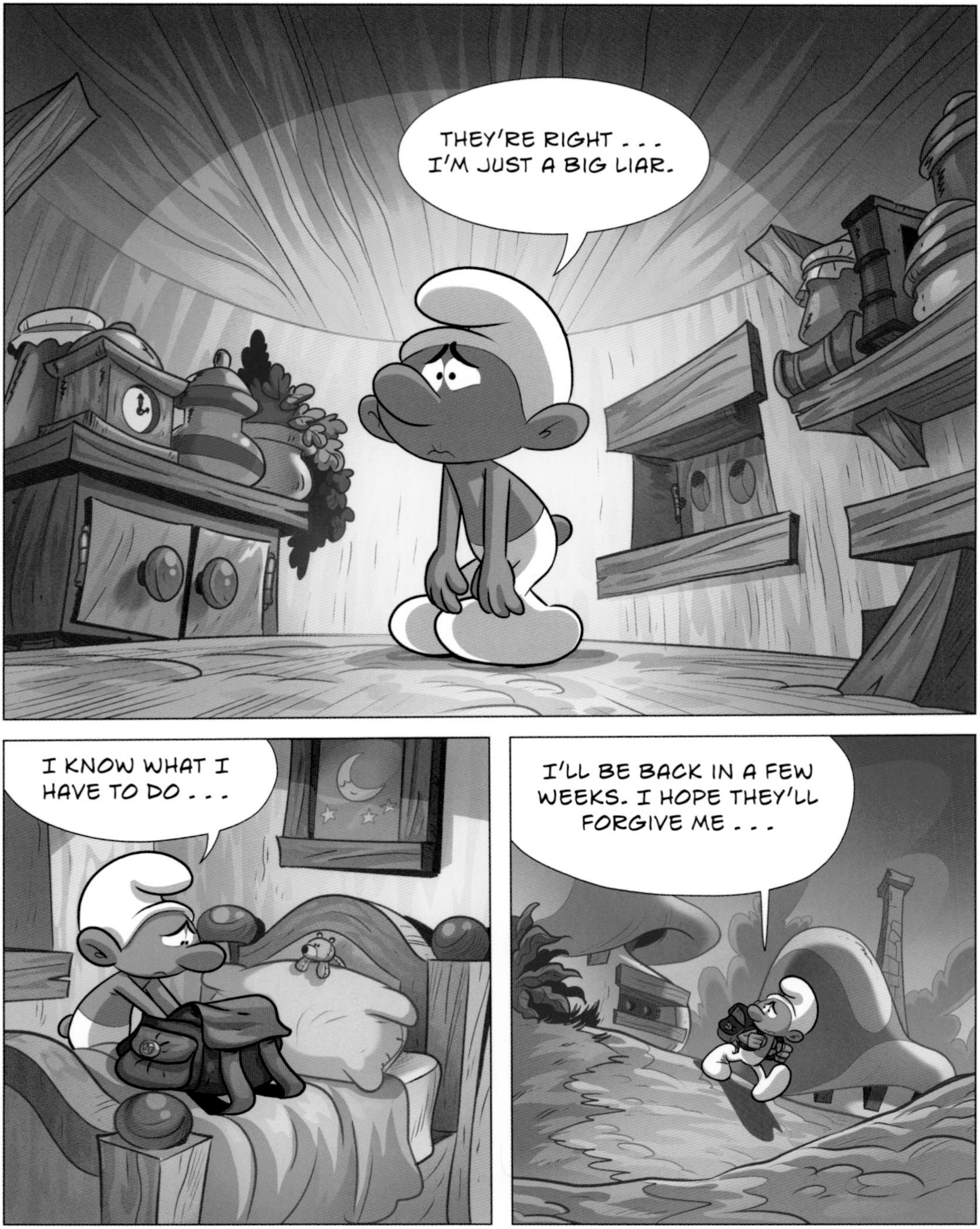
THEY'RE RIGHT . . . I'M JUST A BIG LIAR.
I KNOW WHAT I HAVE TO DO . . .
I'LL BE BACK IN A FEW WEEKS. I HOPE THEY'LL FORGIVE ME . . .

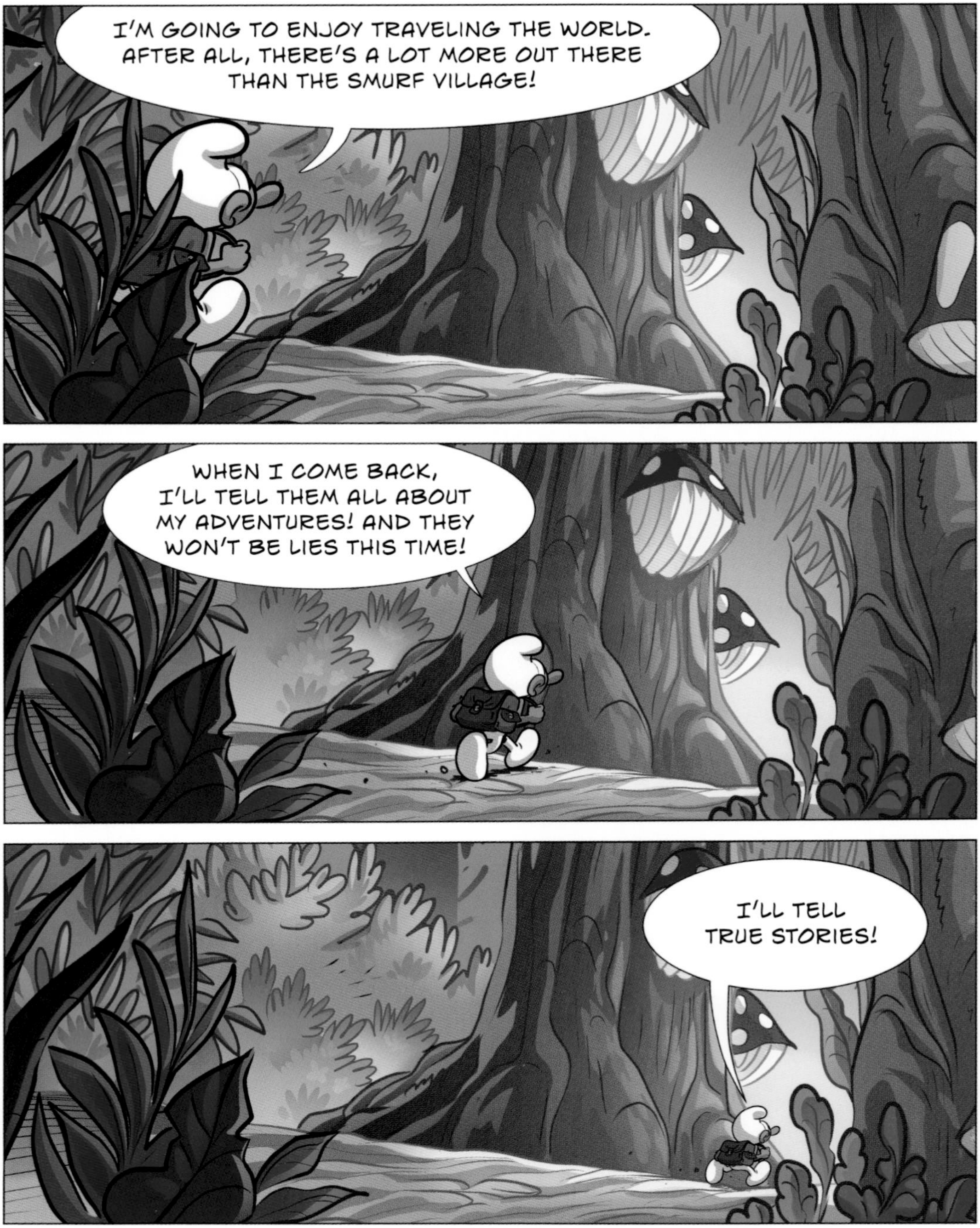
I'M GOING TO ENJOY TRAVELING THE WORLD. AFTER ALL, THERE'S A LOT MORE OUT THERE THAN THE SMURF VILLAGE!
WHEN I COME BACK, I'LL TELL THEM ALL ABOUT MY ADVENTURES! AND THEY WON'T BE LIES THIS TIME!
I'LL TELL TRUE STORIES!

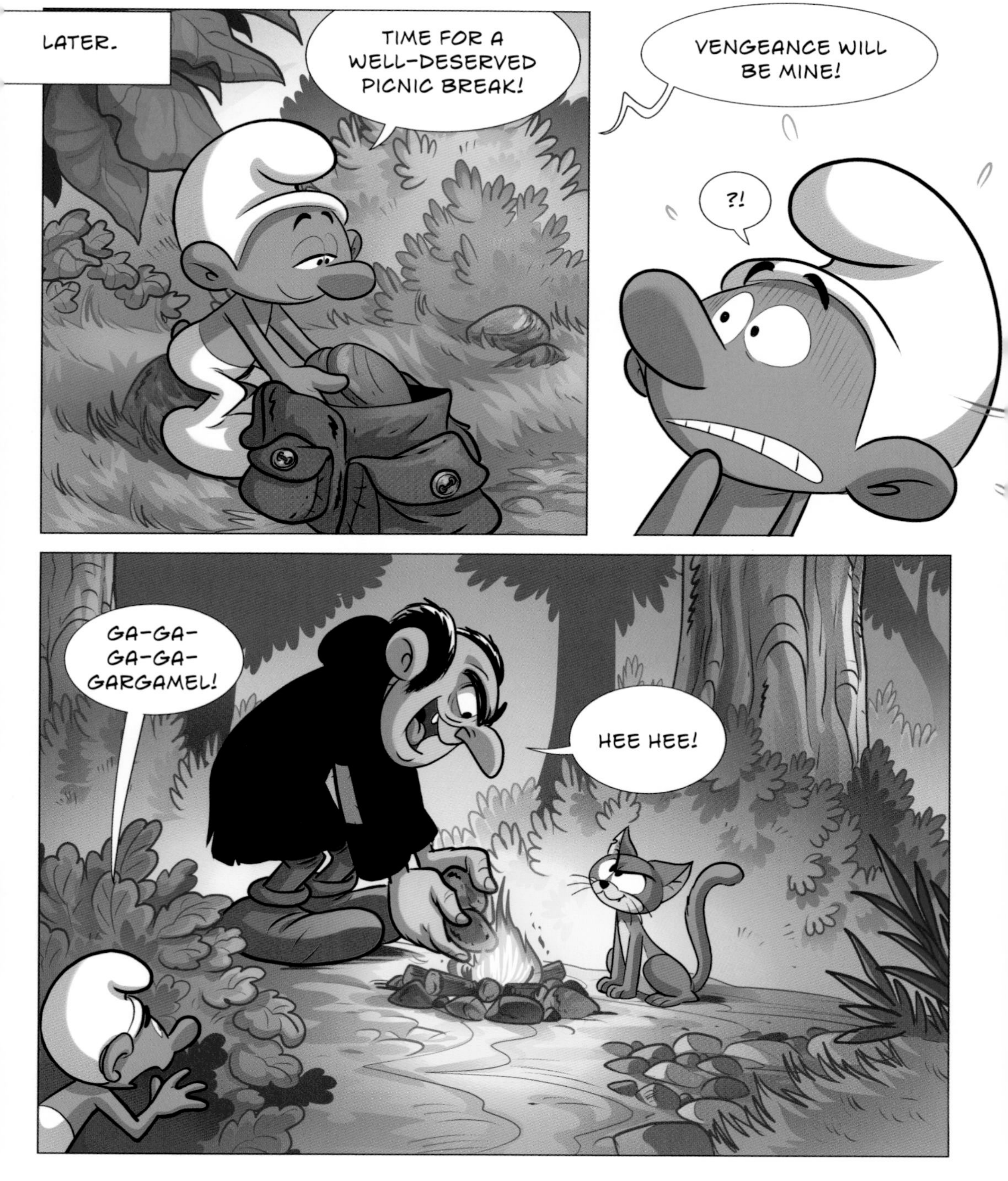
LATER.
TIME FOR A WELL-DESERVED PICNIC BREAK!
VENGEANCE WILL BE MINE!
?!
GA-GA-GA-GA-GARGAMEL!
HEE HEE!

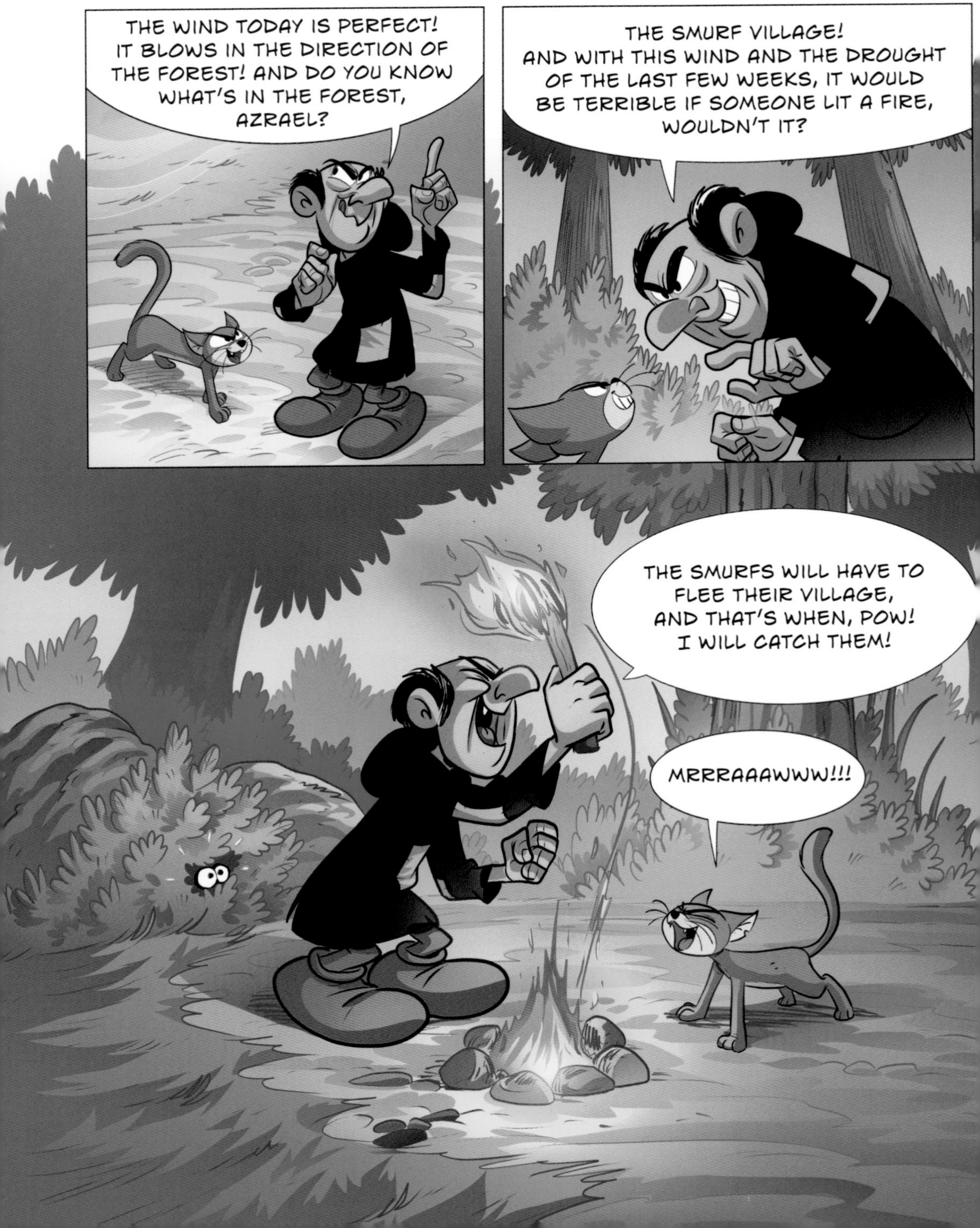
THE WIND TODAY IS PERFECT! IT BLOWS IN THE DIRECTION OF THE FOREST! AND DO YOU KNOW WHAT'S IN THE FOREST, AZRAEL?
THE SMURF VILLAGE! AND WITH THIS WIND AND THE DROUGHT OF THE LAST FEW WEEKS, IT WOULD BE TERRIBLE IF SOMEONE LIT A FIRE, WOULDN'T IT?
THE SMURFS WILL HAVE TO FLEE THEIR VILLAGE, AND THAT'S WHEN, POW! I WILL CATCH THEM!
MRRRAAAWWW!!!

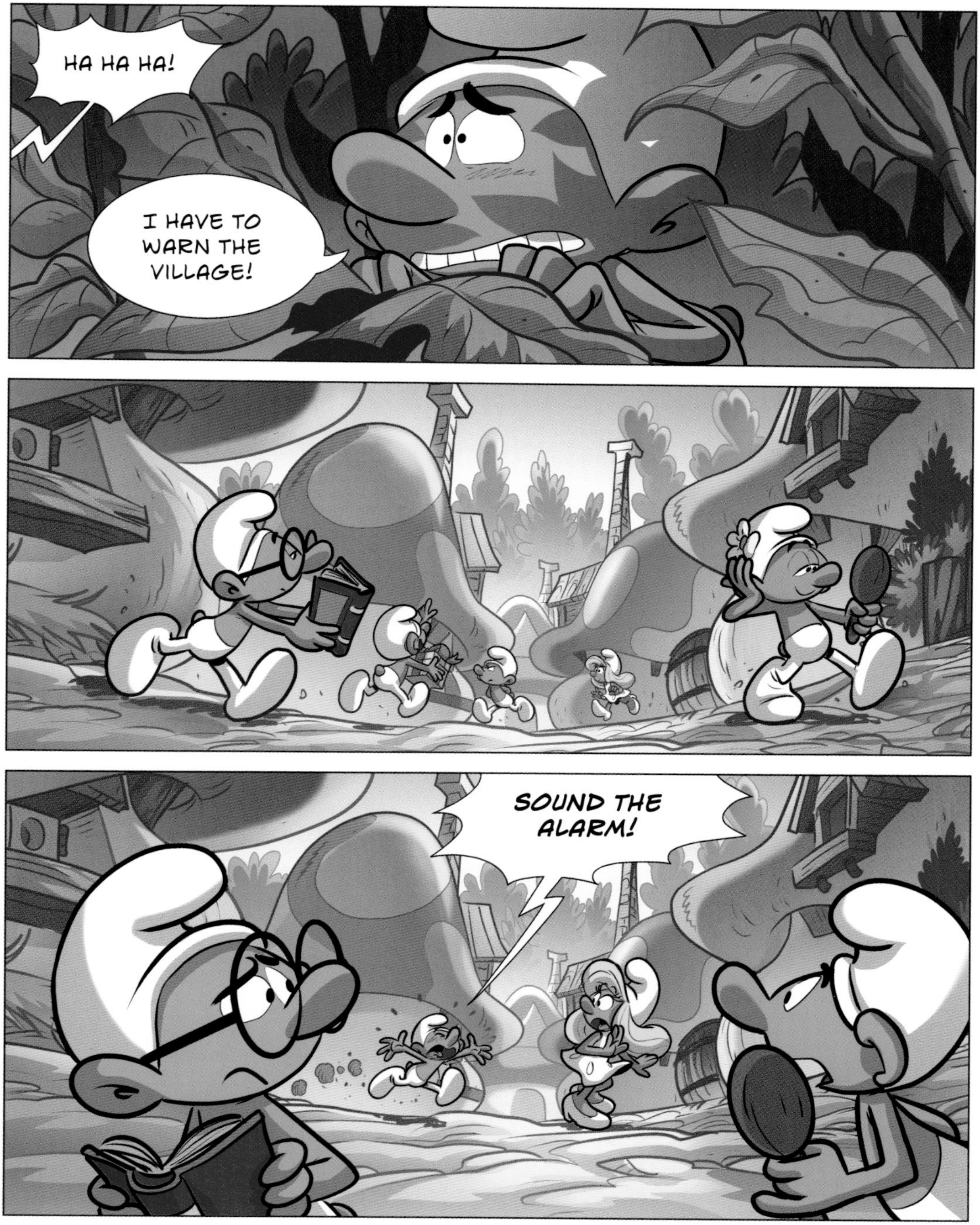
HA HA HA!
I HAVE TO WARN THE VILLAGE!
SOUND THE ALARM!

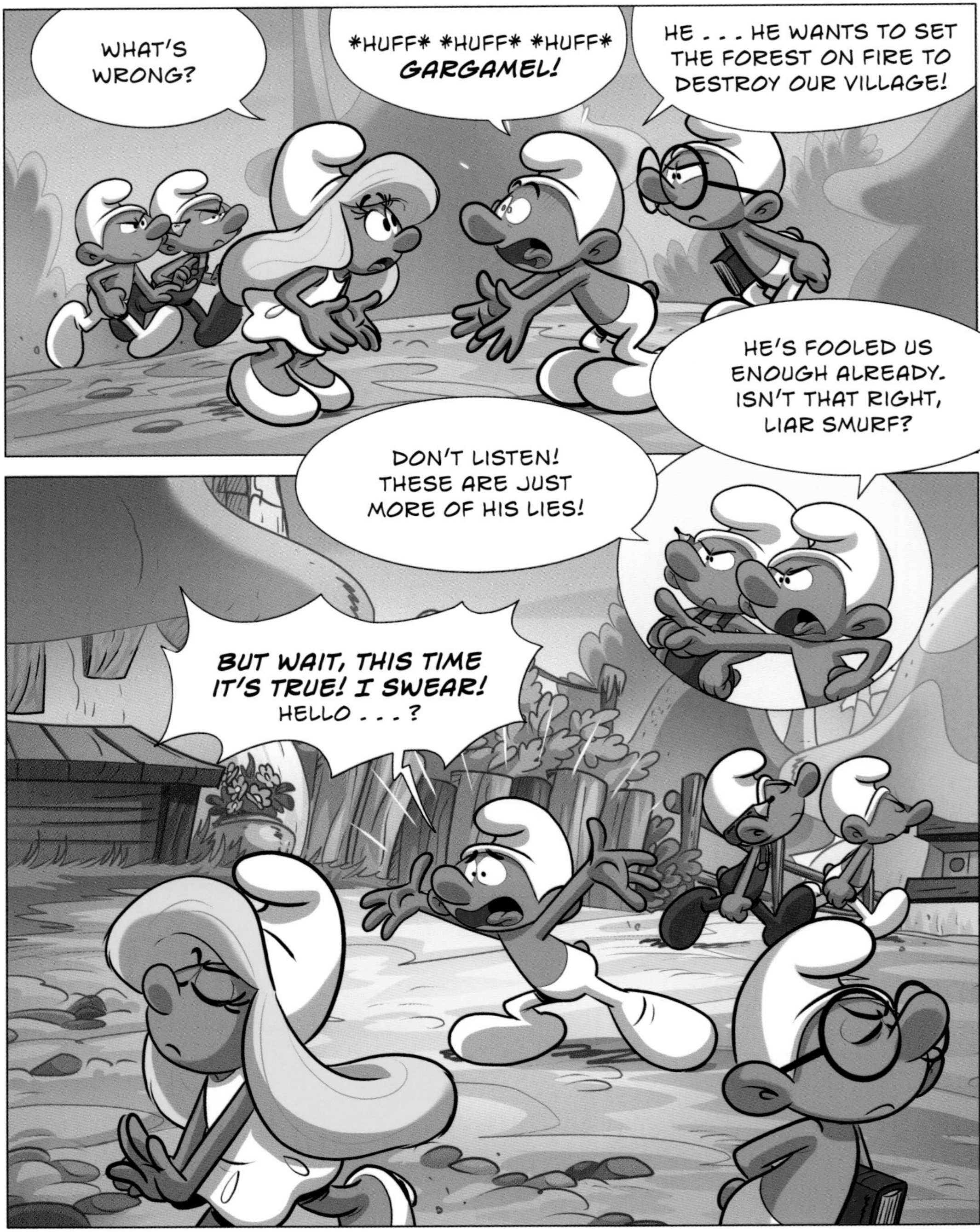
WHAT'S WRONG?
HUFF *HUFF* *HUFF* GARGAMEL!
HE . . . HE WANTS TO SET THE FOREST ON FIRE TO DESTROY OUR VILLAGE!
HE'S FOOLED US ENOUGH ALREADY. ISN'T THAT RIGHT, LIAR SMURF?
DON'T LISTEN! THESE ARE JUST MORE OF HIS LIES!
BUT WAIT, THIS TIME IT'S TRUE! I SWEAR! HELLO . . . ?

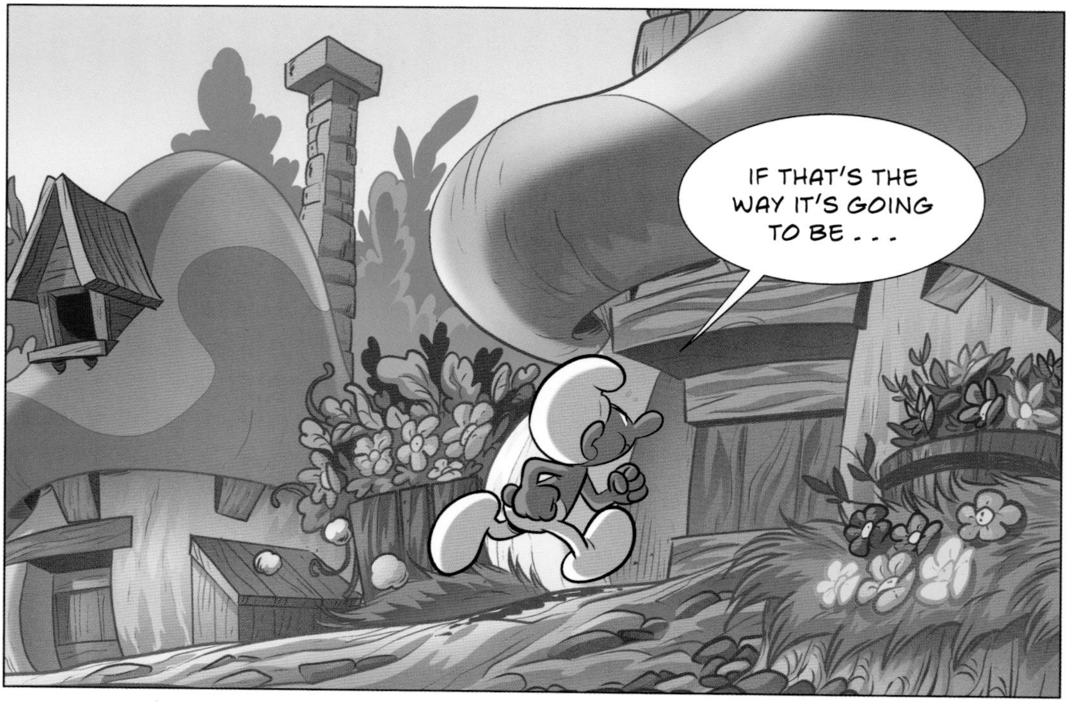
IF THAT'S THE WAY IT'S GOING TO BE . . .

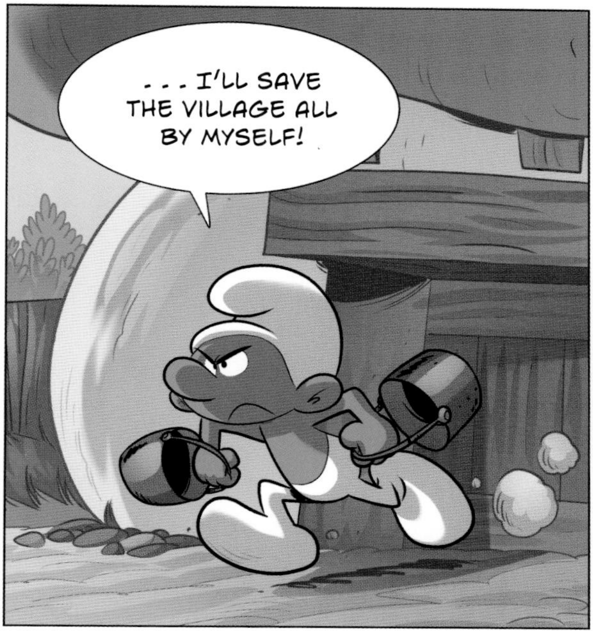
. . . I'LL SAVE THE VILLAGE ALL BY MYSELF!

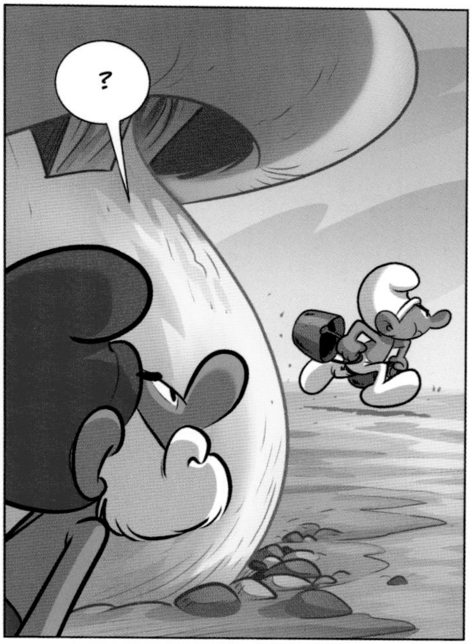
?

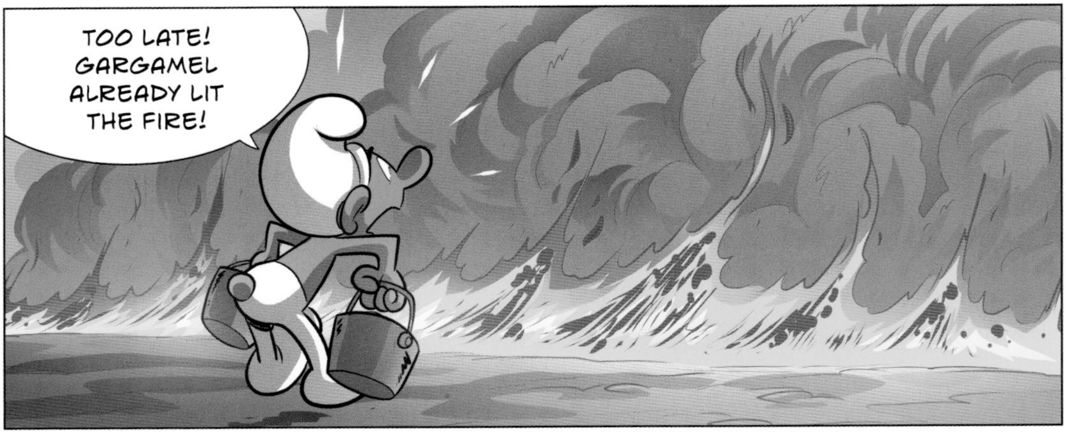
TOO LATE! GARGAMEL ALREADY LIT THE FIRE!

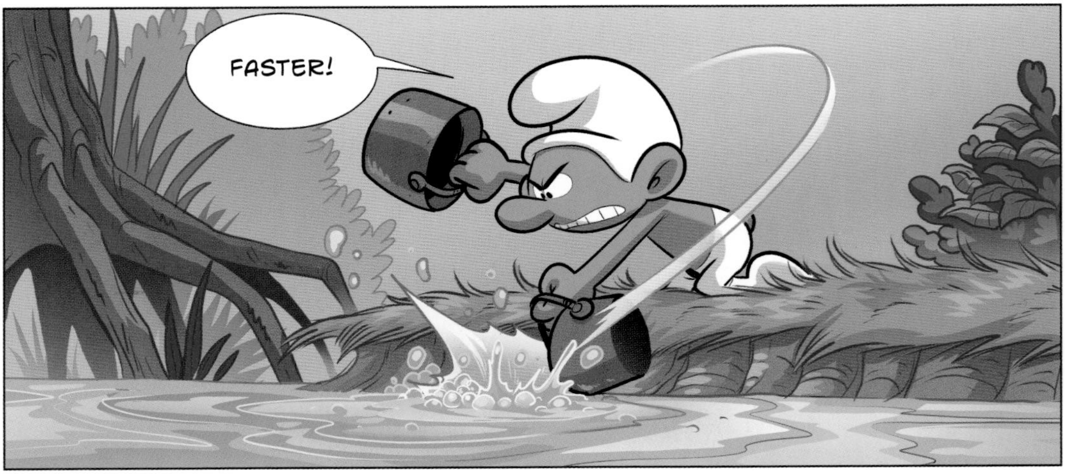
FASTER!

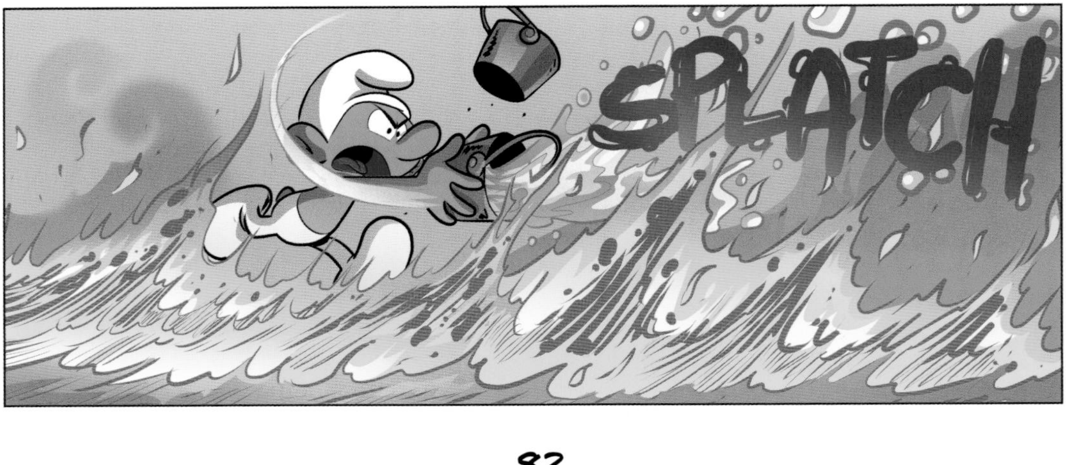
SPLATCH

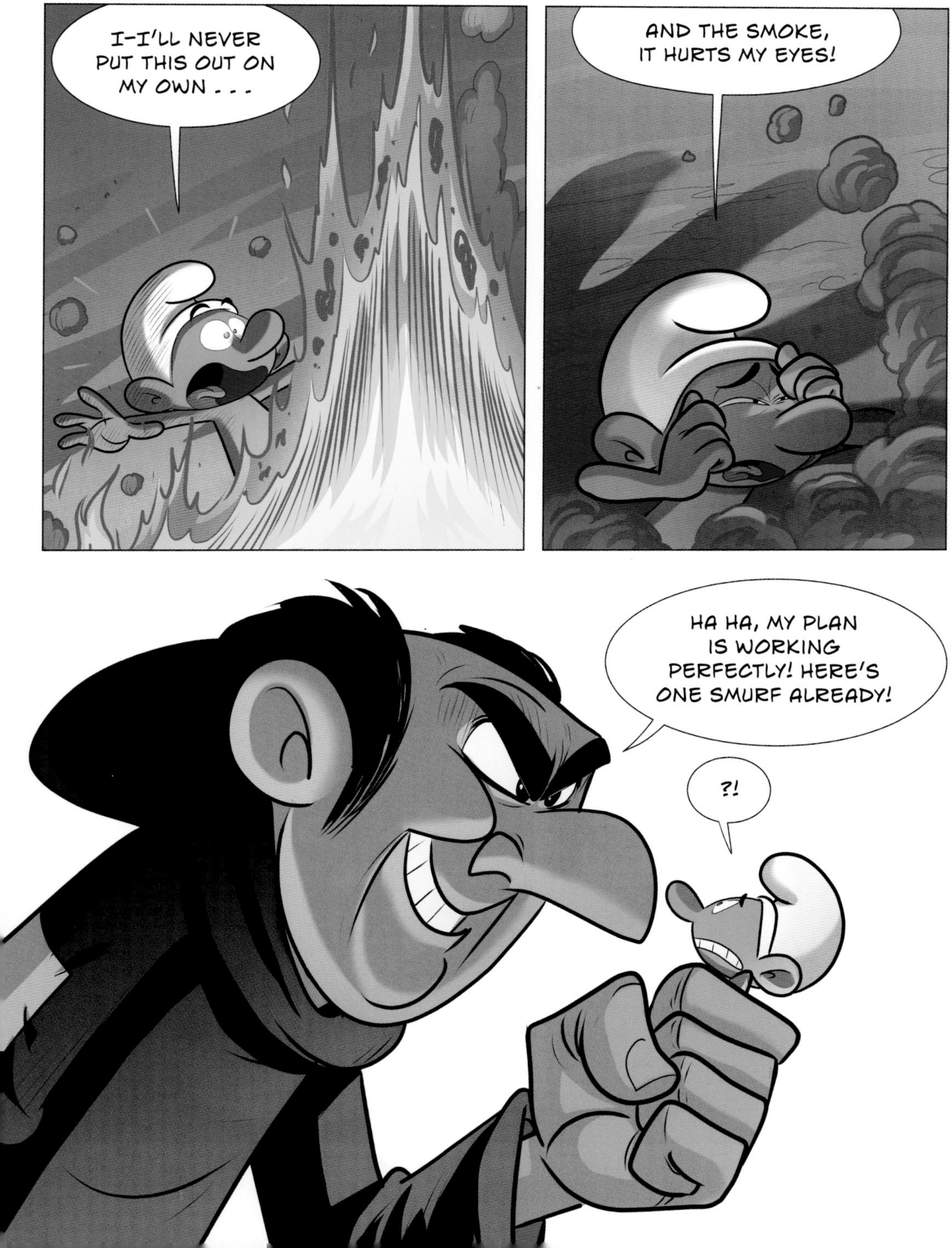
I-I'LL NEVER PUT THIS OUT ON MY OWN . . .
AND THE SMOKE, IT HURTS MY EYES!
HA HA, MY PLAN IS WORKING PERFECTLY! HERE'S ONE SMURF ALREADY!
?!

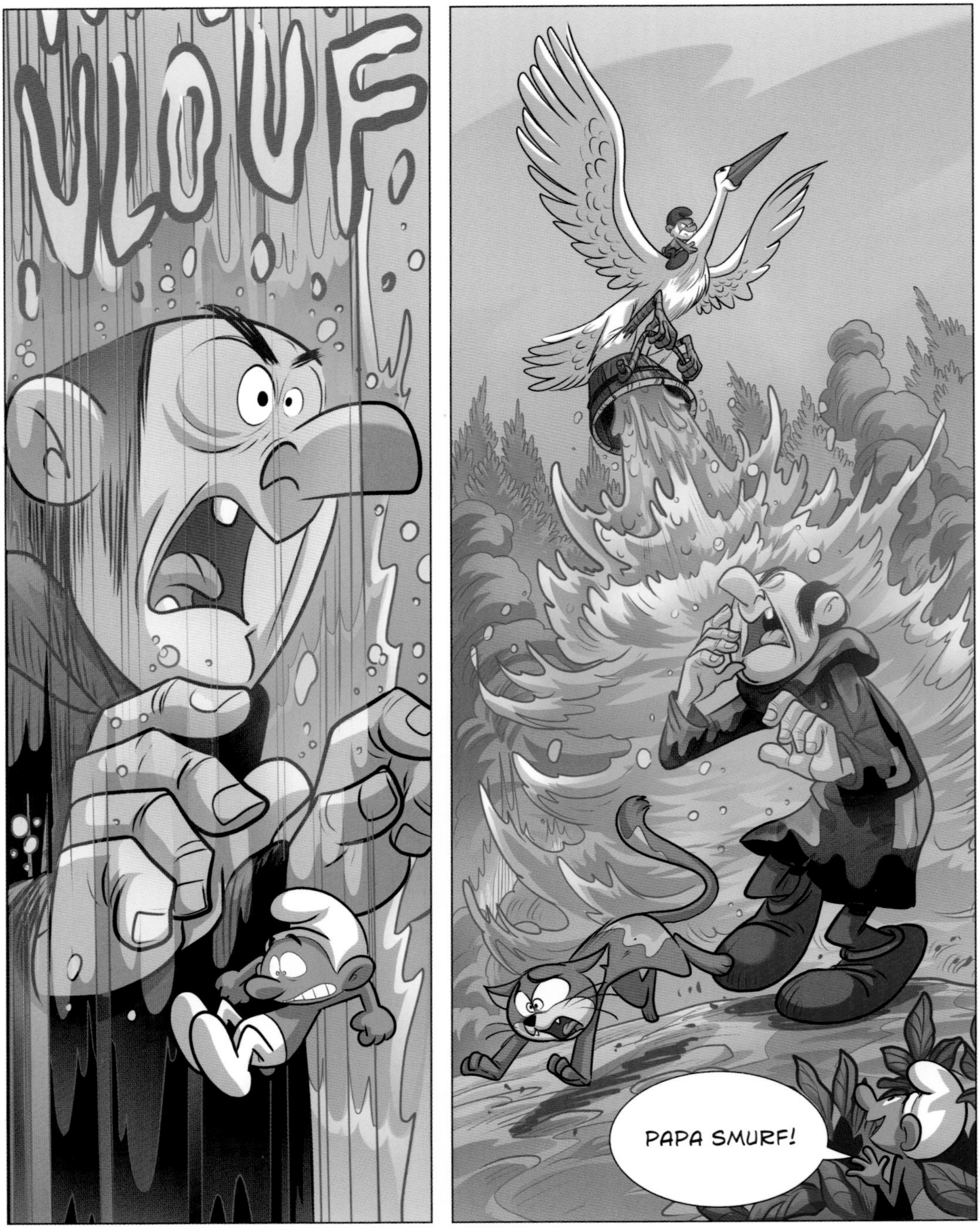
VLOUF
PAPA SMURF!

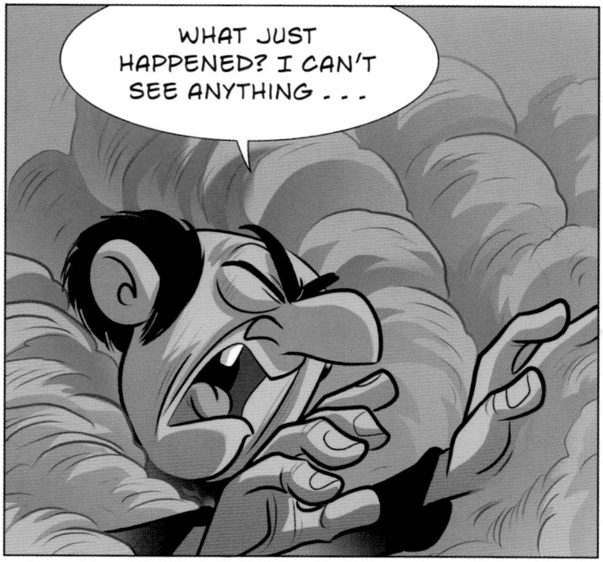
WHAT JUST HAPPENED? I CAN'T SEE ANYTHING . . .

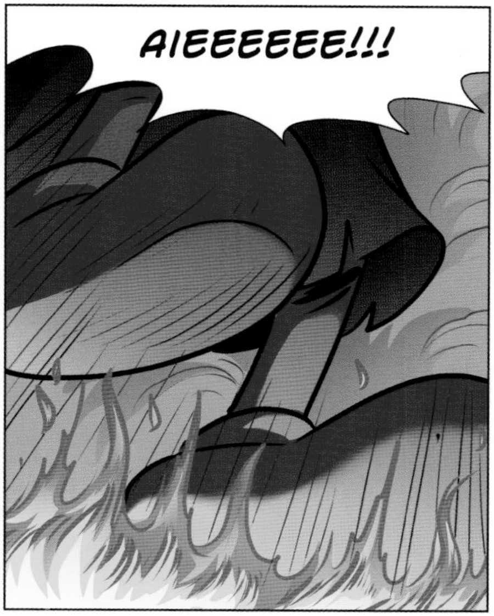
AIEEEEEE!!!

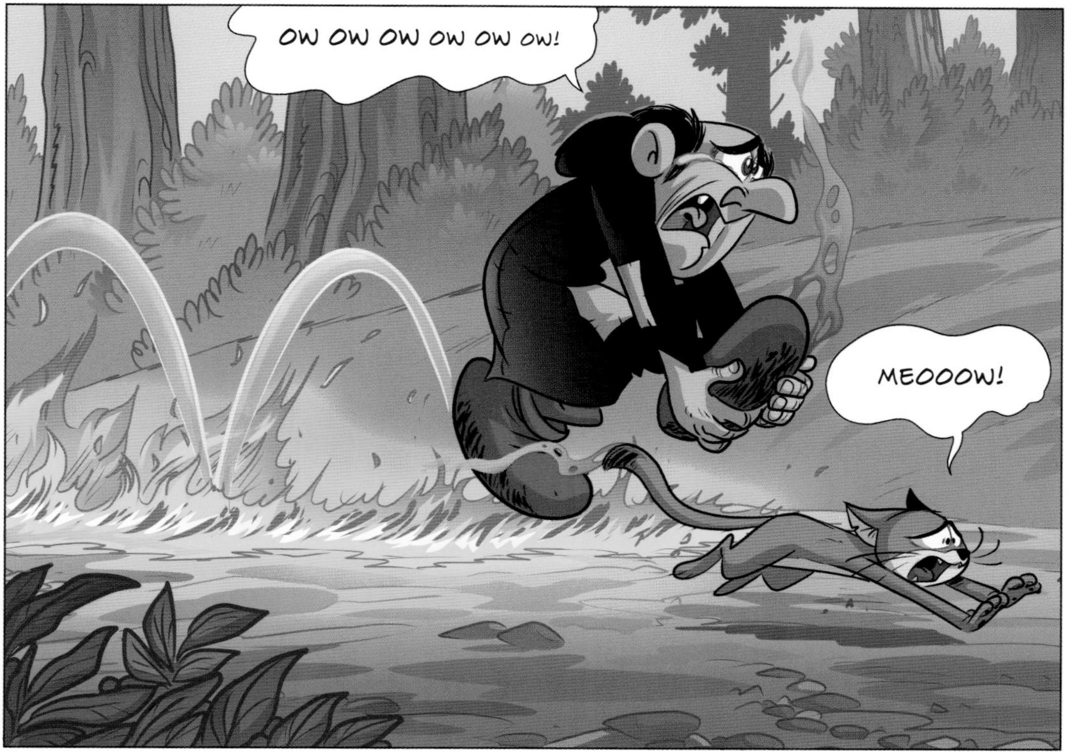
OW OW OW OW OW OW!
MEOOOW!

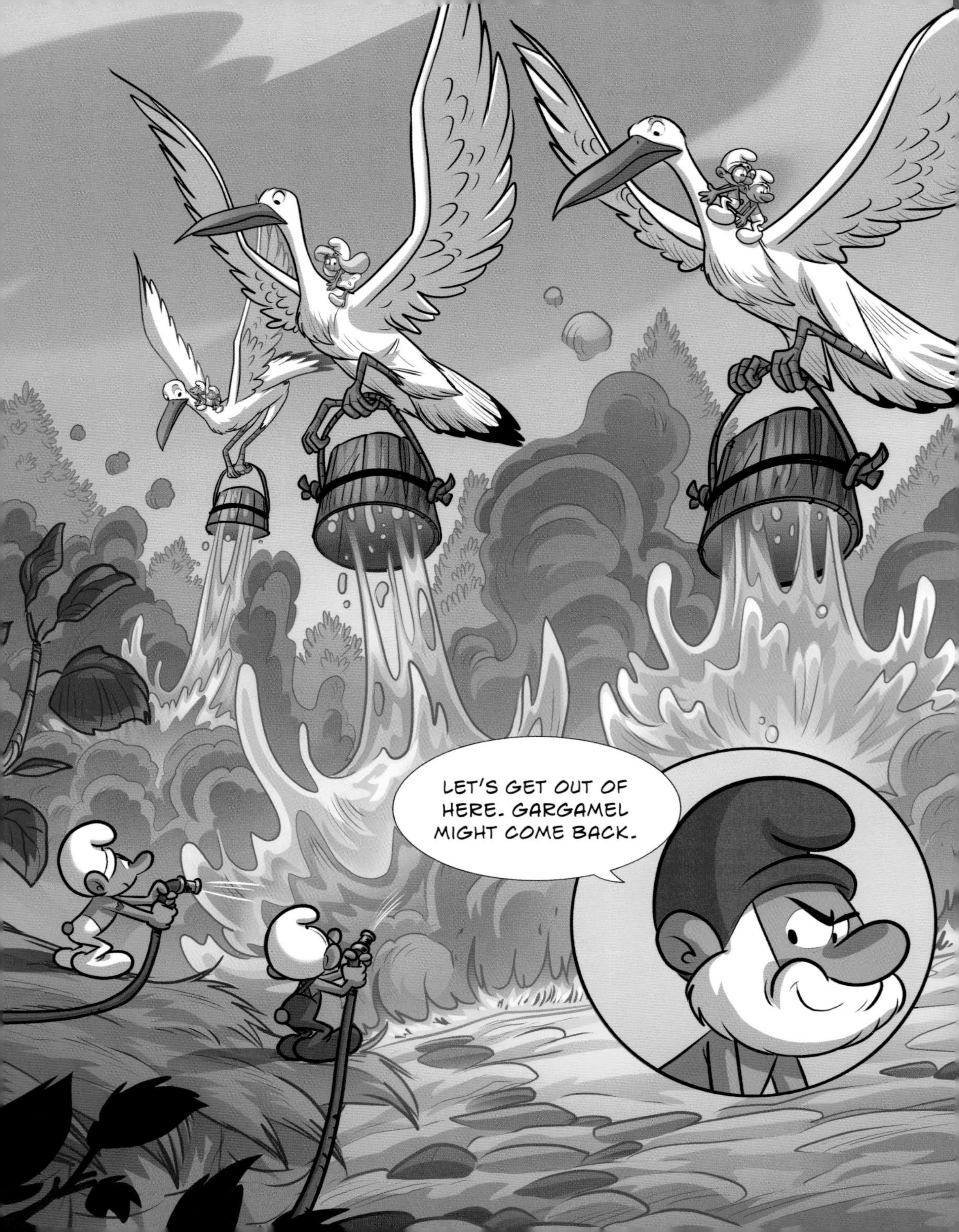
LET'S GET OUT OF HERE. GARGAMEL MIGHT COME BACK.

GOOD WORK, LIAR SMURF! WITHOUT YOU, THE VILLAGE WOULD HAVE CAUGHT ON FIRE!

GOOD THING PAPA SMURF BELIEVED YOU!

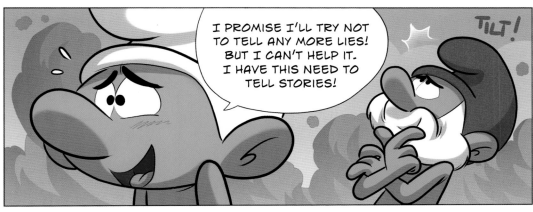

I PROMISE I'LL TRY NOT TO TELL ANY MORE LIES! BUT I CAN'T HELP IT. I HAVE THIS NEED TO TELL STORIES!

TILT!

I JUST HAD A GREAT IDEA!

?

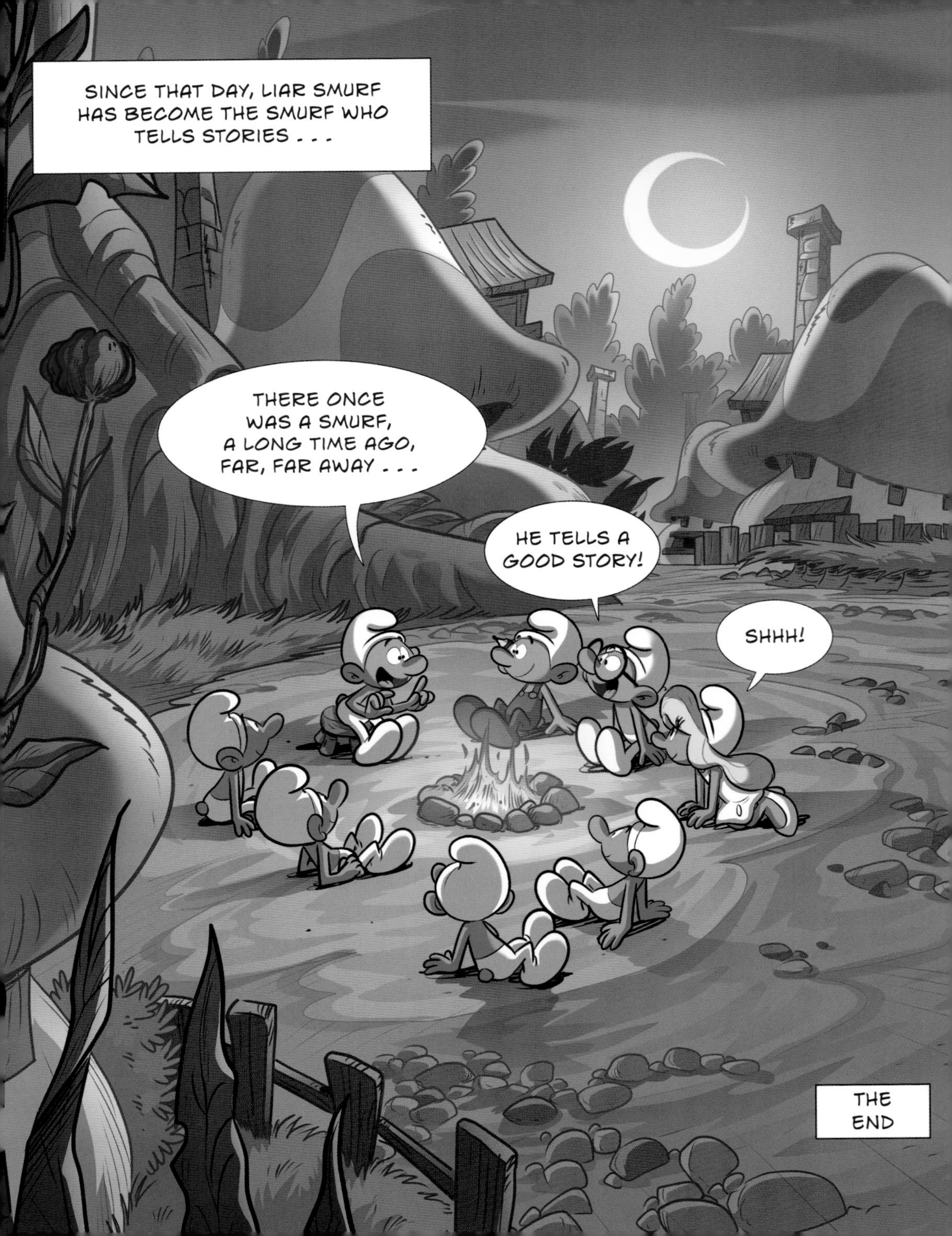
SINCE THAT DAY, LIAR SMURF HAS BECOME THE SMURF WHO TELLS STORIES . . .
THERE ONCE WAS A SMURF, A LONG TIME AGO, FAR, FAR AWAY . . .
HE TELLS A GOOD STORY!
SHHH!
THE END

AND YOU
DO YOU EVER
FEEL DIFFERENT?

A guide written
by Diane Drory

psychologist, psychoanalyst, and
specialist in early childhood disorders

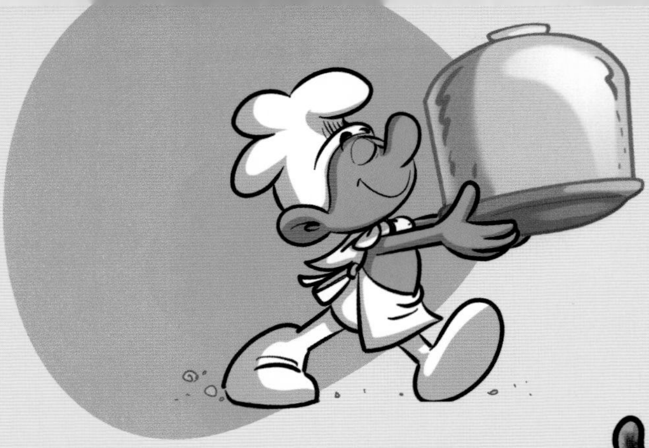

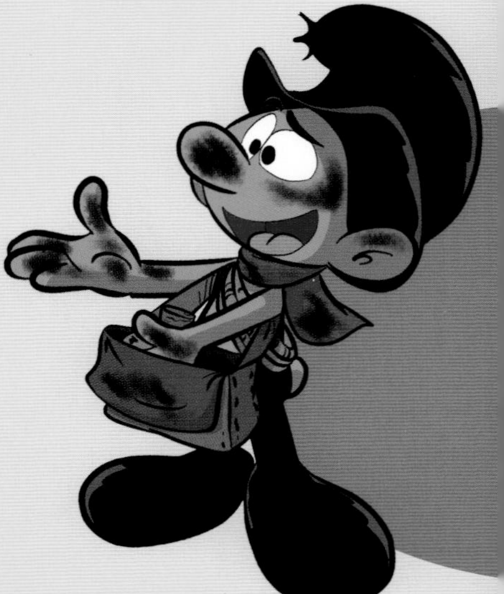

WHO'S TO SAY WHAT'S DIFFERENT?

To be different is to have a trait that's **uncommon or unique**.

We can be very different, like, for example, Sweepy Smurf or Chef Smurf, with special jobs and abilities.

We can all be **a little bit different**, like the way pale green is just a little different from dark green. We can also be **very different**, the way day is the opposite of night.

We're lucky there are **so many differences**, or the world would be very boring!

We are all **unique**. No one is exactly like anyone else.

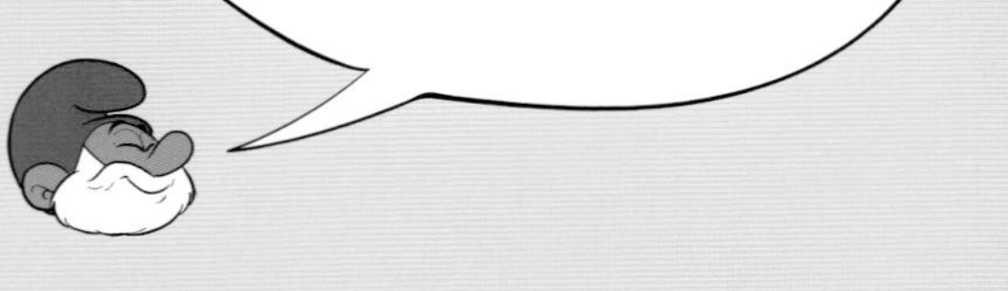
HOW ABOUT YOU? DO YOU FEEL A LITTLE DIFFERENT OR VERY DIFFERENT?

IF WE'RE ALL DIFFERENT, IS NO ONE THE SAME?

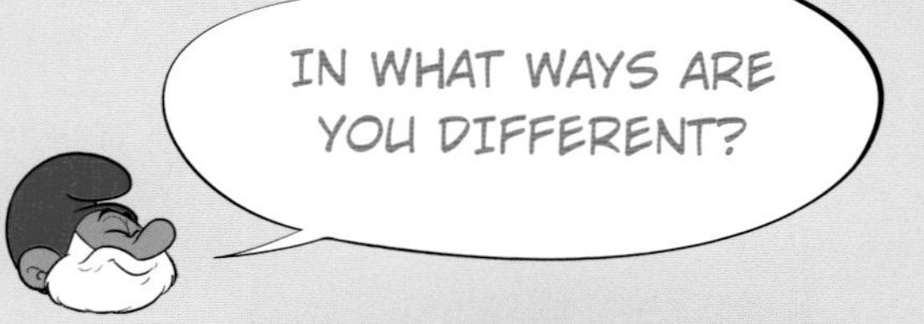
IN WHAT WAYS ARE YOU DIFFERENT?

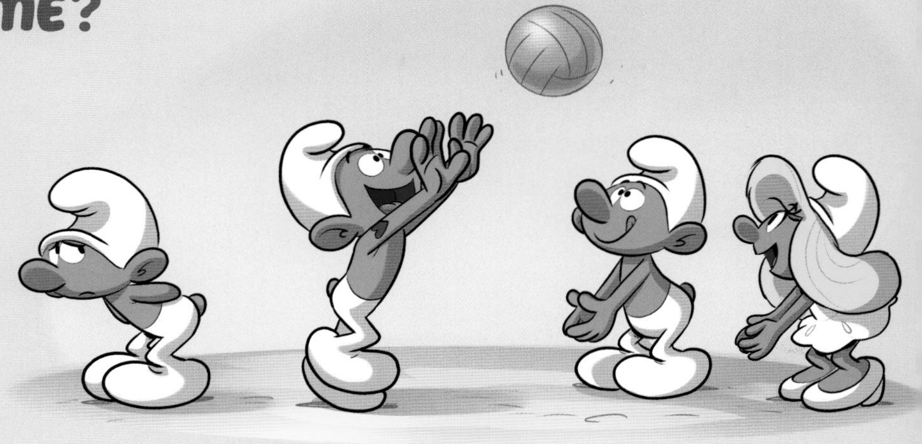

No boy is the same as any other boy, all girls are different, and boys and girls are also different from each other. And some people don't see themselves as a boy or as a girl.

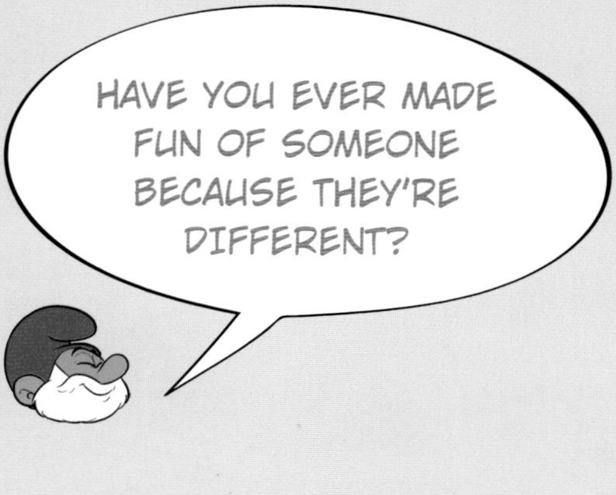
HAVE YOU EVER MADE FUN OF SOMEONE BECAUSE THEY'RE DIFFERENT?

A girl may like to have very short hair, and some boys feel better with long hair. Who knows, under their hats, which Smurfs have let their hair grow long? They might keep it hidden because they're worried people will claim long hair is only for girls . . . or that they'll be laughed at.

Laughing at other people is a way of defending yourself when you **don't understand** something new and are scared . . . We make fun of other people to **hide our fear**.

CAN A SMURF REALLY BE JUST LIKE ALL THE OTHER SMURFS? NO.

The idea that Smurfs **need to be a certain way** is what makes Smurfette feel left out. The other Smurfs think she can't get dirty or go jogging. She's understandably upset about these **false beliefs** other Smurfs have.

In the past, society gave very different roles to men and women. Everyone had one set of ideas for how the "boys" side should be, and a different set of ideas for the "girls" side. A lot of people felt **left out**.

Yes, there are some common physical differences between people who are identified as a boy and people who are identified as a girl. But, as you grow, the most important thing is to figure out **your own ideas** about yourself.

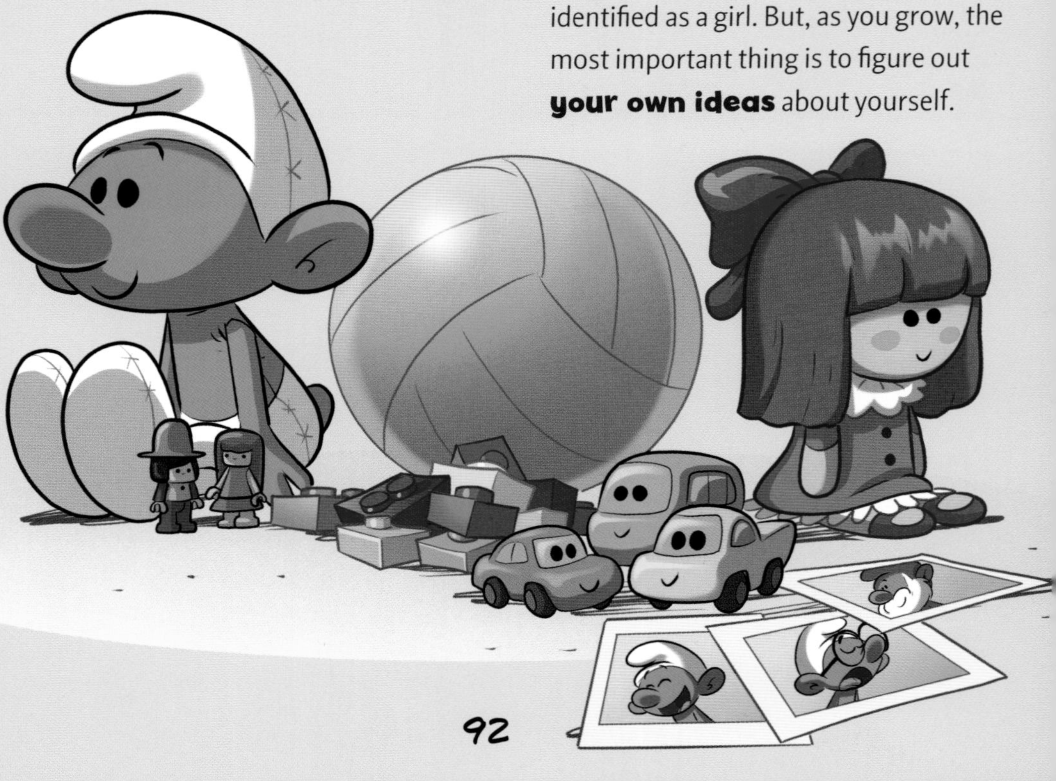

And **nobody** knows everything! Even old people are still figuring out their own ideas about who they are.

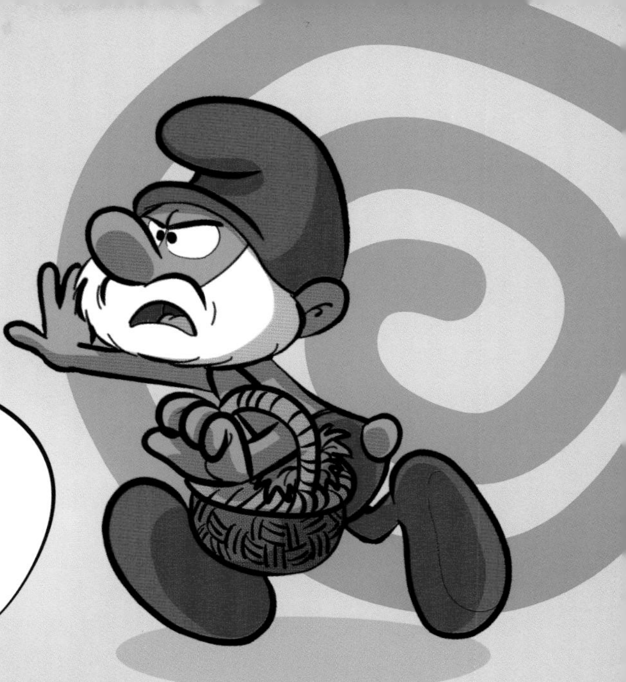

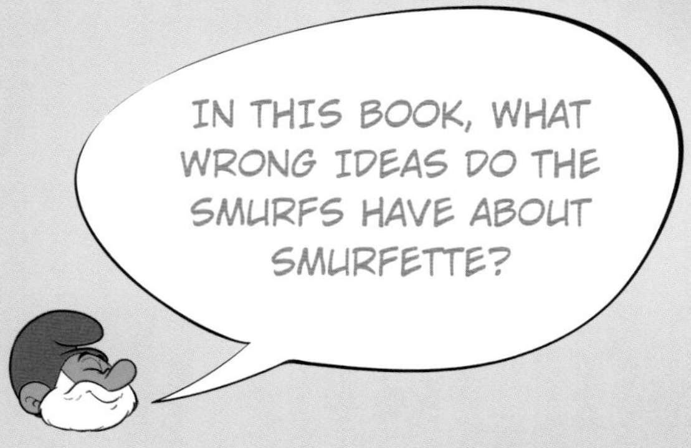
IN THIS BOOK, WHAT WRONG IDEAS DO THE SMURFS HAVE ABOUT SMURFETTE?

DOES BEING DIFFERENT MEAN WE'RE NOT EQUAL TO EACH OTHER? NO!

Anyone who thinks it's better to be a boy or a girl, or neither, is wrong. Yes, we are all different, but we're also all **equal** and deserve to be treated that way.

Whether you're the strongest student in class or the one who takes the most time, we are all **equal**.

Remember one thing above all: While we are all different, every person has the **same value**, from a young child to an adult to an elderly person.

"Which is better, being a boy or a girl?" This question has no purpose. And some people don't identify as a boy or as a girl. The important thing is to understand how you feel about **yourself**, and what you want out of life.

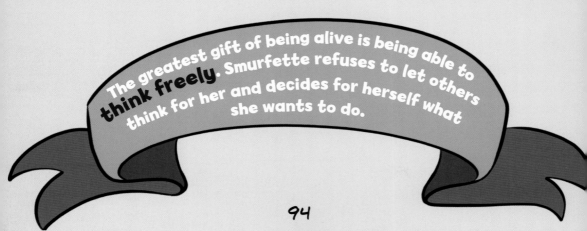

The greatest gift of being alive is being able to **think freely**. Smurfette refuses to let others think for her and decides for herself what she wants to do.

ADVICE FROM PAPA SMURF

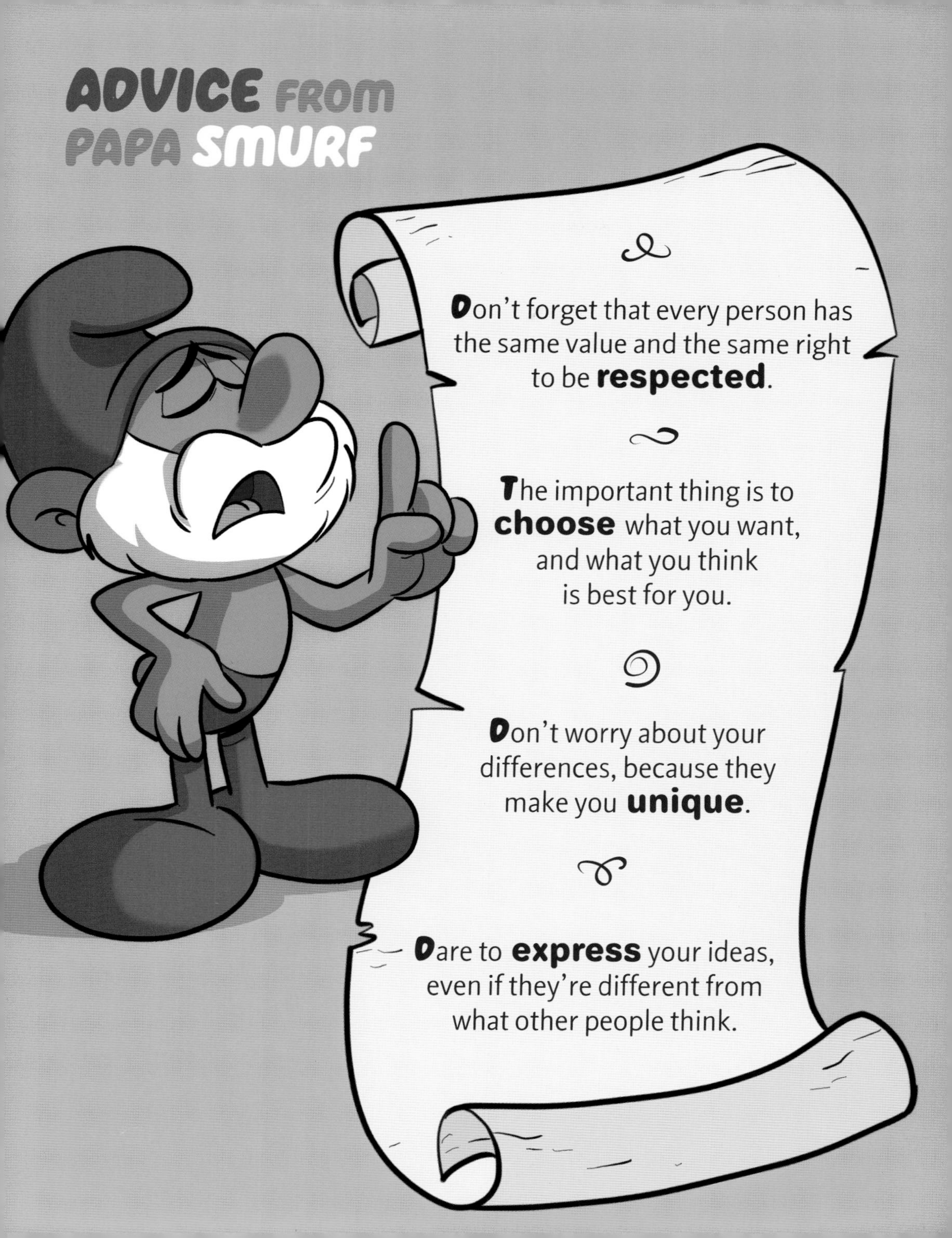

Don't forget that every person has the same value and the same right to be **respected**.

The important thing is to **choose** what you want, and what you think is best for you.

Don't worry about your differences, because they make you **unique**.

Dare to **express** your ideas, even if they're different from what other people think.

AND YOU
DO YOU SOMETIMES FEEL LIKE THINGS AREN'T FAIR?

A guide written by Diane Drory

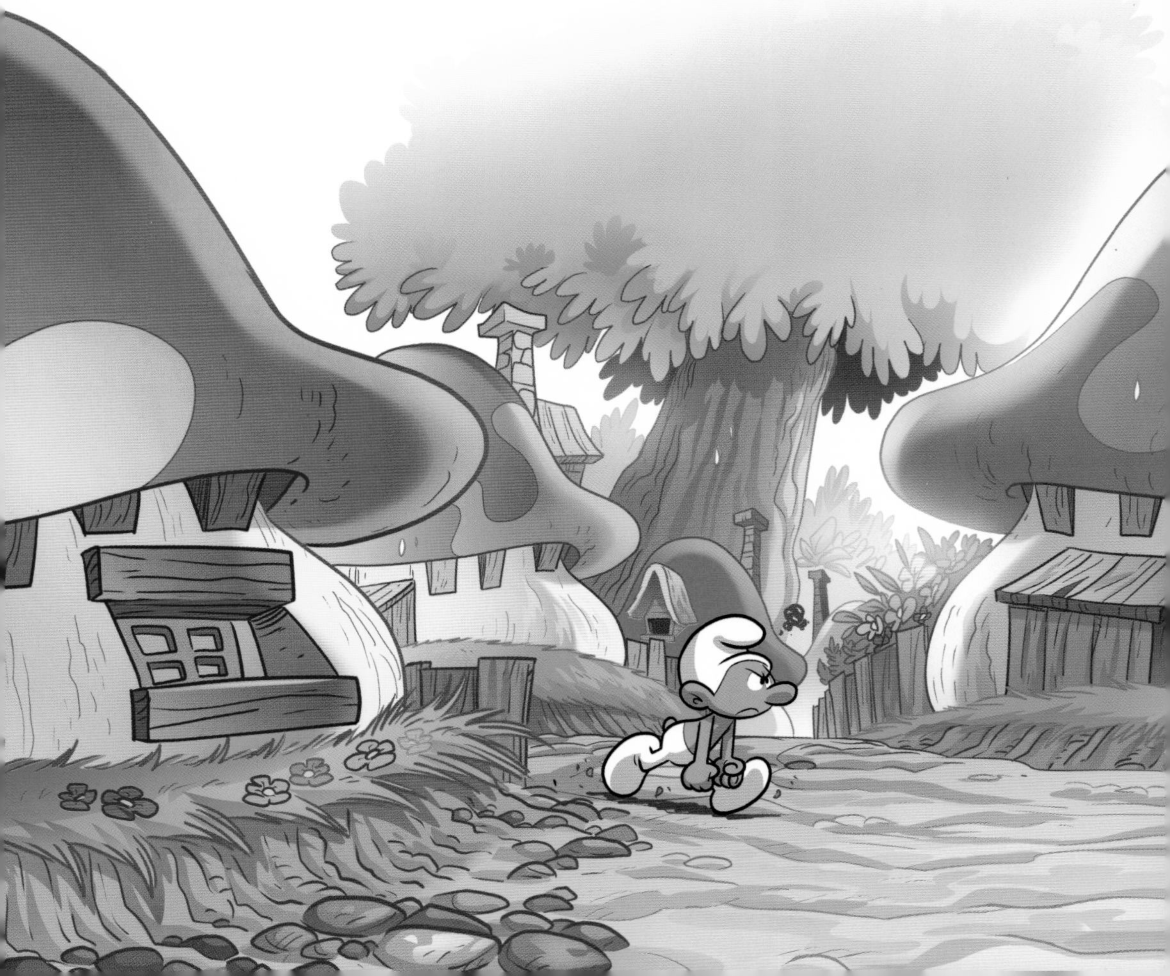

FAIR OR UNFAIR?

In everyday life, we can't all have the **same** things. It's also impossible for all of us to do everything the same way. Most of the time, everyone does their own thing and that's fine. When getting dressed, some people start with their shirts, others with their socks. Everyone is different, and does different things, but it has nothing to do with **fairness**.

DO YOU OFTEN WONDER IF THERE'S A RIGHT OR A WRONG WAY TO DO SOMETHING?

"THIS IS UNFAIR!"

We sometimes say to ourselves, "This isn't fair!" For instance, when you want to go outside to play but it starts raining so hard you have to stay inside. But this doesn't really have anything to do with fairness. It's just the rain, ruining your **plans**!

The idea that "this is unfair" happens when we feel like other people are better off than we are. We compare ourselves to someone else who has more fries or a **bigger piece** of cake.

SOMETIMES WE THINK "IT'S NOT FAIR" WHEN PEOPLE DON'T ACT THE WAY WE WANT.

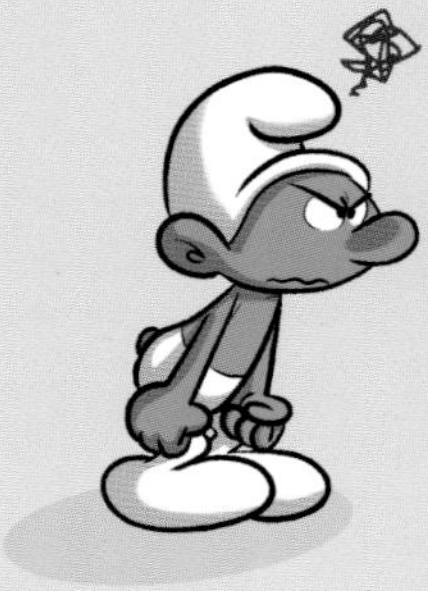

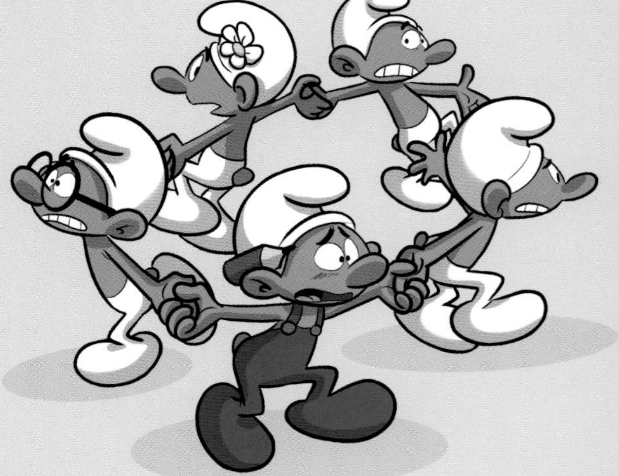

It's fine for Barber Smurf to cut Smurfette's hair. Grouchy Smurf thinks it's unfair because he wants to do it instead. When we **compare** ourselves to others, it's easy to say that something is "unfair" and feel like a victim.

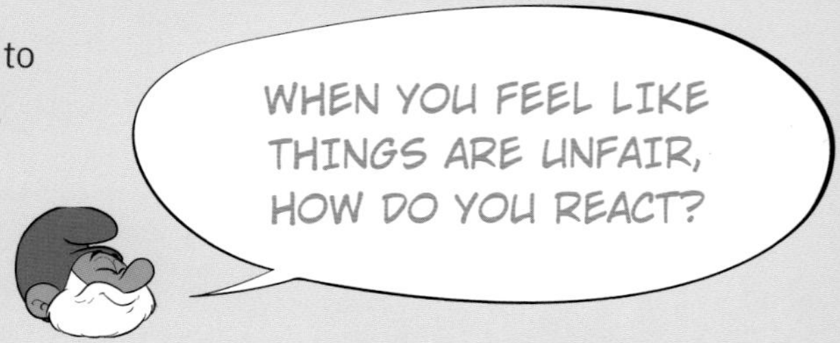
WHEN YOU FEEL LIKE THINGS ARE UNFAIR, HOW DO YOU REACT?

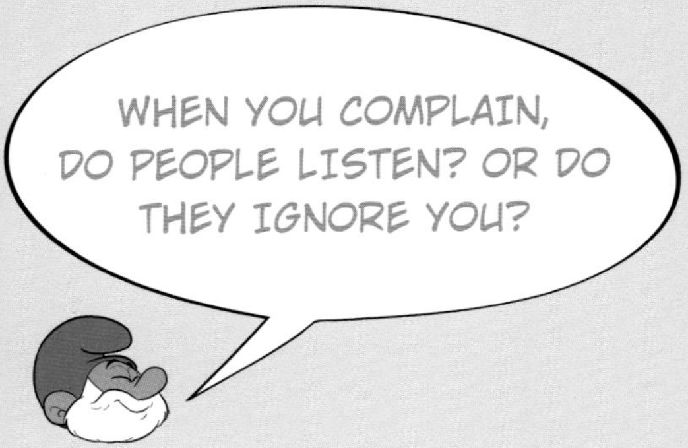
WHEN YOU COMPLAIN, DO PEOPLE LISTEN? OR DO THEY IGNORE YOU?

Sometimes when others don't do **what you want**, it can make you angry, scream, or even run away. Have you been like Grouchy Smurf, **complaining** when people do things their way and not yours?

WHAT IS JUSTICE?

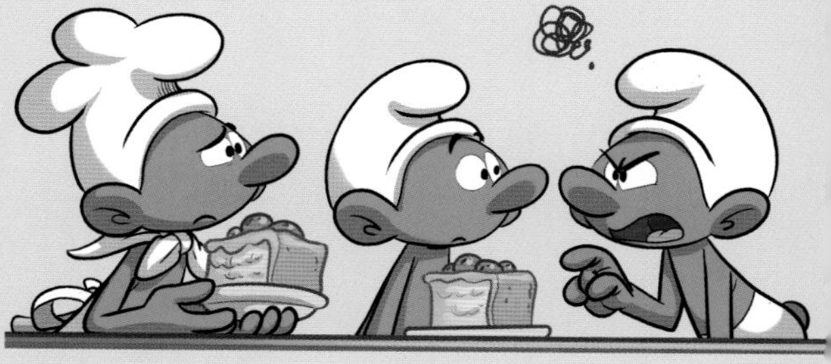

Since everyone has their own ideas about what's fair and unfair, there are **rules** to get everyone to agree. One of the rules of the Smurf Village is that it's Barber Smurf's **role** to cut hair. Each Smurf must accept this rule.

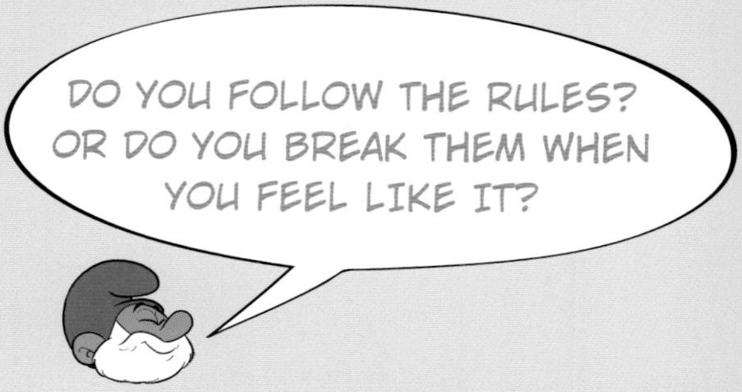
DO YOU FOLLOW THE RULES? OR DO YOU BREAK THEM WHEN YOU FEEL LIKE IT?

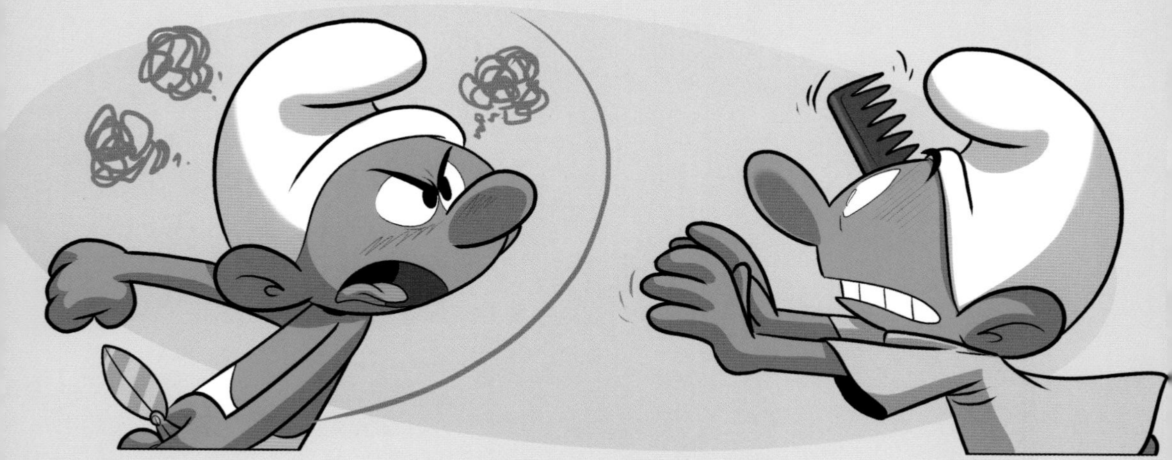

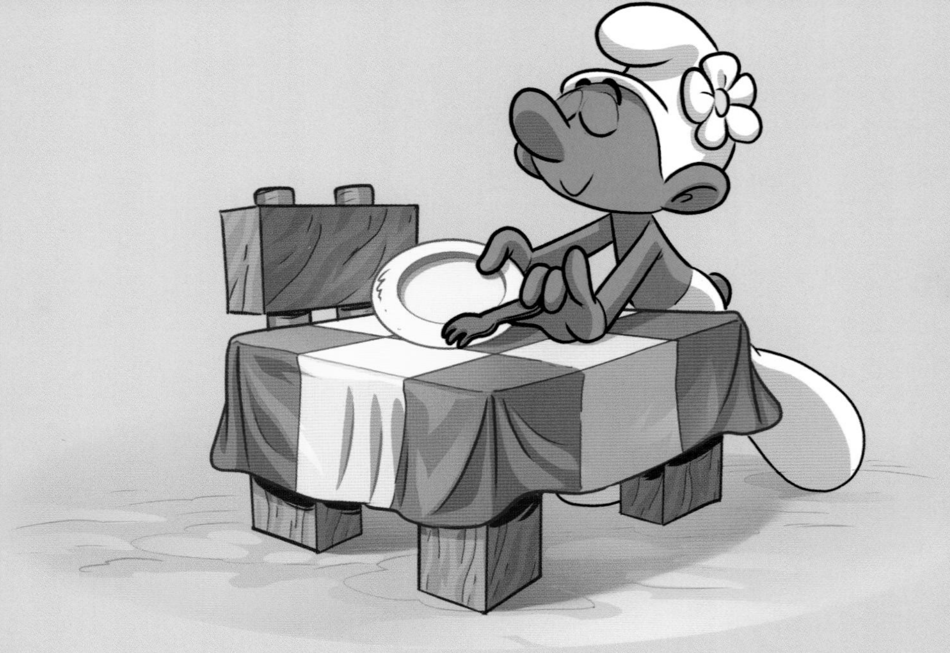

DOES JUSTICE MEAN EVERYONE HAS THE SAME THINGS?

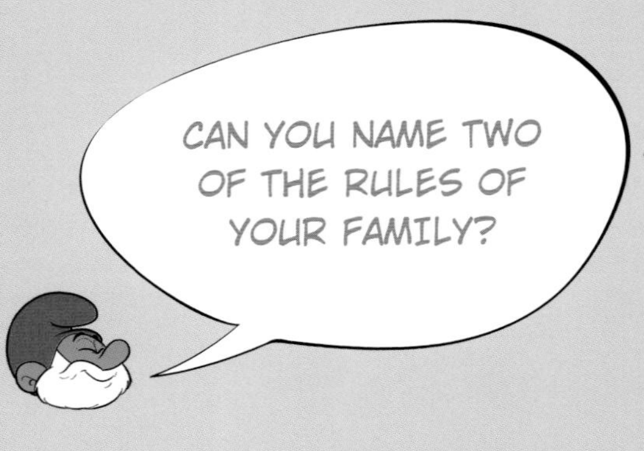
CAN YOU NAME TWO OF THE RULES OF YOUR FAMILY?

No. It would be awful to always have to weigh each smurfberry leaf to make sure every Smurf gets the same amount! Not everyone can always get the same thing. Justice is more about **creating rules** that groups have to follow. A group can be a **family**, and families often have their own rules. For the family to work, everyone has to **respect** the rules.

What seems fair to you might seem unfair to someone else. We don't all have the same **idea** of what justice is. But if you're always complaining about how things are unfair, know that people won't want to spend time with you.

Rules about what is **just** exist so everyone can always know what they are. The rules won't change if someone is in a bad mood or gets confused. They're a **good guide** to what is right and what is wrong.

Without rules everyone would do whatever they want and everyone would trip all over each other. And then no one would be happy . . .

ADVICE FROM PAPA SMURF

Don't spend your time **comparing** yourself to others. Your own life and what you want for it are what matter.

Don't **confuse** difference with injustice. We don't all do the same things and get the same things, but that doesn't mean something's unfair.

If you feel like things in your life really are unfair, tell you parents. Maybe some of your family's rules need to **change**. Your parents might not always remember that you're growing up!

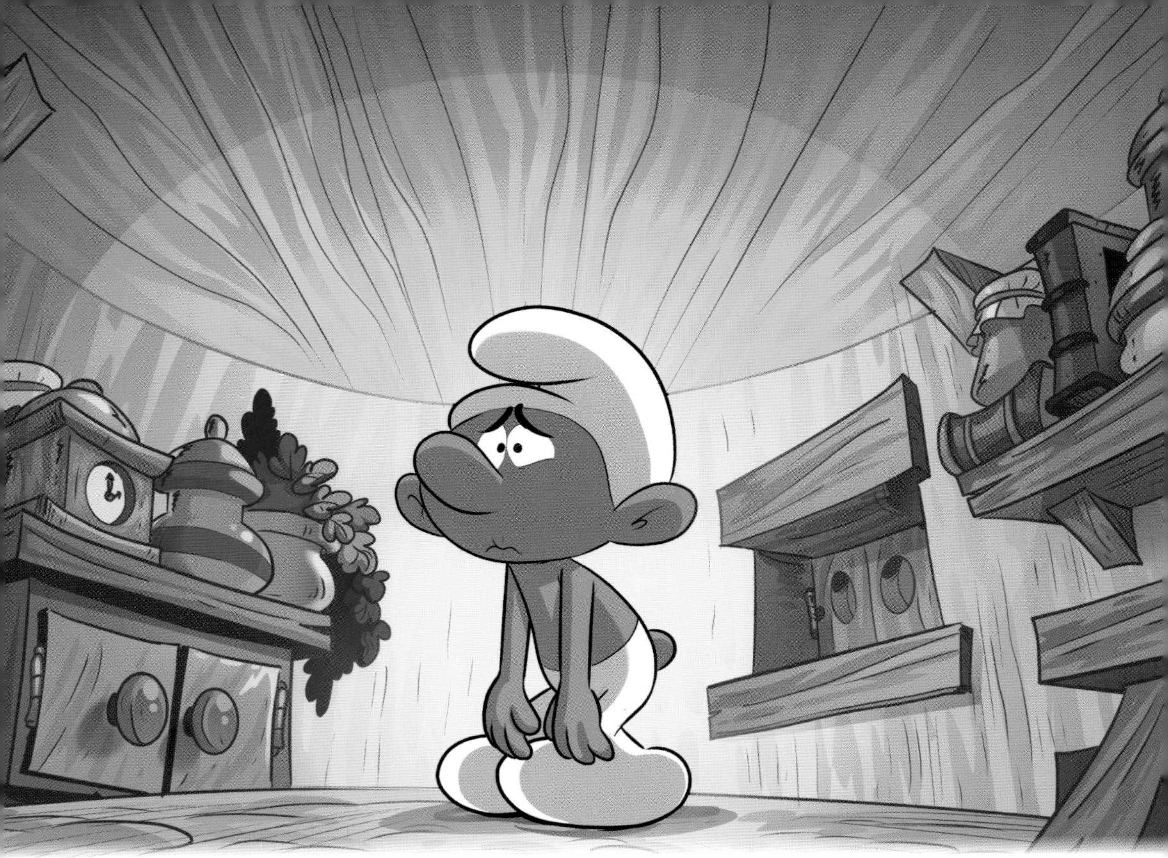

AND YOU
DO YOU EVER
TELL LIES?

A guide written by Diane Drory

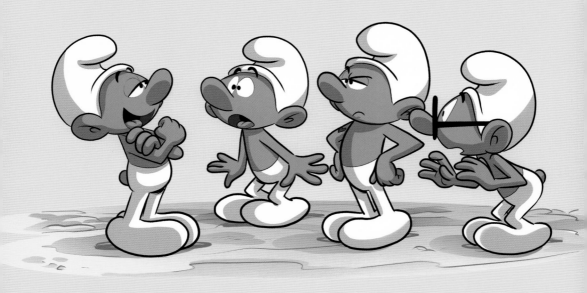

WHAT DOES IT MEAN TO LIE?

It's saying something that's **not true**. It's telling stories, talking nonsense, making things up, and spreading falsehoods.

It's inventing **stories** about things that didn't happen, or even just telling only part of what happened, or exaggerating the truth.

DO YOU REMEMBER A TIME SOMEONE LIED TO YOU?

And it's also **not speaking up** when you know others are lying.

Lying is a bad practice. But sometimes it's too hard to tell the truth, so we tell "little white lies."

DO BABIES LIE, TOO?

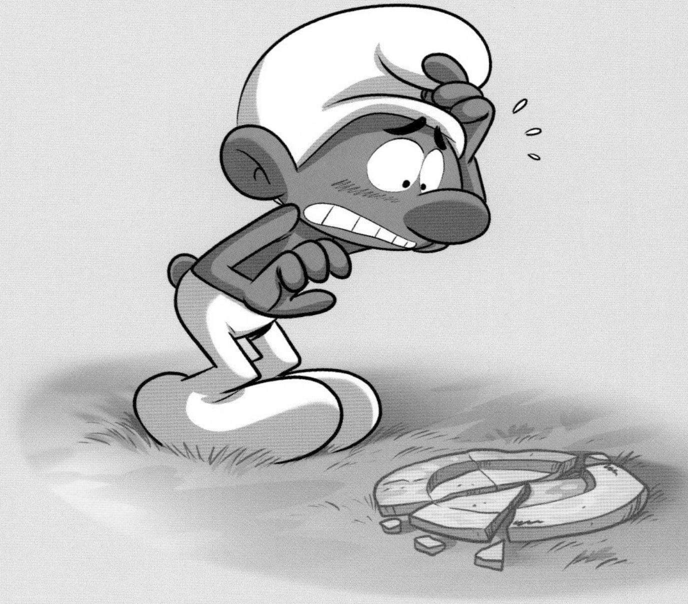

When we're very small, we don't know how to lie. But as we grow up, we **discover** how to lie, and we learn to conceal, to deny, and to transform the truth to deceive other people.

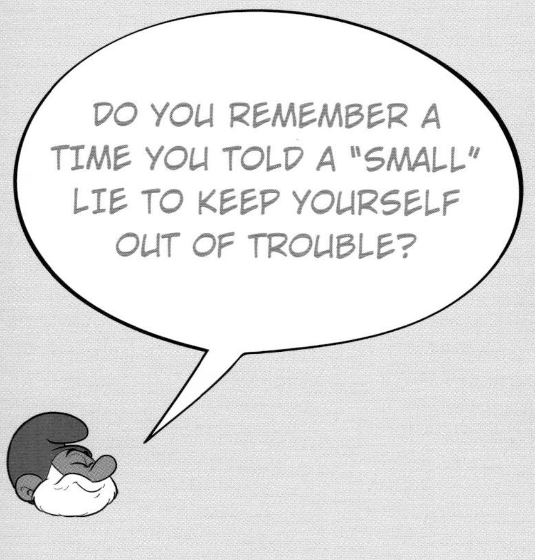
DO YOU REMEMBER A TIME YOU TOLD A "SMALL" LIE TO KEEP YOURSELF OUT OF TROUBLE?

WHY DON'T WE ALL JUST TELL THE TRUTH?

We lie when we find the truth difficult to say. Often it's because we're **afraid**. But sometimes it's because we don't know how to tell a painful truth. We're worried the person we're talking to will get angry and punish us for making a mistake. A lie seems **easier** than telling the truth.

Other times we lie to make ourselves **look better**.

We want to impress other people, so we tell people that we've done things we haven't, or invent interesting things that happened to us. We want to attract **attention** or admiration. And we worry that if we tell the truth, people won't find us interesting.

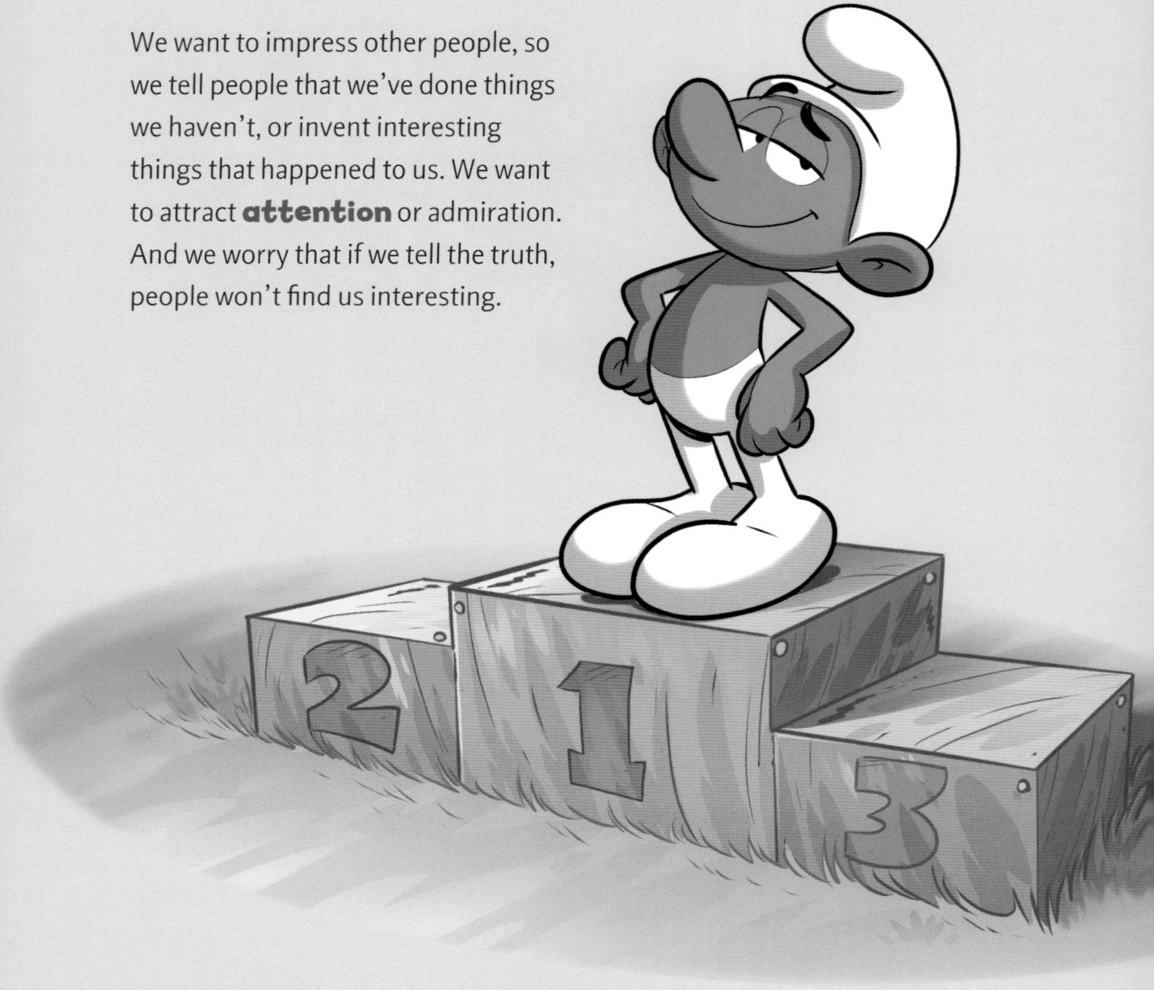
2
1
3

And sometimes we lie to **avoid hurting** other people. For example, if a friend has new sneakers that we think are ugly, we lie and say they look great.

Sometimes we just don't want to tell the truth. We don't want other people to know **our secrets**. For example, we say we're fine when actually we feel sad. The lie is like a **wall** between how we feel and the outside world. It protects our privacy.

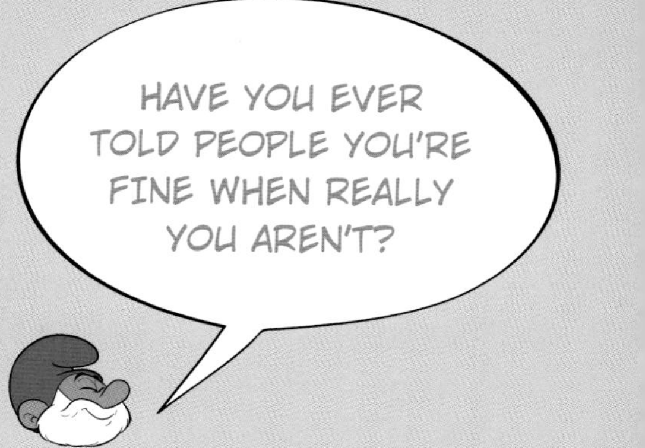
HAVE YOU EVER TOLD PEOPLE YOU'RE FINE WHEN REALLY YOU AREN'T?

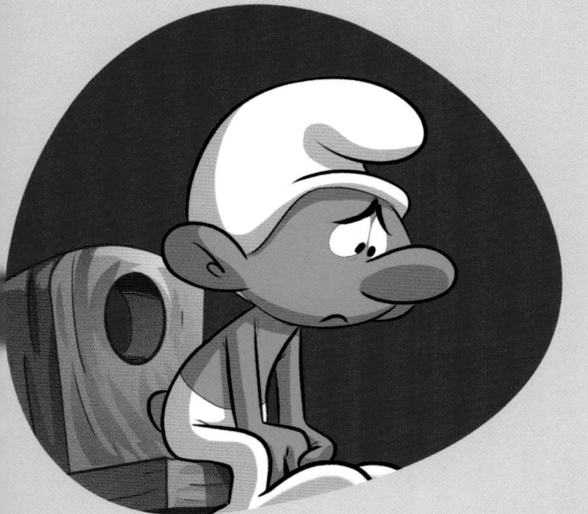

Sometimes we make up stories to make other people **laugh** or feel scared. And we get **caught up** in the stories and forget to tell people the stories aren't true.

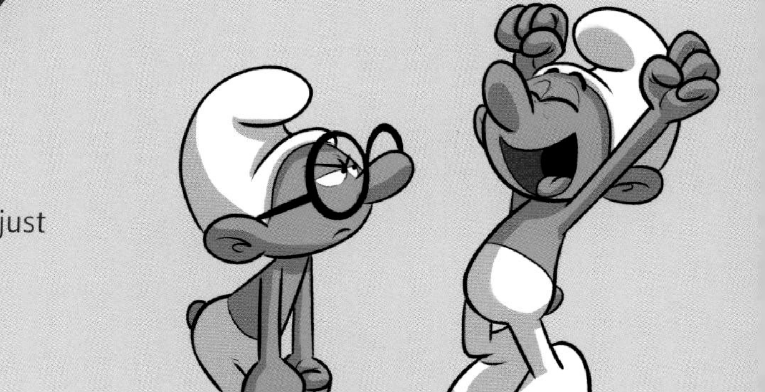

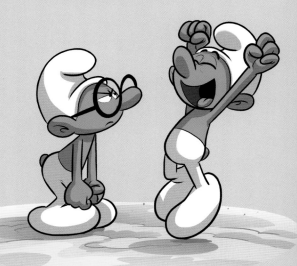

And sometimes we make up stories just for the **fun** of it, to be creative.

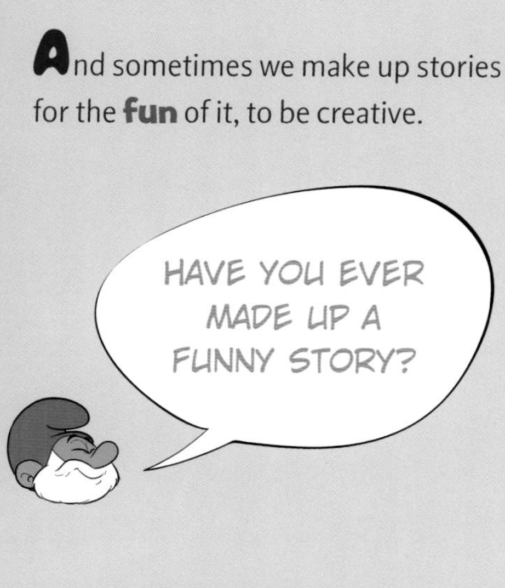
HAVE YOU EVER MADE UP A FUNNY STORY?

DOES EVERYONE LIE?

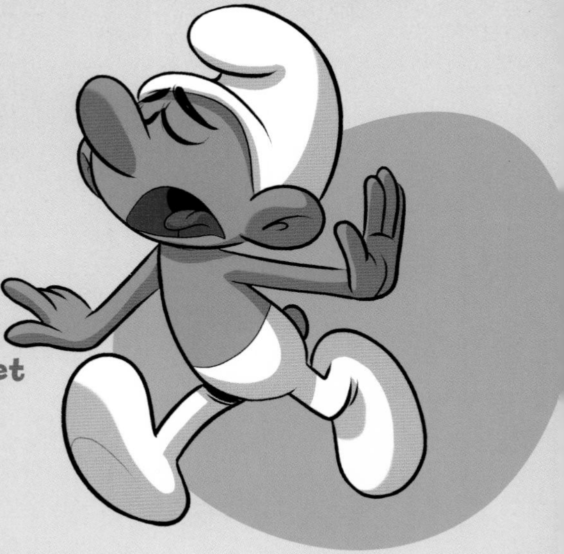

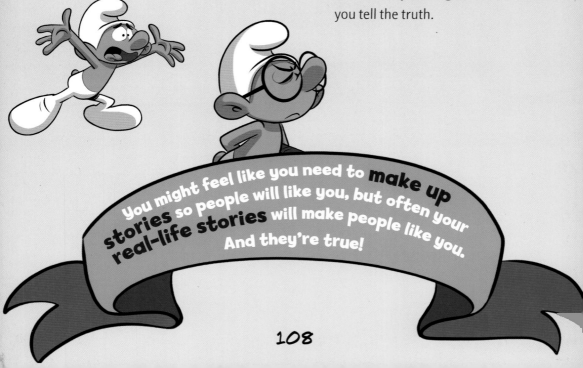

Yes. Everybody makes mistakes, and sometimes people lie without even doing it on purpose. Of course, lots of people also lie to **get what they want**.

Adults **often** tell small lies that play around with the truth, because it makes their lives **easier**, or because they don't know how to tell a specific truth. For instance, if they don't want to do something, they say they're too busy.

Some people tell **funny lies** because they like jokes. A little bit of all of this can be okay, but if you do it too often, no one will believe you **anymore**, even when you tell the truth.

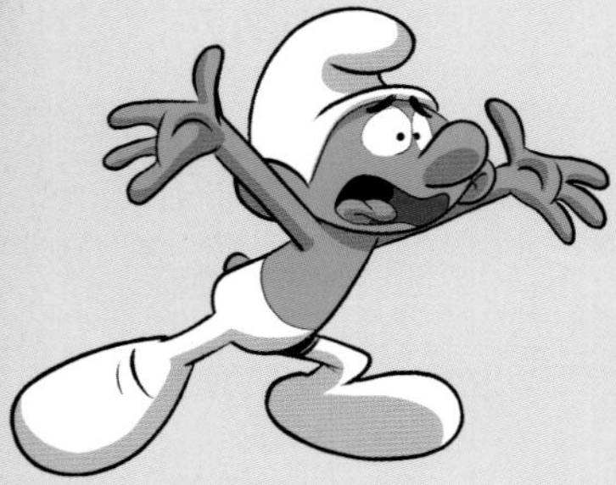

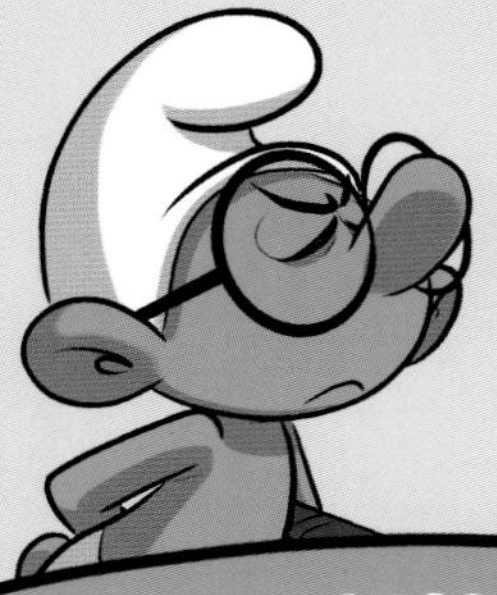

You might feel like you need to **make up stories** so people will like you, but often your **real-life stories** will make people like you. And they're true!

ADVICE FROM PAPA SMURF

Don't be afraid to tell your parents the truth. Sometimes they might get angry about a mistake you made, but they will never love you less because of a mistake. And if you always tell them the truth, they'll trust you.

We all have the right to our own ideas. You don't need to pretend to agree with others just to fit in.

Remember that telling the truth doesn't mean you have to tell everyone everything. It's okay to say, "I don't want to talk about it."